C000225119

SQUARE ONE

www.penguin.co.uk

Also by Nell Frizzell

The Panic Years

SQUARE ONE

Nell Frizzell

TRANSWORLD PUBLISHERS
Penguin Random House, One Embassy Gardens,
8 Viaduct Gardens, London SW11 7BW
www.penguin.co.uk

Transworld is part of the Penguin Random House group of companies
whose addresses can be found at global.penguinrandomhouse.com

First published in Great Britain in 2022 by Bantam Press
an imprint of Transworld Publishers

Copyright © Nell Frizzell 2022

Nell Frizzell has asserted her right under the Copyright,
Designs and Patents Act 1988 to be identified as the author of this work.

This book is a work of fiction and, except in the case of historical fact,
any resemblance to actual persons, living or dead, is purely coincidental.

Every effort has been made to obtain the necessary permissions with
reference to copyright material, both illustrative and quoted. We apologize
for any omissions in this respect and will be pleased to make the
appropriate acknowledgements in any future edition.

A CIP catalogue record for this book
is available from the British Library.

ISBNs 9781787634312 (cased)
9781787634329 (tpb)

Typeset in 11.25/15.75pt Sabon by Jouve (UK), Milton Keynes.
Printed and bound in Great Britain by Clays Ltd, Elcograf S.p.A.

The authorized representative in the EEA is Penguin Random House Ireland,
Morrison Chambers, 32 Nassau Street, Dublin D02 YH68.

Penguin Random House is committed to a sustainable
future for our business, our readers and our planet. This book
is made from Forest Stewardship Council® certified paper.

1

To all the daughters.
And their dads.

1
Keys

Posting the keys through her own letterbox was a pretty rubbish out-of-body experience.

Like finding her name in someone else's address book, seeing her face in the background of a stranger's photo, or really smelling the inside of her elbow; for a second, less perhaps, Hanna was no longer herself. She was witnessing herself from the outside. She was noticing herself, without really being herself.

Hanna had forgotten about the keys until they'd driven to the end of the road. After three hours of loading up a rented Luton van with just enough laundry bags to bring on an attack of self-loathing, she and her father had finally turned the corner and were out of sight when she felt the small prick of recognition. In her thigh. The clutch of keys, held together with a silver ring in the shape of a turtle, was pressing into her leg with an insistence that felt almost like an accusation. She'd put her hand on the dashboard, like a driving instructor preparing to fail a quaking seventeen-year-old, and whispered, 'Stop.' Her dad, thinking she was referring to the cheese and brinjal pickle sandwich he'd started to eat with only one hand on the wheel, slipped the offending item into his door pocket.

'No. Stop the car. I've forgotten something.'

With a small sigh, they pulled in behind a van advertising 'Cranston Scaffolding – Experts in Erections' and Hanna creaked open the door. The day was unseasonably warm and as she lowered her foot towards the pavement, a thick blare of sunshine hit the tops of her ankles, picking out the thin, pale hairs like the feathering around the top of a shire horse's hoof. She couldn't remember the last time she'd done anything to this winter pelt. Through a combination of thick tights, winter boots and unintended chastity, nobody had really looked at her Mr Tumnus legs for months. Not least her. And yet here she was, looking like something ready to be strapped into a harness and made to pull a cart full of apples to market.

Walking back to the no-longer-hers house felt like the longest march in history. Continents had shifted in the time it took her to ease the keys from her pocket. Rivers had changed course quicker than her route round next door's hedge. Glaciers had tunnelled out valleys in the space between her old front gate and former letterbox. At the door, her arms felt heavy, her head stiff. She lifted the flap and, for less than a second, she could smell the air inside the house. A combination of Persil, old coats, coffee and cat, with just a hint of cooking oil and damp, hit her nose. The oxygen of her old life ached through the gap in the door and into her lungs. It was heady. It was intoxicating. It was stale. Before she had a chance to think, she'd pushed the keys through the hole, scraping her fingers on that strange and brittle little moustache that rests across the top lip of so many letterboxes. She heard the dull clunk as they hit the floorboards on the other side and turned. Biting the inside of her cheek – an old habit born of being lacerated by train-track braces and their stray wires during adolescence – she walked past the gate and back down the road. She didn't look back. She didn't know if Joe was watching her. She couldn't bear it if he was. Or if he wasn't.

Four months earlier, Hanna had been chopping an onion and listening to a podcast about weathermen when something started to trickle down her spine like cold tea. A feeling like malign gravity started to leak across her shoulders, down her collarbone and over her ribs. This wasn't a panic attack, not a fever or a stroke. Standing at the kitchen counter, staring into the pine-effect cupboard door in front of her, she had been hit full force with something wet and blank and true. She was lonely. The loneliness that for months had been welling up inside her body had finally breached the watershed somewhere around her neck and now poured through her, unchecked. Those puddles, which had seemed a bit like hunger, a bit like sexual frustration and a little like sadness, suddenly overflowed with a thick, biting ache. She was lonelier than she had ever been in her life. The hours before bed had stretched ahead of her, utterly empty.

Her friend Dom had spent three days suggesting plans and then failed to commit to any of them. Even if by some miracle he was free, Dom lived in Hackney, Hanna in Brockley, meaning it would take both of them an hour to reach somewhere even vaguely central. Her colleagues had all gone straight home from work murmuring about the gym or having a flat viewing. And Joe? Well, Joe had been at band practice. Of course.

Joe's band was, let's be charitable here, awful. Microwave Death had formed when Joe was twenty-one and studying maths at Sheffield University. Their first EP, *Are You F**king Kidding Me?!,* had sold twenty-six copies. They didn't do many gigs. They didn't have a website. They didn't have fans. And yet, they still had band rehearsals four times a week. Because of band practice, Joe had missed: Hanna's twenty-fifth birthday party, every anniversary bar their first, the day Hanna had to be rushed to hospital with suspected appendicitis, her first day at a new job, her appearance as a vox pop on the six o'clock news talking about the cost of Boris Johnson's failed Garden Bridge, all the meetings with all the estate agents, their best friends' wedding, and enough dinners to feed the cast of *Hollyoaks*, past and present. All this would be frustrating enough if the band were brilliant, made money and brought great music into the world. That night, as the smell of onion spread from Hanna's fingers across her hot and sobbing face, it suddenly seemed unbearable. The band was shit. And yet there she was, alone again, because when it came to the crunch, the band always came first.

The loneliness washing through Hanna erupted that night into an argument. One of the few she and Joe had ever had. Standing in their hallway, shoeless and wild-eyed, she'd hurled words at him like thunderbolts: 'selfish', 'childish', 'egomaniac', 'hopeless'. Seeing him standing there, his eyes fixed on the coat hooks, his mouth shapeless, she'd wanted to smack him. She'd wanted to punch him, tear his skin, split him open with her bare hands and force this feeling on to him too. Her loneliness was too great, too heavy, and she demanded that he finally take some of the weight. She was going to make him take responsibility.

'You've made your choice! You chose them! You just didn't bother to tell me!' she'd screamed, trapped in their tiny hallway, hitting her elbows on banisters and radiators as she tried, desperately, to make him listen.

Finally, her fury spent and the tang of onions soaking up her sleeves, he'd held her against his chest and stroked her back with his fingers. He'd shushed her like a baby. Laid his lips on her hair without quite kissing it. In a voice that seemed to come from someone else entirely, she'd told him that she was lonely. Unbearably lonely. She was hanging in space, not going forward, unable to go back. His reluctance to plan the future, to get a mortgage, to even talk about babies, had made her feel cold, dark and remote. It was as though someone had pressed pause on her life. Her self-esteem was at rock bottom, she felt like a bit part in her own life, and she had spent so long having her hopes gently quashed by Joe's ambivalence that she had almost no idea who she was or what she wanted any more. Finally, she'd turned her face – a liquid mask of tears, snot and mascara – up to his and told him that she couldn't live like this for ever. She wanted an entire partner, and Joe was no longer that.

Reaching the passenger door, Hanna swung herself up on to the van's high metal step to climb back in.

'Well, that was great fun,' she said, chewing the inside of her mouth.

There in front of her, sitting on the grey, lightly stained polyester seat, was a sandwich, wrapped in greaseproof paper and covered with her dad's small, unjoined-up handwriting. She looked at the words. *What do you call a man covered in leaves?* There were three little dots in the bottom right-hand corner, slightly speckled with orange grease marks. She turned the sandwich over and read the back. *Russell.*

'I thought you might be hungry,' said Iain, smiling down at her. 'After hoofing all that stuff into the back of the van. And I knew you wouldn't have time to make anything.' Hanna was still balancing on the step, suddenly very tired. 'Do you remember the last time you came to Oxford, just before Christmas? You ate an entire cheese and onion pasty on the walk from the station to town. Well, I thought this would save us buying a pasty.'

'God, those sandwiches you made me every day for school,' said Hanna, her foot in mid-air, the tang of nostalgia in her mouth. 'You'd wake up at, like, dawn, put on some Zimbabwean funk, and assemble a sandwich almost perfectly designed to turn me into a social outcast.'

'Those sandwiches were a culinary—'

'Tuna mayonnaise with sundried tomatoes and sweetcorn?' Hanna interrupted. 'Grated carrot with cheese and peanut butter? Humous and sliced red pepper? Jesus, Iain. If it smelled, stained fabric and would fail a customs exam, you would put it in a sandwich.'

'Hey, my Punjabi pachranga pickle was—'

'Just opening my lunchbox was like an act of chemical warfare!' Hanna's voice was a little more rasping than she'd intended. 'Nearby children would wrap their hoods around their faces to block out the smells. Even teachers would make comments about the drains.'

Iain laughed, a little sheepishly. 'Ah, but the notes, Han. You've got to admit the notes were good.'

Hanna felt her breathing slow, a little. 'Yes, OK. The notes were good.'

'I mean, they were very good. Sometimes I'd be there for half an hour doing you those crosswords or drawing the cartoons.'

'OK, I said the notes were good.' Hanna was quieter now.

'Added Consonants! Guess the Song from the Lyric! Hanna's Adventures in Numberland! They were—'

'Thank you, Iain. Dad. That's really . . .' Holding the crackling parcel in her lap, Hanna gave out a long, juddering sigh.

'No worries.' Iain sniffed, quickly and sharply. 'Now, shall we get this show on the road? I've already finished my thermos, and with my old-man bladder that means I'm going to need to pee pretty soon.'

Hanna tried not to picture Iain standing at the urinal of a service station off the M40; his drooping cock, his age-flattened arse peeping above his sagging waistband, the dribble as he did up his flies. Or worse, to save time, would he pull over in a layby and piss into a bush, the powerful slipstream of passing lorries spraying that urine all over his shoes and the side of the van?

'I'm sorry it took so long,' said Hanna.

'Ah, it wasn't so bad.' Iain was leaning over the steering wheel, craning to see both sides of the junction before pulling out.

'And I'm sorry I haven't been to visit since before Christmas,' Hanna added, surprised to hear herself apologizing. She had never visited much. Even though Oxford was only an hour away, the gravitational pull of London had been too strong. 'I suppose I'm making up for lost time now though!'

Neither of them laughed. Hanna started unwrapping the sandwich. This, she knew, was a four-cornered missive from her father's heart; a token of his support, a dispatch of affection that he would never have been able to put into words. Without asking, he had fallen back to one of the useful services he had performed throughout Hanna's childhood. Where her mum would have screamed obscenities about Joe or fired a machine-gun attack of questions about her future into the side of Hanna's head, her dad had made a sandwich. Brie, mango chutney and yellow pepper. And why not?

'Do you remember that bike ride to Abingdon?' asked Hanna, looking down at the joke on the back of her sandwich.

'I do,' said Iain, grinding the van into the middle lane to overtake a minibus with the words 'Inspector Morse Tours' painted along the side in gold.

'What do you call a man covered in chain grease . . .?' said Hanna, turning back to look at her father.

'Ollie Hans!' Iain laughed as if it was the first time he'd ever said it. 'And what do you call a woman covered in type?' He was chancing his arm and he knew it.

'Rita Book,' Hanna replied, tasting the salt from her tears across her top lip. 'I was, what, thirteen?'

'Yup. About that. You were going to start upper school that September.'

That day had been one of the happiest of Hanna's younger life. An uncomplicated day of joy as she leaned over the precipice of adolescence and decided, just for now, to stay a child. It was also, she now realized, a memory that Iain had held close all these years too.

'I'm really only planning on being at yours for a month, tops,' said Hanna, after a brief pause. 'Once I've got a job, I should be able to start renting a room somewhere. Maybe Cowley or Rose Hill. They're still a bit more affordable, aren't they?' Hanna thought of the two-up, two-down terraces she'd walked past on her way to middle school.

'They're still the more affordable areas, sure,' said Iain, before taking an enormous bite of his sandwich. Chunks of red pepper and bits of cheese started to crumble out of his mouth, like a dog trying to eat sand. It was revolting to watch.

'I could probably find a shared house or something,' Hanna said, as much to herself as to Iain. Hanna had been applying for jobs, rewriting her CV, going to job interviews and Instagram-stalking potential bosses for months before moving, but to no avail. Her last temping job, for a construction firm who were looking to invest in social enterprises as a way of greenwashing their more harmful practices, had come to an end a couple of months after that big, hideous, relationship-ending argument with Joe. It was hardly surprising; like so many of Hanna's jobs up until that point, the work had been dull and moderately paid and only tangentially related to what she really wanted to do. Her dissertation had been on microfinance and environmental conservation – at one point she really thought she knew how to save the world. Today, she wasn't sure she could even save herself. Sharing the rent in Brockley had torn through every scrap of Hanna's savings while she'd tried to decide what to do.

Though she was unsure where to go, all the jobs Hanna had initially looked for had been in London. Jobs that might just pay her enough to be able to afford her own one-bedroom flat, somewhere very quiet, far from transport links. Then jobs that would mean she could become somebody's lodger, somewhere very quiet, far from transport links. Then jobs that would qualify her for housing benefit, somewhere with no transport links at all. When these had all turned to ashes in her inbox, and Iain eventually offered to put her up for a few months while she found her feet, she'd started looking for jobs in Oxford. A free flat was, after all, a free flat. She'd started to fantasize about a new life, miles away from Joe, in the small, golden stone city. She'd begun to think of her move to Oxford as a sabbatical: she'd get a job, earn enough to rent her own place, maybe start growing vegetables in the garden, and rebuild her self-esteem, away from the piss and chicken bones of London. As the date she'd given Joe for moving out approached, a gnawing anxiety had started to spread through her intestines. She needed work, a job – any job – that could pay enough for her to rent a room. She'd applied to work on the reception of a local refugee housing charity; she'd applied to be a private maths tutor; she'd applied to do admin at the local art school; she'd applied to manage a coffee shop; she'd applied to be a marketing assistant at the local paper. She'd spent so long looking on the city council jobs website that she'd ended up applying to manage a weekly local car boot sale, despite having absolutely no relevant experience, not owning a car and not being able to drive. There had been a couple of promising interviews – one at a museum, another at a local PR agency – but nothing had come of either yet. Maybe things would be different when the new financial year kicked in. Even so, with her bank balance wilting like a bag of supermarket salad, she'd had to accept that, until she got a job, sleeping in Iain's spare room was her only option.

'Sure,' said Iain, spitting a tiny bit of lettuce on to the steering wheel. 'Something will come up, I reckon. Why don't you eat your sandwich and we can talk about the flat when we get back to Jericho.'

Hanna felt the weight of the greaseproof paper parcel in her lap. It didn't make her pain go away. It didn't make life any more certain. It didn't make her feel any less adrift in an unknown future. But, as they drove down the A40, soaring above London on the Westway and out into the green of the Chilterns on the way to Oxford, the sandwich in her lap did remind her of something. That she was a person. A whole person. And if that person smelled like an ungodly combination of brie and mango chutney then, well, so be it.

2

Jungle Book Duvet Cover

In the days immediately preceding her period, Hanna would often find herself standing at an open cupboard eating like a stray dog. Raw anchovies, dry cereal, spoonfuls of peanut butter, biscuits, fingers dipped in Marmite, or handfuls of raisins while waiting for her toast to finally pop up from the toaster. For a day, maybe two, she would eat like a log flume – entire meals disappearing through her body with no apparent impact on her revving hunger. Eventually, she would feel that familiar wetness, that unfurling of gravity between her legs, and immediately it would lift. She would look across the kitchen tops like a general looking over a battlefield after a particularly bloody assault. And she would stop eating. For a bit.

But while hormones could flip her appetite like a switch, her heart and stomach seemed to work on entirely different systems. Sadness, anger, grief; they did nothing to her hunger. And so, barely an hour after walking away from her boyfriend, home and former life, Hanna was sitting in a van, staring out of the window, crunching through a bag of Bombay mix on her sun-warm seat. As she and Iain soared over High Wycombe – a town apparently made up entirely of storage units and shopping centres – she pushed dusty fistfuls of puffed rice and spicy peas into her mouth like a conveyor belt. Red kites circled above them like paragliders. Crows flew from their treetop nests, ready to have a go at the other corvid big boys.

'Are you ready?' Iain said quietly.

'Ready for what?' Hanna replied, pushing a bit of pea out of a tooth gap with her tongue.

'Are you ready?' said Iain, louder this time.

'What are you talking about?' said Hanna, louder this time, wondering if he was about to do a bargain basement *Thelma & Louise* and zoom off the flyover on to an ASDA.

'ARE. YOU. READY!' Iain screamed. He was like a man blowing the whistle for a bare-knuckle fight. His hands were white, his eyes staring, his voice genuinely frightening.

'NO!' Hanna screeched. 'Stop. What are you doing?! NO!'

And suddenly there they were – driving through the Aston Rowant Cutting. Two huge chalk cliffs rising up on either side of the motorway like the sides of ocean liners. The white stone, like a thousand paracetamol tablets, was dazzling in the midday sun.

'ROCK TUNNEL!' Iain roared, pumping his hand in the air like a cowboy whirling a lasso. 'Roooooooock tunneeeeellllll!'

During the unending drives back from visiting her Auntie Molly in London, this motorway cutting had always signalled to Hanna that they were nearly home. As a child, long car journeys had brought on a kind of boredom that was actually physically painful. Beyond an itch of irritation, it was like having every limb pulled apart. Her joints would ache. Her chest would feel tight. Her eyes would dry out and her sphincter would pulse like an overtired eye. Reading made her sick. Drawing made her sick. Her parents would lose interest in playing games. Even making friendship braids out of knotted lengths of thread would eventually wear thin. And so this zoom through an actual hill had become something of a ritual bloodletting in the family. As they passed through it, Hanna, Iain and even occasionally Julie would bellow at the top of their lungs: 'Rock tunnel.' A motorway cliff. The gap that heralded the home stretch. It was like driving along the bottom of Beachy Head, but here, in the Chilterns.

'Christ, Dad. You could have warned me,' Hanna said, pulling her eyebrows back down from the roof felt.

'I did warn you!' Iain chuckled. 'I warned you just back there.'

'Screaming like the referee from *Gladiators* isn't exactly a warning,' Hanna shot back. She was trying her best to look cross but her face wouldn't behave. Her mouth kept curling up at the sides.

'Had you really forgotten?' asked Iain, checking his

rear-view mirror as they were overtaken by yet another lorry.

'Yes, funnily enough, people don't tend to scream "rock tunnel" on the Oxford Tube very often,' said Hanna.

'I bet they'd feel better if they did,' Iain said, his face creasing into an origami smile.

For a few more miles, they drove along in silence. Not an uncomfortable one. Hanna ran her fingernail along the gap between the passenger door and its window. Iain listened to the radio. Hanna tried to remember how it had felt to be that child, sighing in the back of a family car, rather than single, unemployed, heartbroken, and zooming towards middle age in a van full of old saucepans.

As they came into Oxford, through Summertown, past the giant houses and leafy gardens, Hanna was struck yet again by just how ludicrously beautiful the city was. They drove past Gee's, a restaurant that had always epitomized sophistication to Child Hanna, because of its conservatory seating and string of outdoor lights. She used to tell herself, aged twelve or maybe thirteen, that when she was an adult – something she was desperate for – she would eat in places like Gee's. She had pictured herself wearing platforms (of course) and a lycra minidress (*bien sûr*), with hennaed hair (this was the nineties after all) and smoking at a table in Gee's, being attended to by a waiter wearing – and why not – a bow tie. Strangely, now she thought about it, Hanna had never actually pictured herself with anyone at that table. Only her. Just a perfect picture of adult sophistication on the Banbury Road.

They turned into St Margaret's Road – Iain was really showing her the scenic route – and for the first time, from her Luton van height, Hanna was able to see over the hedges and front walls; the tasteful Farrow & Ball front door colours, the heavy curtains, the bee-kissed gardens. These people were her neighbours of just a few streets but seemed to live in a different city entirely.

Hanna and Iain manoeuvred their way into Cranham Street like a heavily pregnant woman trying to navigate the tables of a crowded restaurant. The great girth of the van seemed to wheeze and spread even further as they clipped wing mirrors and sighed up the kerb. On their right was the small block of ex-council flats in which Iain lived. There was a single municipal willow tree on the front lawn, and the metal railing along the path was encrusted with bikes.

'And that's a wrap!' Iain said, turning to face Hanna for the first time in nearly two hours. He was clearly enjoying his van driver role play. Hanna had felt a little twist in her heart when, after finally reaching the motorway, Iain had triumphantly produced two Yorkie bars from the glove box for them both. He'd even bought a coffee in a service station – an act of extravagance and eco-unfriendliness that marked this day out as almost otherworldly.

'Can I have a wee before we start unloading?' Hanna asked, delaying the inevitable.

'You can if you take a bag in with you,' said Iain, leaping down into the road and only narrowly missing a cyclist.

Iain's favourite part of moving his daughter out of her home and away from her ex-partner was clearly the buttons that operated the rear door of the van. She could see the childlike joy on his face as he lowered the footplate and unlocked the grille. He watched with something like awe as the hydraulics hissed and the cooling engine hummed. Then he jumped up and threw open the van like a magician whipping away a silk handkerchief. Seeing her belongings squished between the hard sides of the rented van made Hanna feel extremely small. The contents looked like a packet of cereal – shaken to dust across a potholed road. Nothing had really broken; it was all just flattened and sagging with exhaustion. *You and me both, pal*, thought Hanna, grabbing a plant pot and satchel full of old laptops. The stuff at the back was destined for a storage unit by the Cowley Carworks – another delightful family outing to come, no doubt – so everything in view was, pretty much, Hanna's life. For the foreseeable.

Nothing good ever happened in a flat with a Salvador Dalí print on the wall. This Hanna knew and yet here she was, carrying another forty-litre laundry bag past a print of *Swans Reflecting Elephants* in her dad's hallway.

It wasn't even framed – just hanging by a bulldog clip looped over a baton pin.

'So this is your room,' said Iain, striding proudly into a pale blue box with sanded floors and Blu-tack stains on the walls. It was almost empty but for a huge shelving unit across one wall and a single bed, made up with a Jungle Book duvet cover and dark blue pillows. Until Hanna's life zoomed down a U-bend, this had been Iain's office. Except Iain didn't really need an office – he never worked from home – and so instead the room had been used to store his enormous record collection. Metres of vinyl, at least a ton of CDs both bought and copied, guitars and drums, as well as his most prized collection: the compilation tapes.

'Thank you, Dad,' said Hanna, strolling over to the window and looking out at the pastel-coloured flats on the other side of the road. The ones painted to be an echo of the postcard cottages on nearby Observatory Road. One of them had a child's bicycle on the balcony. Another a can of Tyskie. 'I really am grateful to you for putting me up like this.'

'And putting up with you!' said Iain, clearly thrilled at his speedy wordplay.

'Hm,' Hanna nose-laughed. 'Where shall I put my stuff?' They both looked over at the pile of laundry bags heaped in the corner like Jabba the Hutt.

'Well, ah, on the shelves, I reckon,' said Iain, brushing his hand along one of the huge wooden slabs that had, up until now, held Rock and Pop J–L of his vinyl.

As with much of the rest of the furniture in the flat, Iain had made these shelves himself, in just a weekend. His sheer capability with building, fixing and designing was one of the few areas in which Iain drew complete respect from his daughter. His ability to think in 3D, his exacting patience in lining up the weight-bearing angles, his unquestioning faith that he could do it best himself, seemed like a superpower when the rest of the world had to hire strangers to come and erect their new flat-pack furniture. That Hanna had inherited precisely none of this skill was made worse by the fact that she'd never taken a single moment to try and learn any of it either. Her apprenticeship to Iain consisted almost entirely of one botched attempt to build a brickwork compost heap together at her granny's house in 1996, during which she'd managed to drop a brick on her toe and split open the nail.

'But, like, my kitchen stuff and bathroom stuff. Am I OK to just put them in with yours?' she asked, thinking of her large stainless steel cooking pots and bottles of shampoo.

'Oh sure, sure. If we double up on stuff then we can just bung yours over to the storage unit another day.'

So that's it, thought Hanna. *My stuff. Bunged.* Just like her future. And her self-worth.

'But let's have a cuppa, before you start to unpack Mount Rushmore,' said Iain, nodding at the red checked bags. 'I might even have some of that dried mango left.'

Walking into Iain's kitchen, the first thing Hanna

noticed was the square, black plates on the drying rack. What precisely was it with single men and black, square plates? Every student house, every bachelor pad, every bedsit: they'd be there. God knows where they bought these things – surely production stopped around 2004 when *Changing Rooms* finally came off air. But they were there. They were always there. Who actually wants to pretend they're eating everything off a slate? Off a matte-finish iPad? Off a chalkboard? Answer: a man.

Iain stood by the kettle and gestured towards a small shelving unit full of boxes of tea.

'What do you fancy? Builder's? Peppermint? Willow bark and spit? Clog heel and the whisper of moss?'

'Just regular for me,' replied Hanna. Then she slammed her hand on the table. 'Actually, fuck it. Let's have a blend.'

There was a pause.

'A blend for the lady,' said Iain, doing a little mock bow that made his knees click, before reaching for the teapot on top of the boiler. The blend – one bag of lapsang souchong to two bags of Yorkshire Tea – was what Iain, Hanna and her mother Julie had drunk on Saturday mornings. Usually sitting on the kitchen floor reading the paper or while eating pancakes. The smokiness always reminded Hanna of camping trips, and the colour – just grey enough – had got it dubbed 'John Major's piss' by Julie, even though she happily drank it too.

Like someone on autopilot, Iain flicked a switch beside the kitchen window as he waited for the kettle to boil.

There was a satisfying 'pock' followed by a hum. He then reached for a remote and pointed it towards a black, blinking mass in the corner. The strains of 'Worried About You' by the Rolling Stones poured out from the walls, coating Hanna like mist. Iain rarely did anything around the house without accompaniment. Like a man living in a film, his every move, his every thought was soundtracked by music. Whereas Hanna was fully addicted to podcasts, Iain had always switched between radio, records and CDs. Switched, literally. Since moving into this flat seven years ago, Iain had rewired every room in order to have a unified system of speakers, hi-fi, CD players, tape decks and record players so that he could listen to anything, anywhere, at the flick of his self-made switch. When Hanna pointed out last Christmas that he could now achieve the same with just his phone and a wireless speaker, he'd looked at her as if she was suggesting he could have his kidneys replaced with dishwasher tablets. Creating those switches, drawing out the plans and threading those wires had occupied Iain for the first two months after his marriage with Julie finally came to an end. They had become his life, if not his home-engineered wife.

'So, love, here's a thing,' said Iain, after a few minutes of busying himself suspiciously at the kitchen counter. He'd produced a packet of oatcakes and a handful of dried mango and put them out on one of the black square plates like an airline snack. 'I downloaded an app.'

'Tinder?' interjected Hanna, her eyes twinkling at her hilarious joke.

'Ah, actually . . .' There was a dreadful pause. Hanna felt the chair against her buttocks. 'Yes. Um. I downloaded Tinder.'

Hanna's jaw twitched. What the hell was happening? Did her dad just say he was on Tinder?

'Yes, a few months ago actually. It's funny, you know – I heard them talking about it on Danny Baker's show. It sounded a hoot. People going on there pretending to be Garfield. One man found his old piano teacher. Anyway. So I, umm. Well, I put it on my phone.'

Hanna was holding her cup of tea like a handbrake.

'And I actually met some really nice people. One lady, Deborah, who makes her own ice cream.' Hanna hated the way her dad still called women 'ladies'. Amazing, really, that out of the horror of this whole sentence, his use of the word 'lady' could still set her teeth on edge. 'And I got invited to this party down at Aston's Eyot during the full moon by a lady called Ruth?' Iain was starting to incline his voice at the end of these sentences, like questions. 'It was fun?' Hanna wasn't taking the bait. Her jaw was clamped shut so hard that it was now both physically and psychologically impossible for her to respond, even if she wanted to. And she did not want to. Iain ploughed on. 'Anyway, none of those really worked out. Not even a fumble.' Hanna felt her head implode like those sinkholes that suddenly suck up entire streets in China. Her face collapsed into the pits that had been her eyes and ears. 'But I've got a date tonight with a woman. Her name's Mary.'

Hanna sat as unmoving as a loaf of bread. In her head, something was unravelling. Her dad was on Tinder? She now lived with her dad. Her dad was dating? She was single. She might go on Tinder? But no, now she couldn't. Because her dad was on Tinder. Wait. Her dad had swiped right on someone called Mary? On Tinder? And Hanna was sleeping in his spare room? She was temporarily trapped in a two-bed flat with her keen-to-have-a-fumble dad, with no obvious escape. This. This was a disaster.

Without saying a word, Hanna stood up and walked – incredibly aware of the bones in her legs – out of the kitchen and into the front room. Going into the room, she managed to somehow trip over a drill and a small bag of nails. What the fuck were they doing in the middle of the floor? She heard Iain throw his teaspoon against the metal side of the kitchen sink behind her. Clang. And then the creak of a kitchen chair. Somehow the voice in Hanna's head seemed to have got stuck on the words 'swipe right'. Instead of processing any of what Iain had just said, instead of a stream of filth or shock or horror, instead of some reasoned debate, the only thing that her internal monologue seemed able to produce at the moment were the words 'swipe' and 'right'. *Swipe right, swipe right, swipe right*, it went, over and over again.

Hanna looked around the room. It was, in every sense, the room of a single man. There were two clamps attached to the walls, holding Iain's prized guitars. There was a pile of trade magazines with thrilling titles like *Fire and Arson Investigator* or *Fire and Materials* sliding into the side of the sofa, like a drunken tired vicar. The sofa itself was black, faux leather and – perish the thought – wipe-clean. There were no cushions. No blankets. It was just a large, squeaky bench, squatting at the edge of the carpet. One entire corner of the room was taken up with a music system that looked more like the cockpit of a fighter plane than part of a home. Blinking lights, sleek black oblongs of various depths, disc drives, equalizers, Scart leads, speakers, and something that looked a lot like the timer on a B-movie bomb. In the centre of it all was Iain's fourteen-year-old Apple Mac, on the top of which was stuck a Danish troll doll, a novelty plastic turd from a joke shop, and a tissue-thin but fully intact snake skin. The walls of this techno hole were papered with old gig tickets, shopping lists, completed crosswords, printed-out emails and *Private Eye* cartoons. The carpet was mauve and grey. There was a dirty pair of socks on the back of a chair and a pile of ring binders stacked against one wall. Hanna turned back towards the window. There on the sill was a large potted spider plant. Its pale striped leaves were spread against the glass like fingers. Sunlight glowed through the green fronds and there, on the right-hand side, was a little clump. A baby, hanging off its plant parent like a tiny botanical firework. Attached, but trying to put down its own roots. Hanna looked at it for a second. Then watched as her fingers came up and pinched around the offshoot. Her nails bit into the adjoining stem. She gave a sharp tug and heard a snap.

The kitchen was silent, but for the milky guitar of *Tattoo You* still coming from the speakers – of course, it would never occur to Iain to turn the music off in the middle of an argument. *Although*, thought Hanna, *was this even an argument?* If neither of them was actually arguing? She walked past the bathroom and into her bedroom. The sun didn't reach this side of the flat in the afternoon. The pale blue of the walls looked slightly mottled – chalky outlines of recently dismantled shelves were etched across the surface like murder victims. Her pile of bags sat in the corner.

Hanna walked heavily over to the bed and sat down. She pulled out her phone. There was a message from her old friend, former flatmate and platonic ideal, Dom: *How's the castle?*

Hanna lifted the phone slightly above her head, so as to fit in the great landslide of laundry bags. She gave a thumbs up and pulled the exact face she'd last used when having her coil removed with a pair of medical tongs. *My dad is on Tinder*, she wrote as a caption. Send.

A couple of seconds passed. Hanna patted Baloo absentmindedly on the snout and rubbed her big toe across the floor.

OK. But no threesomes, Dom replied. Then: *Sorry. That was crass. I'm glad you got there in one piece.*

Giving in to the inevitable, Hanna lay back, her eyes

open but blank. She felt her feet hot against the cold of the bedding. Immediately, the unmistakable smell of Febreze sighed out from the pillow and across her face. She lifted a corner of the duvet cover and held it against her nose. She gave a tentative sniff. Of course. Of course he'd Febrezed the bed. His bed. This bed. Her bed. Whatever.

Ping.

The sound of a message arriving on her dad's phone rang out from the kitchen down the hall. Why was it that middle-aged men always had their key tones and notifications on maximum volume? As if it weren't bad enough that they kept them in those sad little flip-open leather wallets, like Avon ladies.

'Hoooooeeee!' Iain let out a long, low whistle. Then a chuckle. 'Very saucy.'

Hanna wondered if she was about to vomit on Mowgli. This couldn't work. It might only be a few weeks but she was not going to listen to her dad slavering over his matches the whole time she was staying here. She wasn't going to be held hostage by her father's newly liberated libido. She had to say something.

'Iain,' she said, standing in the doorway, her hands stuffed into the pockets of her jeans to hide the shaking. 'I can't ask you to delete Tinder . . .' She left a long pause, just in case Iain wanted to offer to do precisely that. He didn't. 'But if we're both going to be under one roof, and both dating, I think we need to set some ground rules.'

'Oh, Hanna,' said Iain, peering at her over his pound-shop reading glasses. 'Don't you think it's a bit soon for you to be dating?'

Hanna let out a snort, somewhere between fury and derision.

'Well, don't you think it's a bit late for you to be dating?' she replied, staring at the eyebrow hairs that were curling over the frames of his glasses.

'Fine.' Iain sat up straight in his chair and braced his shoulders. 'I'll take Tuesdays, Thursdays and Saturdays. You have Mondays, Wednesdays, Fridays and Sundays. No overnight guests unless previously agreed.' Hanna contemplated throwing a ladle into his face to stop him talking. 'And nothing that might wake the neighbours.'

Checkmate. He'd got her. He'd absolutely got her. While she'd hoped her father might shrink away from discussing the logistics of his sex life with his only daughter, Iain had apparently been preparing a rota. He'd thought it all out. She was prisoner of circumstance in this flat, and if that meant listening to her dad sexting at the kitchen table on a Saturday night, then apparently she had no choice.

'OK, fine,' Hanna mumbled, turning back into the hall. She needed to get out of this flat. She already felt like a worm, curled in on herself from the scorpion sting of rejection after her slow break-up with Joe. It was somehow far worse to be forsaken while your elderly father got his rocks off in the room next door. Pulling her laptop out of a nearby rucksack, Hanna dropped down on to her bed and started scrolling Gumtree.

Hi, I am the Rent Guru and I have a Great 4-Bedroom Student House Available for next academic year! Hanna tried to look past the frantic use of capital letters, to the useful detail. *Fully furnished with washing machine, fridge/freezer and cooker. It has 1 shared bathroom with shower.* The single photo was of a large, arched brick porch and a red front door. *Rent excludes utilities, total cost to include Gas, Electric, Water, Council Tax, and Wi-Fi.* She looked around at her piles of bags. Maybe there would be a shed. *Please call/email to arrange a viewing.* Pushing away visions of shared Lynx shampoo bottles, threadbare carpets and black mould, Hanna hit the email button.

3

Tin Foil

Hanna stared at the corner of the ceiling as morning light pushed into the room like lecherous fingers. She was doing maths. *If the room is square*, she thought, *then there would be ninety-degree angles at the corners of all the walls. But when you look in the corner, the very corner, of a room, there are three ninety-degree angles all meeting. Side wall meeting end wall, meeting the ceiling. All the walls are touching, and yet all the angles are ninety degrees.* Hanna was lying in her bed, wearing a pair of medium-size maroon paisley men's pyjamas from Marks & Spencer, her fingers teasing through the tangles of her curly brown pubes, staring at those three ninety-degree angles, meeting in 3D space. *When a corner meets a corner meets another corner, that makes, what, 270 degrees? That's not a thing. Is it? 270 degrees isn't a known total. It's just three quarters of a circle. But then, of course, this corner is itself just one corner of the whole.* She accidentally pulled too hard and plucked out a pube with a ping. *Within a sphere there would be eight of these little corners, all meeting on the axis. Which is—wait.*

She started to do the long multiplication in her head: *Eight times seventy is 560, carry the five, so eight times two is sixteen, plus the five – is 2,160. Wait, that's not a thing. 2,160 isn't anything.* She must have got this wrong.

She rolled over and picked her phone up off the floor. It was 5.56 a.m. Calculator. 8 x 270 = 2,160. Hanna's phone was still, strictly speaking, on bedtime mode and so did not automatically show her any of the notifications that had come in overnight. Hanna had always, ever since school, woken up before her alarm. It didn't matter what time it was set for – she would beat it by at least ten minutes. If she had to catch a train, she'd wake up a cool half-hour before her alarm. If she was going to hospital or to a wedding, it could be as much as an hour. This early morning superpower – inherited no doubt from some teat-squeezing dairy farmer in her ancestry – was of almost no practical use whatsoever.

'So, this is Sunday morning at the Bunkhouse,' Hanna said, walking into the kitchen ten minutes later, her phone tucked into the handkerchief pocket of her pyjamas, making her breasts look cockeyed.

'Yep,' replied Iain, turning to face her. 'How have you survived your first night *chez Papa*? I hope I didn't wake you when I got back in last night.' Iain left a significant pause. Then added, 'Alone. As per our agreement.' He was at the kitchen counter in a pair of cargo shorts, a cashmere jumper and nothing on his feet. Iain's personal thermostat was fixed somewhere around the Siberian tundra – no doubt a result of growing up in a big house with no central heating – and his love of fresh air knew no bounds. Including through his leg hair. It was only April but Iain wore shorts whenever he could, all year round. He'd wear them to work, if they let him. Twinned with a fleece and thick woollen socks. Maybe a clipboard. Iain's knees saw more of the world than most commuters'.

'Well, it's nice to be able to put the radio on in the shower,' replied Hanna, aiming for breezy. She didn't want to bring up Tinder before breakfast and, while she'd spent two hours last night trawling property listings on Gumtree like a bounty hunter, she hadn't actually heard her father's bedsprings banging yet. In fact, after he'd left at 8 p.m. for his illicit hook-up, she hadn't heard a whisper. 'With Joe I was always too scared to flush the toilet before eight, in case I woke him up,' Hanna added. 'I even used to brush my teeth with my mouth closed to try and deaden the sound.'

'What?' said Iain, pulling a large glass jar of nuts off the shelf. There was a mixture of concern and anger on his face. 'You worried about brushing your teeth too loudly?'

'Ah, well, you know. Not worried . . .' Hanna felt suddenly annoyed. 'I was just always aware that I woke up before Joe. And I didn't want to put him in a bad mood by waking him up too early. I used to bring a thermos to bed so I could have a cup of tea in the morning without the noise of the kettle.' She faltered. Iain was looking something like stern. Typical of him, thought Hanna, scuttling away from her own hurt and turning it into anger at Iain.

He was making a mountain out of a molehill, just to give poor Joe a kicking. 'It wasn't a big deal. Joe was just a really bad sleeper and never kept regular hours. So I had to creep around a bit.' Hanna tried to give Iain a withering stare. But she was aware that under her anger was a grain of something that felt more like shame. Had she really once been so scared of upsetting her boyfriend that she'd stopped boiling the kettle in the morning, stopped humming, stopped running before work? Had she really compromised herself so much while expecting so little in return? Had she really been brought so low by that relationship?

'Dad, does the number 2,160 mean anything to you?' It was the conversational equivalent of throwing a sausage across the room to distract a humping dog. But it worked.

'Hm . . . Can you give me a clue?' said Iain, unscrewing the jar and grabbing out a handful of mixed nuts. 'Is it something to do with six circles?'

Hanna quickly strode over to the fridge and pushed her head deep in the recesses of the butter and mayonnaise shelf. For reasons that simply did not make sense, Iain had taken to cracking nuts with his teeth and then spitting them on to the top of his muesli. The trails of spit that sometimes hung between bowl and bottom lip were enough to turn the stomach of a sailor. The first time she'd seen this happen, during her last visit, Hanna had dry-retched, then begged Iain to let her crush his nuts with the edge of a kitchen knife. Or chop them. She'd even shake them to pieces with her bare hands if it meant not having to watch him dribble out spit-moist chunks of hazelnut on to his cereal every morning. But Iain 'didn't want to bother her' and promised not to spit on to her breakfast. Not wanting to embark on a passive-aggressive kitchen campaign so early into their cohabitation, nor wanting to actively call her father revolting to his face, Hanna decided to do nothing.

'Oh, it's nothing really. I was just thinking about corners and angles. The rules of trigonometry still apply in 3D, don't they?' said Hanna, waiting behind the fridge door to hear if Iain could reply or was still spluttering nut clusters into a bowl.

'Even more so,' Iain replied. His voice sounded clear, his teeth empty, so Hanna chanced a peep. He was carrying a bowl the size of a cauldron to the table. Iain was one of those men who could somehow ingest meals the size of large family pets and yet never put on weight. When she was eighteen, Hanna had found a pair of his old shorts – true 1970s originals covered in patches and burn marks – and discovered to her horror that not only did they fit her, but after carrying them downstairs to show her dad, they still fitted him.

'Anyway, what are you doing this morning?' said Hanna, snapping open the neck of a banana, while walking away from the fridge.

'I'm off for a swim,' said Iain, nodding towards the dry bag and set of goggles sitting on the kitchen table.

'Should be a good one – it hasn't rained since Tuesday so some of that flooding will have eased off.'

'Do you do that every Sunday?' asked Hanna, pulling her cardigan a little tighter across her collarbones.

'Pretty much. Come rain or shine!' said Iain, before lifting another spade's worth of muesli to his mouth. 'In winter it's really still dark at six thirty, but it's amazing how your eyes adjust to it.' She could see the muesli falling around his mouth as he talked, like the contents of a cement mixer. 'The outline of the trees, the light on the horizon—'

'I'd be afraid of rats,' Hanna said. It wasn't true – she had loved swimming in the river as a child – but just now she wanted to cut him off before the oats started to escape on to the kitchen table.

Finally, Iain swallowed. Then smiled. 'I reckon they'd be afraid of you. So anyway, what are your plans this fine Sunday? Teaching nuns the lambada? Nice walk around a landfill site? A bit of amateur parkour up a pylon?'

'I'm going to buy some tin foil,' Hanna replied. 'Then maybe a quick whistle-stop tour of the local fatbergs, if I'm lucky.'

'Are you making another crack pipe?' asked Iain, chewing on a bit of dried apricot like a horse.

'Sure,' smiled Hanna. She'd forgotten what it was like to do this. To talk nonsense with someone who knows you better than you know yourself. 'But then I was actually going to make us a roast. If you like?'

'Ah, the traditional Sunday spit-roast,' said Iain. 'No, that would be lovely. With meat?'

'If that's OK?' Hanna asked. She'd been looking for an excuse to go to the Covered Market, to see if they still hung whole dead deer and sheep from the rafters like in her childhood memory. To spot the puddles of blood and sawdust that would gather beneath those strangely gaping, hollowed-out bodies. She'd always liked the shop sign: M. Feller and Daughters. Just some old feller and his daughters. That still passed for radical feminism in the early nineties.

'Fine by me,' said Iain. 'Just make sure you get something on the bone so we can make stock.'

'To pour on the advancing army? From the battlements?' added Hanna, pushing down on the cafetière.

'Precisely. You can never have too much hot oil. I think it was Abraham Lincoln who said that.'

Stepping out into Cranham Street, Hanna felt the cold swoop down her neck like guilt. She gave a little shiver before wondering if she should go back in and change her coat. April was like that – always dressed for yesterday's weather. But she decided to press on. As much out of pride as grit because, as always, she was too aware of how she might look to any watching stranger. She didn't want anyone thinking she was indecisive or puny or weird. The fact that the only other person on the street was a white-haired man in a padded gilet carrying a copy of the *Telegraph* – a man who would hardly have noticed if Hanna had stepped out wearing a dressing gown and pair of rocket boots – didn't matter. Hanna didn't want to be judged. She'd rather be cold.

Just before she got to the Co-op, Hanna passed the familiar black railings and wooden benches of Jude the Obscure. The bile in her stomach gave a sympathetic twitch in recognition of all those Tuesdays she'd spent at their hazardous pound-a-pint nights, trying to enjoy large glasses of cold piss and pretending to be, according to her fake ID, a nineteen-year-old foreign language student called Esther. It was from here that Iain had once had to walk Hanna home after she'd misguidedly tried to stage-dive on to her friend Kevin and ended up dislocating her knee. Of course, Iain had turned up after just six minutes, carrying a length of wood with a support strut drilled in halfway down to act as a handle, and a pillow nailed to the top, that he'd just whipped up for Hanna to use as an ad hoc crutch. Of course, he'd got so swept up in the drama that he'd let Hanna's friend Luke buy him a brandy and had then treated a group of fifteen drunk seventeen-year-olds to a demonstration of how to blow smoke rings. Of course, he'd shown them the shark bite he'd got in Australia. Of course, Hanna and Iain had both tacitly agreed to tell Julie none of this and, as they'd walked through the door, had both blurted out, 'Slipped over on some soap in the toilets,' while somewhat suspiciously sucking Polos.

Hello, Han. I have a question.

Standing in the home baking aisle, Hanna looked

down at her phone with a sort of cold numbness spreading up from her rectum through her body. It was a message from Joe. Her Joe. Who was no longer Her Joe. Her heart thrashed wildly between hope, fear, affection and dread. Was he going to ask her to come home? Had he slept with someone else? Had he finally realized what they'd lost? Was he suicidal? Had he guessed her login and found her old G-Chats to Dom about fancying Ricardo from work? Would he be angry? Would he be proposing via text? Like someone giving up their gun in front of Bruce Willis, Hanna slowly sunk to the floor and dropped her shopping basket on the ground. She needed to think. On one knee, beside the bicarbonate of soda, she typed out a reply.

Hit me, sergeant.

Well, she had no idea where that had come from.

Joe is typing . . .

Three of the worst words in the world squatted across the top of Hanna's screen.

Joe is typing . . .

Medieval peasants knew nothing of purgatory. With their Black Death and terror of hell and ignorance of germs and their illiteracy, they had it easy. The millennial woman, on the other hand – her life spent hovering in the pauses between speech, her everyday existence hanging in the known silence of words coming – she really knew about limbo. She was in it every day.

The night after the big hallway argument, Hanna and Joe had lain in bed so far apart that the duvet settled in the hollow between them like a lake. Their rent had been due in a week and both had known they couldn't afford it on their own. Both had known that any of their friends who were wealthy enough to have spare bedrooms had recently filled them with howling babies and overstuffed feeding chairs. Both had known that they had two months' notice with the landlord. Both had known that Joe's parents lived in Newcastle, in a bungalow in the suburbs that smelled of fish fingers and Camel Lights. Both had known that Hanna's mum – the only parent based in London – lived in a static caravan in the middle of Epping Forest that you could only reach by car or bicycle. Back at the beginning of their relationship, Hanna had joked that if Joe ever wanted to break up with her, all he'd have to do would be to sit her down and sing, entirely a cappella, 'The Long and Winding Road' by the Beatles. They had laughed at the image of a man earnestly and dolefully singing into the face of his unsuspecting partner. But that night, the memory had pinned Hanna to the bed with grief. There had been no song, no private joke, no mutual understanding. They had been breaking up. And she, in part, had done it. But neither she nor Joe could have walked away from this. This was post-recession London and neither could afford to leave. They'd been ripping apart and yet, for weeks, they would still be sleeping together. But not sleeping together.

The message finally came: *I need the login details for the gas bill.*

This wasn't, Hanna couldn't help but notice, a question. Joe didn't 'have a question' at all. What Joe had was a complete inability to perform basic household tasks. And so, for years, Hanna had taken sole charge of every account, every renovation, every appliance, every guarantee, every meter reading, every bill. And here he was, just a week after she'd moved out, and still getting her to be Mummy and sort out his gas bill for him. *Wow.* She was furious. She hadn't quite expected this. She was raging. And bored. And disappointed. And heartbroken. Again. Lifting her basket with shaking hands, she threw a box of Bacofoil the size of a toaster on to her shopping and marched towards the checkout. What had she expected? A love note? A WhatsApp letter of apology? A bleeding heart? A little fourteen-line sonnet? No. Not really.

And yet, somehow, this message about the gas bill both confirmed and confounded all her worst feelings about the break-up. God, their life had been boring. God, he had been rubbish. God, they'd made each other unhappy. But God, she missed him. She missed the arch of his eyebrows, the weight of him on the mattress, the cups of tea he had brought her when she'd been on the phone to Southern Electric, the smell behind his ears, the surprise train tickets to the seaside he'd buy, and the way he could talk to her mum. She missed being loved and loving in return. What she'd wanted was a message saying, *I miss you warming your feet on my legs in bed.* Something tender and sad and their own. Instead, the gas bill was the perfect reminder of just how banal heartbreak could be. Losing your partner wasn't all waves crashing on harbour walls and cold baths in twilight. Sometimes it was just spare keys and gas bills and cat food and passwords. Hanna rested the shopping basket on a stack of Stella Artois.

It's my email address, she typed. *And the password is Hanna_i5_W1cked.*

She slipped the phone back into her coat pocket, determined not to look at it again until she was actually out of the shop. She felt it buzz just as she tapped her card on the reader. Hoicking the tote bag over her shoulder, she just made it on to the pavement before turning the screen up to her face.

Thanks.

Then another green bubble.

I'll try to put it in my name today.

And then a third.

But you might need to ring them and do it. It's registered to your account.

Surprise, surprise.

Outside the Jericho Café, Hanna saw a man holding open the door for someone with a buggy. His grey hair was neatly cropped. He was wearing a navy blue Harrington jacket. His legs were obscured by the buggy. In his hand was a copy of the *Guardian* and a wallet. He was probably in his late fifties. If he lived round here and bought his morning coffee from a café then he was probably pretty wealthy. The thought was spooling out of Hanna's brain like dental floss, almost entirely without her input. It was a familiar daydream. He was probably a widower. Probably lived off Waitrose ready meals and Lidl red wine. Probably knew a lot about local history and making marmalade. Fuck Joe. Maybe she could become a trophy wife. Maybe she could go live with a man like this; no mortgage, no difficult ex-wife, probably not much of a libido. They'd only need to have sex once a month. If that. They would have a big house – maybe on Southmoor Road. Too big for him to clean by himself. Far too big now all his children had moved out of home. He'd give her housekeeping money and fall asleep at 9 p.m. and listen to Brahms and do the crossword and quote plays she'd never seen, and just be thrilled to have someone young and soft around the house to make him feel like he still mattered. It would be so easy. She wouldn't have to work. He would order for her in restaurants. She wouldn't have to worry about him cheating. He would suggest books for her. He would buy her clothes. God, she might never have to make another decision again. She'd be totally looked after, totally adored, totally freed from the grinding mundanity of work, dating, hope, anxiety. She'd have someone to look after her, take away her choice, put her in a nest and just admire her superficially. Heaven.

She looked again at the wallet. Brown. Old. Oh. Strangely familiar actually. Oh dear. She'd seen that wallet somewhere else. The man glanced over his shoulder to check that the buggy lady had made it on to the pavement. A wave of ice swept across Hanna's skin. Sweet mother of suffering clots. It was Iain. Iain in a new jacket. He'd had his hair cut and bought a new coat. She hadn't recognized him. Now the pram had moved away she could see his stupid hairy legs and those disgusting cargo shorts. Iain had been the lonely widower with a massive house and overstuffed bank account. She'd been unknowingly contemplating having once-a-month sex with her father in return for a clothing allowance and canal-side garden. Great. Now she'd have to give herself a lobotomy with a kebab skewer when she got home. Just after she'd wasted all that money on tin foil.

Iain caught her eye and waved. 'I'm just getting you one of those custard pies you like!' he shouted.

What a clown.

Hanna's phone vibrated in her coat pocket, like the twitch of a tired eye. Maybe it would be Joe, she thought, so quickly there was no time for her rational brain to intervene. Maybe the whole gas bill thing had been a cover for his failing courage in the moment. Maybe he was about to ask her to move back; to zoom away from her hobbit-legged, Tinder-swiping, nut-crunching father, and come home.

Hello, Hanna. This is Dave, from the room advert. Hanna blinked. *Did you want to come and look at it? A few other people have been in touch.*

Yes. When were you thinking? Hanna typed, before her indecision could crystallize into inaction. Then she deleted the second sentence of the message and wrote,

What time? More assertive. More professional. She stood outside a fancy dress shop, beside a stand of Prince Philip and Boris Johnson masks, and watched the screen for a reply.

Well, I'll actually be at the flat until 3 p.m. if you want to come now? Dave was keen. Or perhaps Dave was a murderer.

What's the address please? Hanna's texting tone of voice seemed to be sliding away from professionally assertive and into angry teacher.

14 Regent Street, OX4 7JD. Just ring the bell. Or call – in case I don't hear it.

If she dropped the food off at Iain's and walked over now, calculated Hanna, she could get to the flat in twenty-five minutes. Within half an hour she might just have found a way out of Iain's spare bedroom. She started running.

4

Wooden Bangle

'Oh hey, are you Sarah?' The man standing at the door was wearing a pair of red batik trousers with a folded gusset that hung, nappy-like, around his knees. The infamous Thai fisherman trouser – an article of clothing loved by gap year students, post-partum mothers, middle-aged festivalgoers wading through a particularly nasty case of haemorrhoids, and nobody else.

'Yes. I mean, no. Sorry if I'm a bit out of breath,' said Hanna, holding her side like a teapot. 'I got a stitch at Merton Street that's been pinching me the whole way here.' She was trying very hard not to look at the small crop of pubes edging out over the man's low-slung waistband. 'I brought you a packet of Hobnobs.'

'Ah-mazing . . .' There was a small, awkward pause. 'My mum always buys these.'

Hanna walked to the top of the stairs, holding the biscuits like a dagger.

'So, are you Sarah?' he repeated.

'Oh, right! No. I'm Hanna. You just rang me about fifteen minutes ago, saying I could come and have a viewing?' Dave hadn't moved back into the hallway as Hanna had expected, but stayed stock still at the top of the steps, meaning they were now standing so close that she could smell his coffee breath. There was a slight tang of something beneath it that could have been onion and could have been marijuana.

'Oh, sorry, right. Sarah was the woman who was meant to be coming this afternoon, too.' Dave scratched the line of pubes absentmindedly. 'But actually the room's just been taken?' The moronic inflection almost annoyed Hanna more than what he was saying.

'Taken? But it's been . . .' She checked her watch. 'It's been seventeen minutes.'

'Oh yeah!' Dave chuckled as though 'seventeen minutes' was an old private joke the two of them shared. 'But my housemate's boyfriend, Caspar? He just said that he'll actually take the room? Which is great, actually. Caspar's a legend.'

At which point, Hanna grabbed Dave by the pubes and dropped him into the nearest wheelie bin, followed by a sack of cold baked beans. At least, that was the image that clicked over in her head as she walked home, the sweaty patch from her rucksack turning cold against her back. The injustice, the disappointment, the shame. Had she really just run across the city to try and secure a poxy little room in a dank, probably vermin-infested dosshouse, full of people who listened to Mr Scruff, burnt joss sticks and used lemon juice to bleach their fringes? She wiped a tear off her red cheek. Her first chance of escape from her dad's flat and it had already been whipped away before she'd had a chance to take off her jacket.

'Life is much harder for my generation,' Hanna said the next morning, whipping a pair of black trousers through the air like an angry matador. 'Trawling property sites, preparing for job interviews that go nowhere, dating apps.' She accidentally slammed a shirt against the side of the bath, possibly cracking a button, before hanging it, and a pair of orange knickers, over the wooden rack. 'You spend hours every day just trying to push open the doors that everybody else has already walked through ahead of you.' She wrenched at the rope that lifted the drying rack above the bath on a pulley system. The whole thing – designed and of course installed by Iain when he first moved in – rose into the air to hang like a particularly unlikely set of bunting.

'I'm sorry, pickle,' said Iain, who had been leaning on the doorjamb, watching the whole dhobi wallah impression unfold. 'I'm sure something will turn up. When I first graduated—'

'That's just it!' interrupted Hanna. 'Your generation never went through this. You don't understand. Job hunting, flat hunting, dating; they're all much more depleting emotionally, psychologically, physically and financially than the end result. Flat hunting is way harder than paying rent and dating is much worse than being in a relationship. But you never did any of it.'

'Well, I th—'

'When you graduated you could basically buy a house for the price of a cheese and pickle sandwich, and there were loads of jobs – or at least, the jobs that were available were real jobs, not internships in Dubai masquerading as employment. And you didn't date. You just, I don't know, "took someone to the pictures", bought them a port and lemon, and then six months later got married.'

'I met your mother at a Grace Jones concert where we were both trying to score cocaine,' interjected Iain.

'OK, fine. But my point stands,' said Hanna, after taking just a microsecond to add this Grace Jones story to her list of Dinner Party Parent Anecdotes. 'It's much, much harder now.' Her phone buzzed flatulently on the side of the bath. It was an Oxford number she didn't recognize.

'Hello?' said Hanna, trying to sound both enthusiastic and enquiring. She body-slammed past Iain, suddenly embodying Jed Bartlet in *The West Wing*; hoping that some corridor momentum might make her sound authoritative and give her the auspicious boost she needed. She only managed six steps before she hit the front door, but as she turned around and walked back to Iain, her face was breaking out into a cautious smile. She swept past him, power-walking towards the kitchen in a pair of tracksuit bottoms and one of his old New Order T-shirts. 'Yes, of course. I can post the originals to you if you like. Or bring them in in person. I'm only around the corner, in Jericho.' He watched her slow down towards the kitchen, then, like an Olympic swimmer executing a perfect flip turn, she lifted one leg, pushing through with her foot, whirled 180 degrees and started marching back past the bathroom. 'By the end of the week. Great! Lovely. Ah, thank you so much, Annabel, for letting me know.'

She stopped just before the coat rack and spun round.

'Dad! I think I've got the job!' she cried, not sure whether to jump in the air, run to her dad for a hug, bow or knee-slide down the corridor into the toilet.

'Hoooooooeeeeeee!' Iain cried out, like someone shouting an echo under a motorway bridge. 'Which one?' Hanna wondered if he was about to lift her up in the air and catch her like he had when she'd done her first poo in the potty.

'Events at the Natural History Museum!' said Hanna. 'It's the only one I actually wanted.' The two of them were now standing in the hallway, three metres away from each other, shifting their arms awkwardly and unsure what to do with their hands.

'Gadzooks!' shouted Iain, resting one hand on his shoulder and the other on the top of his head.

'Yeah,' said Hanna, pulling at the hem of her T-shirt and holding the other hand just above her head in a sort of semi-fist. Iain stepped forward and – without either quite knowing what was coming – slapped his hand on her shoulder in congratulation. Hanna, misinterpreting that initial gesture as an oncoming hug, scooped her arm through the air only to find Iain still standing at her elbow.

'Thanks,' said Hanna, taking a step back, suddenly very aware that she wasn't wearing a bra. 'Yeah. It's great. I did the interview before I moved but because I hadn't heard back, I just assumed I hadn't got it.' Her smile started to fade. 'The only thing is, they want a copy of my degree certificate and birth certificate before I can start. They say it's university policy – the medieval weirdos need to see original copies. I suppose I'm lucky they don't want them on vellum. But I have absolutely no idea where they are. I'm not even sure if I have them.'

Iain frowned. He'd given up his place at Hanna's graduation so Julie's elderly mother Ethel could go and watch her only grandchild graduate. They both knew the degree certificate was unlikely to have made its way back to his flat.

'I might have a copy of your birth certificate. I know we got quite a few done, in case.' Iain stepped into the lounge and headed for one of the black ash veneer bookcases. He pulled down a blue box file labelled 'Certificates' and flipped through to the section marked H. 'Yep. Got it here,' he said, pulling out a small square of brown paper with a red stamped crest at the top. *Hanna Electra Markhouse. Sex: Female. Date of Birth: 17 November 1987. Place of Birth: Headington, Oxon.* 'But I'm afraid there's no degree certificate.' They both looked up from the box file. The deep furrows between

Iain's eyebrows became momentarily more defined. 'I think you're going to have to ask Julie.'

'Ask Mum to find my degree certificate?' Hanna's voice turned shrill with panic.

'She might know where it is,' said Iain, unconvincingly.

'Are you joking? Mum can't find her own feet in that caravan, let alone my degree certificate.'

'Well, you could call back and explain that—'

'No,' interjected Hanna. 'I'm not risking this job by being difficult. I can't start pissing about before I've even had my induction. I'll just have to go to Mum's and look for it myself.' She ran her hands through the hair, scraping it off her face. 'It'll be fine. I need to see Mum anyway.'

Stepping off the train at Chingford, Hanna walked straight into the smell-cloud of a middle-aged man in a pair of chinos and pale blue shirt that looked like it had been sprayed on to him as he bench-pressed a moose. Over the shirt was, of course, a waistcoat – no, let's be honest, a grey polyester corset – with a plunging neckline. His hair was dyed, his shoes stuck out like trowels, and he was vaping on something that looked like an MS-DOS computer. The smell was a mixture of disinfectant, caramel, and the squeezed anal gland of an unsuspecting mammal. He must have poured his aftershave on from a tap. Hanna forced a polite smile, flicked a quick look up to his sandy-coloured roots and walked on past him to the ticket barrier.

When she had rung Julie, asking her mother to look for her degree certificate, Julie had sounded particularly distracted and dreamy. It had been like trying to hang a coat on a marshmallow. Every time she thought she'd got the request and its urgency across, her mother would say something like, 'So darling, did I tell you about Mary's wonderful new sculpture course?' and she'd have to start again. Eventually, tears of frustration pricking at her eyes, Hanna had barked, 'Mum. Do you have my degree certificate: yes or no?'

'Oh, I don't know, darling. Maybe you could come for the weekend and have a rifle through the loft yourself. Wouldn't that be lovely? To finally spend some time together.'

The 'finally' had nearly ripped Hanna's molar in two. It didn't matter how often she rang her mother, how frequently she visited, how long she stayed; every time Julie would act like someone stranded on a North Sea oil platform, hearing only from loved ones twice a year.

And so here she was. Setting off to walk across two miles of ancient woodland to retrieve her degree certificate. Hanna always chose to walk to the caravan park where her mother currently lived rather than catch the bus from nearby Loughton. Just to remind herself that there was some positive to having a parent living in a field surrounded by chalets, every one in three of which was hung with a Union Jack. At least the racists and septic tanks were surrounded by beautiful trees, grassy hills, holly bushes and secret streams. Julie called it a 'park home', of course. But frankly, if it looks like a caravan, creaks like a caravan and flushes like a caravan, then it's a caravan. And this was a caravan. Julie had moved to the Falcon Park Home Estate the year she divorced Iain. She'd wanted, in typical oxymoronic fashion, to be closer to London and also closer to nature. She'd wanted to live in a community but not to have any neighbours. She'd wanted a garden and a wood-burning stove and also to be in Zone 1 in less than an hour. Most importantly, she'd not wanted a mortgage. And so a pale blue box in the middle of a wood in Essex, beside a gastro pub and the helipad for London Ambulances, had been, to her alone, the obvious choice.

'Darling! You came! I thought you might have got lost.'

Julie threw open her arms, setting off an earthquake of clonking wooden bangles. She was wearing a pair of solar system print leggings, white men's Donnay sports socks with a greenish silver ankle chain, and some bright red Birkenstocks.

'Nearly. But then I trapped and saddled up a muntjac deer, and when I whispered your name in its ear, it brought me here,' said Hanna, stepping on to the patio between two giant pots of rosemary.

'Did you really catch a deer?' Her mother's eyes were sparkling.

'Mum. Come on.' Hanna could never quite be sure if Julie was truly credulous or just not really listening.

'Oh, don't be like that, darling. You've just got here,' said Julie, looking crestfallen. Hanna felt a stab of guilt and irritation. 'I've just made some nettle tea – to cleanse the blood – or there's white wine.' It was 10.27 a.m.

'Do you have any regular, heterosexual, semi-detached tea?' asked Hanna.

'I might have a bag of Yorkshire kicking about.'

'Peace be upon you.'

Julie's kitchen was a mixture of a storage container, nursery, ashram, wholefood shop and Francis Bacon's painting studio. There was a row of seedlings along the windowsill, interspersed with costume jewellery, crystals and hand-carved wooden idols. There were photos of Hanna everywhere: stuck to the fridge, in frames on every wall, tucked into the seams of kitchen cupboards, printed on to aprons. There was even a baby photo of Hanna with her mouth open in a scream sellotaped to the bottom of the dustpan.

'So, to what do we owe the pleasure?' said Julie, handing Hanna a mug covered in butterflies.

'We?' Hanna was genuinely unsure if her mother was lapsing into the royal use of the plural, or if this was her way of telling her that there was a strange man asleep in the other room.

'Well, me and Max,' said Julie. Max was a Burmese cat so decrepit and toothless that for the last six months Julie had been feeding him salmon paste off a teaspoon and carrying him to a litter tray five times a day. He was more of a memento mori than a pet.

'Oh, OK. I thought for a second you were going to announce that you'd met someone,' laughed Hanna. 'Some twenty-five-year-old Brazilian mindfulness tutor who lives in a horse box next door.'

'Who, Paolo? He's just a friend.'

Hanna's nostrils fluttered in panic. She shot her mother a look.

'You're not the only one who can make jokes, Squidge,' said Julie, triumph spreading across her face like sunshine. 'But really, is this just a social call?'

'Mum, I told you on the phone!' said Hanna, sounding like an exasperated primary school teacher bollocking the class for not putting the lids back on their felt tips. 'I've been offered a new job but they need to see my birth certificate and degree certificate first.'

'Certificates?' Julie said the word like someone asked to hold a mouse dropping in their mouth. 'Oh God. We're going to have to go up to the loft.' She tucked a wisp of her curly brown hair back into its bulldog clip and ran her hands down her face. 'You know I'm terrified of going up there on my own. And it's hard having to climb up through the shower.'

'It's fine, I'll do it,' said Hanna. 'It's my fault for leaving it with you anyway.' Julie smiled.

In the small lavender bathroom Hanna looked across the wicker baskets of Julie's toiletries. She slowly unscrewed the lid of some Pond's cold cream. Suddenly, she was standing in her granny's bedroom, in Herefordshire. Hanna breathed deeply into the pot. Hosepipe fights, Golden Retrievers, raspberries from the garden, pop socks, meat gravy, court shoes and *Channel 4 Racing*; the smell brought her grandmother to her and around her and in her. Another single woman. This time due to widowhood rather than heartbreak. Uncomplaining, undemonstrative, unbreakable; Ethel had had self-esteem. True self-worth. Not a sense of comfort tethered to a man, or a relationship. No wonder her eldest, Julie, could live in a tin box in the middle of nowhere; she had learned what independence really meant. And it didn't mean having your own bank account and occasionally going away for the weekend with a group of girlfriends. Independence meant sitting up against the raw, grinding edge of loneliness, for years, and not letting it beat you. It meant plumbing in your own washing machine, checking your own back for moles, booking your own train tickets and writing your own will. It meant crying into a handkerchief, washing it in the bath, and pegging it outside on a line you had strung up yourself.

Hanna needed to find that grit. Knocked off-kilter by the long, slow break-up with Joe, her sense of self, her confidence and her self-worth had been dragged into the mud. She felt lost. But she needed to find herself. Without Joe's company, support, conversation, tastes, irritations, cooking, music and dislikes, she felt blank and unsure about the world. She'd applied for twenty-seven jobs because, without a counterpart there to tell her otherwise, she didn't really know what she wanted to do. She'd eaten half a block of cheddar and two apples for lunch yesterday because, without a partner to suggest something, she hadn't known what she wanted to eat. It was heartbreak, she knew. But she needed to get over it. At least Julie was a whole person. It had been seven years since she'd divorced Iain, in which time they'd never fallen out, never squabbled about money, and never contemplated getting back together. Hanna had to work out who she was, in order to stop feeling like just somebody's ex. Like Julie and Ethel, Hanna would never be truly free until she became truly independent.

'I found it,' said Hanna, walking back into the kitchen forty-five minutes later, dust tickling down the back of her neck. 'It was folded in an ice cream tub with "Boring Shit" written across the lid in felt tip,' she added, brushing cobwebs from her shirt. 'So thanks for that.'

'Oh, you're welcome, Squidge,' said Julie, either ignoring or unaware of Hanna's tone. 'Now, are you sure you can't stay for tea? I could read you P. G. Wodehouse and we could play cards?' Hanna was sorely tempted. To lie on her mother's sofa and be read to would be so lovely, but the trip back across London and out west to Oxford was already going to take at least four hours.

'Sorry, Mum, but I should probably leave now if I don't want to spend hours stuck in traffic outside Hillingdon.'

'Well, please take these for the journey then,' said Julie, handing Hanna a tote bag full of old takeaway boxes.

Hanna had a look at the top two – cold lasagne, carrot sticks, cucumber sliced into batons, homemade apricot and almond biscuits, grapes. God knows what would be on the bottom tier. Homemade humous? Spiced rat? Magic mushrooms?

'Oh my god, are you sure? Mum, this looks amazing. It looks like you've made my lunch for the week.'

'Well, you're probably not going to have time to do much cooking with the new job,' said Julie, her lipstick bleeding into the wrinkles around her mouth as she smiled. So she had been listening, after all.

'Mum . . .' Hanna felt the words tumble out of her mouth before she'd had a chance to form them in her head. 'Do you have any, um, spare money?'

Julie looked confused. 'For the train?' She reached towards a coat hanging on the back of one of the kitchen chairs.

'No.' Hanna knew she was blushing now. 'I really don't want to stay at Iain's any longer than I have to, but to rent somewhere I need money upfront . . .' Julie's hand rested on the hood of the coat. 'I'd need about three thousand pounds: so I can pay a deposit and the first month's rent. And the signing fee. And I'm not going to get my first paycheque for a month and . . .' Hanna's eyes fell to the floor.

'I'm sorry, darling,' said Julie, in a great whooshing-out breath. 'I don't have that at the moment. I had to spend seven hundred pounds getting a leak fixed in the roof this winter, and since I lost my regular Thursdays at the Purple Temple I've had to use my savings to live on.'

Hanna felt horrendous. She shouldn't have asked her mum for money like this, over a carrier bag of crudités and homemade dahl. Actually, she shouldn't have had to ask her mother for money at all. She was thirty, for God's sake. She was meant to be an independent woman.

'But I do have this pair of candlesticks, from Iain's mother,' said Julie, walking over to a set of shelves covered in jam jars and china dogs. 'You could try selling them? They're probably tat but maybe at an antiques auction?' As she lifted the brass candlesticks, one of the bases rolled off the shelf and hit the floor with a metallic ring.

'Oh shit, that's right,' tutted Julie. 'They're broken actually. Probably not worth much any more.'

Walking down one of the great tree-lined avenues back to the station, gritting her teeth with the effort not to look at her phone, hair tucked behind her ears to better hear the birds above her, Hanna's eye was caught by a shaking patch of leaves to her left. A large brown lump lolloped out through the branches. Head like a mouse, body like a dog, legs and flashing white tail like a hare; muntjac deer, thought Hanna, looked like the kind of animal that would result if she were asked to draw a deer from memory. Suddenly, catching Hanna's scent, the deer looked up sharply. Their eyes met. And for a few seconds, there in the middle of the forest, the two little brown-haired mammals stared at each other. One panting, the other too scared to breathe. Hanna could hear sticks creaking above her head as squirrels leaped from branch to branch. She could smell the faint sweetness of blossom as it started to push through the sticky buds. She felt the grass lumping and slippery beneath her feet. She smiled. And, catching the movement on Hanna's face, the muntjac threw its head over its shoulder and bounded back into the trees.

Time to go home. Whatever that meant.

5
Swimming Towel

A pink dawn was breaking over the rooftops of Oxford like strawberry milk. And some thundering middle-aged wanker in a green batik waistcoat was playing a fiddle on the steps of the Bodleian Library.

Disdain surged through Hanna. She heard herself tutting like a dentist examining a particularly nasty bit of plaque. What was it that brought out this feeling in her? While the rest of the city was thronging with spring fever and good grace, she was cycling through town like some disapproving member of the Politburo. She loved May Morning. Loved the dawn chorus, the singing on Magdalen Bridge, the children turning up to school wide-eyed with insomnia and cider, the bacchanalia of people kissing in the streets. It was just the cheesecloth shorts and penny whistle brigade that brought her out in hives. Clive, one of her dad's folk-night friends, had once spent an entire May Morning standing just a little too close to her, talking about poetry and not so subtly staring down her top. He'd been playing one of those stupid drums that you're meant to thrub-a-dub with something that looks like a child's rattle, and was wearing a CND badge on a T-shirt just tight enough to show the nipple piercing on his flaccid man tit. His earnest, wholefood leering over her adolescent body had left her feeling somehow greasy, like she'd been sprayed with sunflower oil or slid over by a snail. He was revolting. It was revolting.

Passing under the Bridge of Sighs and wheeling around the corner of Radcliffe Square into Broad Street, Hanna passed a group of university students in mud-smeared ball gowns throwing up gang signs to a friend with an iPhone the size of a tea tray. Barely registering their satin folds and glossy hair, Hanna kept pedalling and turned left into Beaumont Street. She was going to Port Meadow for a swim. When she'd been a teenager, and too frightened of hallucinogens to really throw herself into the free party scene, this had become her little May Morning ritual. Wake up before dawn, listen to the singing by Magdalen Bridge with a can of gin and tonic, then cycle through the city to have a dip in the bracing, duck shit-coloured river. She hadn't been in Oxford on May Morning for over a decade but cycling through the city now, she was excited. Picking up the old habit was both an act of nostalgia and adventure. By now, the streets of Jericho were bathed in a golden morning light, and people in linen aprons were scraping garden tables out on to the pavement or shaking out ashtrays.

She freewheeled the last hundred metres down from the old Lucy ironworks and manoeuvred her bike through the kissing gate on to the grass. Looking out across the flat green plain of Port Meadow, small twists of smoke rising from the few boats moored along the western bank of the river, Hanna felt that nagging need to share the moment with someone. For six years, Joe had been her person. Like so many post-Millennium couples, Hanna and Joe had used each other as part archivist, part audience, part hype man. Any moment of drama or achievement, any site of particular beauty or interest, any thought, any view, she had shared it with him. And he with her. They had sent each other thousands of photos, voice notes and messages over the years. And received praise, admiration and attention in return. In Joe she'd had a repository for her life, as it had happened. She'd had a witness, a companion, a record. He'd been there to reinforce and recognize the tiny details of her existence. Without this, she felt at a loss. What was she meant to do with this view now? This moment? Just walk through it? Breathe in the air, watch the birds, and tell nobody? Was that how other people lived? Carrying the incidences of their lives around in their pockets, privately, to be forgotten or put down when the next one came along? Bullshit. She wanted this fleeting experience to mean something. And it would only mean something, surely, if other people knew it had happened. And so, she took a photo. And when she'd had her swim, she would post it on Instagram, alongside a wet-haired selfie. And people she didn't know would double tap it. And her brain would release a little squeeze of dopamine. And that would do. She didn't have a boyfriend any more. But she did have 1,378 followers.

Clanking through the cattle gate, Hanna saw the swimming spot she'd had in mind. A little bay between two trees, lined with unripened blackberry bushes, it was one of the few parts of the bank that slid down gently into the water. Sand coated her feet as she tried, with all the elegance of a mule, to pull off her knickers under the Ariel the Mermaid towel she'd found at the bottom of the airing cupboard. It had been her beach towel when she was about twelve and, like anything that wasn't actually on fire or eaten by stray dogs, her father had kept it as a back-up. Iain had in fact invited her along to join the Dodo Club this morning for their group dip, but Hanna wanted to swim on her own. Not to spite Iain – well, not entirely – but because she didn't want to feel the pressure of other people's chutzpah. She didn't want to be chivvied into the water by some uni-bosomed headteacher with a voice like a foghorn and shoulders like roofing beams. She would swim. She knew she would. But she would do it in her own time.

The cold hit her like a whip. As her heart slid under the water, a jolt ran through her body, along her scalp, through her lungs and over her neck. It felt like panic, like pain, like joy. A pair of ducks skidded in to land just metres away and she realized that her inner monologue had finally fallen silent. For a moment, she thought of nothing. Not Joe, not starting her new job, not her luscious crop of neck hairs. Nothing. She felt her muscles tense and stretch, the blood rush to the surface of her skin, and the air in her throat squeeze out. *Well, look at me*, she thought. And then her foot brushed against something pulpy, the vision of a dead hand filled her brain and she scrambled out, retching.

Just as she was towelling off her hair, standing on the grass in a bra and jeans, a topless man walked past. There is a particular curve at the bottom of a man's stomach that, on the right body, acts like a giant arrow. Strictly speaking, it's called a groin. But for Hanna, who'd had the pleasure of studying the history of medicine for GCSE, it was hard ever to say the word 'groin' without immediately then thinking of 'buboes', followed quickly by 'the plague'. But this groin. This groin was something else. The man had the sort of thickened body that spoke of carbohydrates, whole milk, camping, toolboxes, rolling tobacco and salted butter. His neck and shoulders were large, defined and smooth. A thick fuzz of warm brown hair lay across the two large pads of his chest, tapering to a point above his belly button. She could see freckles on his arms, a Casio watch at his wrist and, God help her, a scar like a crooked smile across his shoulder. Hanna threw her hair back in a pond-water approximation of a hundred shampoo adverts and met the man's gaze.

Well, hell. It was Tom Moss. From Year 10 English. Tom Moss, who had taught her how to roll cigarettes, dared her to climb a tree in Shotover woods in the dark, and had once made her a mixtape titled *Into Your Arms*. Tom Moss, who had suddenly in Year 12 taken up running, sculpted a new and perfect body out of his soft childish dough, aced all his exams despite appearing to listen to nothing a single teacher said, and then had disappeared to Spain to grow tomatoes. Tom Moss, who had once carried her home from a house party over his shoulder after she'd got accidentally white-wine drunk and cried. Tom Moss, who had never had a girlfriend but had once turned up to the Turf Tavern with a twenty-three-year-old Classics student called Eleanor who had stood with her hand in his back pocket the whole evening, drinking whisky, and then was never seen again. Tom Moss, who had once held Hanna's chin between his finger and thumb and told her she was far prettier than she knew. Tom Moss, who had let her sleep in his bed on New Year's Eve and had woken her with a cup of tea and a samosa but had never kissed her. Tom Moss. Tom. Moss.

As their eyes met, Tom ripped out his headphones and shouted, 'Hannacopter?!'

'Tomato!' she replied, suddenly aware that this was not her best bra and that her waistband was probably creating an overspill around her belly button.

'What are you doing here?' he asked, bounding over to her in three long, lolloping strides.

'I've just moved back!' Hanna said, throwing her arms high into the air, both in excitement and an attempt to stretch out her concertinaed midriff. Tom had clearly misread the arm signal and so grabbed her around the waist and lifted her off the ground in a hug. Her nipple edged up the lace cup of her bra and she felt her areola brush against his hard, slightly damp collarbone. When he put her down, there was an unreadable smile across his mouth. Had he felt her nipple? Was he smirking? Was he embarrassed? Pleased? Totally unaware? 'What are you doing here?' she asked, bending down to pick up her jumper, unthinkingly rising up on to her toes.

'I work in Jericho. At Jericho Bikes? So this is my walk to work. Pretty sweet, right?' He swept his arm across the horizon, like a laird displaying his estate. A Friesian cow on the other bank started moving down to the edge of the river, swinging its hips with the funny, ungainly walk of something with fourteen litres of spare milk storage hanging between its legs.

'Wow, lucky you. I've just been for a swim!' she said, as if trying to one-up him on the topless rugged front. She waited for his exclamations of awe. Wasn't that why people swam outdoors? For the praise and approval?

'Hannacopter, you were always so gnarly,' he said. 'Like, none of the other Cheney girls would ever go swimming in here.' Hanna disliked being told she was 'unlike other women'. It was usually said by men who had never taken more than thirty seconds to get to know an adult woman. It was usually said after she'd done something fairly prosaic like carry a bike up a set of stairs or grouted some kitchen tiles. It was usually intended as a compliment, but only really had the effect of making her feel slightly freakish or seriously misunderstood. Men who told you that 'you're not like the other girls' needed to spend some time with the other girls and get a bloody clue. And yet, somehow, the way Tom said it was different. Something about the way he called them 'the other Cheney girls', used her old nickname, separated her out from their secondary school contemporaries, felt like a mark of affection, nostalgia, shared history. In his eyes, Hanna was both the topless, wet-haired woman in front of him and the eleven-year-old, fifteen-year-old and eighteen-year-olds she'd once been. In that way, it was more an act of recognition than a hollow compliment.

'Are you walking back this way?' he asked. Hanna nodded vigorously. 'Then let's walk together! Unless you're, like, in a rush or something?' he said, gesturing towards the crumpled Ariel the Mermaid towel beside her feet. Thanks to a strategically placed fold, it now looked like the flame-haired siren was trying to sniff her own armpits.

'Ah, no. No rush,' Hanna answered, wondering if she needed to explain the towel. If now was the time to mention that she was living in her dad's spare room and sleeping under a Jungle Book duvet cover on a single bed. If Tom would be pleased or disinterested to hear that she had just broken up with her boyfriend. If she should mention that last night she'd played Scrabble with a fifty-five-year-old man and gone to bed at 8.47 p.m. Probably not.

They walked back along the towpath, Hanna pushing her bike, Tom walking beside her, bouncing a little in his skate trainers. At Bossoms Boatyard the path thinned and he stepped behind her, falling into single file. *I wonder if he's looking at my bum.* She wouldn't know what to do with it even if he was. After so many years with Joe she'd almost forgotten what it was like to have your body studied by another man; well, a man you liked. She had no idea what combination of tensing or pushing would make her bum look best. For most of her life, her bum was just something that followed her around. Suddenly, she pictured the half-moon curves at the bottom of her buttocks curling up in a creepy smile at Tom as she walked. Where had that come from?

It was just then that they saw the pony. Walking slowly along the thin strip of towpath by Fiddler's Island, it had no harness and no saddle. It was entirely alone, swaying its head back and forth and whinnying in distress. How the hell had it got here? Surely it hadn't pushed open the two gates at either end of the bridge? And not even the worst kind of Bullingdon Club mega-melt would bother kidnapping a horse, only to leave it here, on a strip of gravel, out of sight and miles from the nearest road. Could it really have walked over the high red arch of Medley Footbridge? But why? If she'd been on her own, Hanna suspected that she might simply have walked past this unhappy horse. She would have looked around, assumed somebody else was in charge and sloped guiltily off to work. But with Tom there, she felt a call to act. Bravado, sympathy and adrenaline gathered into her muscles, and she quickly leaned her bike against the chain-link fence to her right.

'Poor thing. I'd better move it,' she heard herself saying, as if she were the obvious candidate for such a task. 'Don't worry, my grandad was a vet,' said that voice again. Who was this person? What was she planning? The pony was only little but it was looking Hanna right in the eye, its tail swishing in the dust motes of the morning sun. Hanna very calmly took off her jumper and walked towards the horse. She started talking gently, making the soft, clicking noises she remembered from trips round the field at the bottom of her grandad's garden, and stroked a firm, if slightly shaky, hand across its thick, fuzzy neck.

'You a bit lost, are you, pal?' she said in that funny sing-song questioning voice people use when talking to an unknown animal, or a potentially dangerous stranger on a night bus. Quickly, but without flapping, she pulled one sleeve of her jumper over the neck of the pony and under its chin, making a loop around its head. It gave a little snort, shook its mane and did a quick two-step back and forth.

'Come on then, petal. Let's be moving,' she said in that same voice, which seemed touched with an accent that wasn't quite her own. She gave the jumper a gentle tug, leaned into the horse's shoulder with her own and, miraculously, it got the message. It started to walk, casual as a Saturday morning supermarket shopper, back towards the bridge. 'Open the gate, please, Tom,' she said, just before they got to the wooden gangway. A look of awe flashed across Tom's face and he raced ahead, pulling open the swing gate. Hanna and her new fetlocked friend walked calmly up the ramp, squeezed through the gate and on to the bridge. The wobbly planks seemed to slightly unsettle the pony and, as it tugged its head and gave a stamp, Hanna realized that physically she would be no match if it bolted. But she held the sleeves firm and, after a few seconds, she and the pony started to clop evenly across the bride.

As her feet hit the soft, spongy ground on the other side of the bridge, she let go of one of the sleeves and slid the jumper back off the pony's neck. It stood there. It turned its head into Hanna's elbow, then turned back. They both stared at the spindly paths that led to Walton Well car park and the miles of Granny Smith green on their left-hand side.

'Go on then!' said Hanna. 'Off you go!'

The pony didn't move.

'Come on,' she said, and gave the pony a loud, triumphant slap on the bum. It worked. The pony gave a grunt and trotted off to join the rest of the herd munching around on the meadow. For a second Hanna had a pang of guilt – she really hoped it was a Port Meadow horse and not somebody's prize pet that she'd just accidentally set loose. Oh well. At least it wasn't trapped on a riverside corridor with no food any more.

She turned back and strolled towards Tom, trying to keep her cowboy swagger to a minimum.

'Sorry about that,' she said, her face a picture of faux modesty.

'That was . . . Fuck. That was the coolest thing I've ever seen!' said Tom. 'Hanna . . . that was . . .' He followed her back across the bridge, his hands raking through his curly brown hair, his biceps bulging around his ears.

She smiled. The absurdity of the situation started to hit home; her wet hair, bumping into Tom Moss, the gin now tickling through her veins, her exposed bra, the lost pony. It was ludicrous. She had just stripped to the waist and walked a wild animal across a rickety bridge before breakfast. She had just shown her bra to Tom Moss twice in twelve minutes. Her hands started to shake and her teeth rattled. It was just the delayed shock from the cold river, she knew. But when she went to pick up her bag, her fingers slipped across the strap and it landed in a pile of dust.

'Here,' said Tom, lifting the bag up for her.

'Thanks,' said Hanna, turning round so he could slip it on to her shoulders.

'Umm, don't you want to put your top back on first?' said Tom, the bag hanging in mid-air.

They both burst out laughing. Hanna laughed so hard she could feel the lace cup of her bra start to creep dangerously lower. She laughed so much her eyes filled with tears. Tom's heavy shoulders and broad stomach shook. She remembered how they'd laughed together during those endless, hideous lessons on electromagnetism in Dr Erdem's freezing science classroom; sitting so close that she'd been able to feel the entire length of his thigh against her own. She remembered how he'd laughed like a drain when she'd tried to do a cartwheel aged seventeen, and ended up ripping open the flies of her school trousers. She remembered how he'd then taken out his shoelace and helped her tie the waistband back together, his fingers brushing against the top of her knickers, a smile curling at his lips. She remembered the way he'd laughed when she'd called him a misogynistic piece of shit because he'd bought a copy of *FHM* to read on the coach the day they went to London to join the march against the Iraq war. She remembered the way that his face used to crumple when he laughed, so his freckles would almost meet his eyelashes.

Still reeling at the turn her day had taken, at the wild, unlikely flavour of this May Morning, she turned back to Tom and pulled on her jumper, feeling its neckline pop over her forehead and tear-damp eyes. She tilted her face up to meet his. God, he was tall. He'd been tall at school, but never like this. Now he was big. Fulsome. Sturdy. She felt a powerful urge to bury her face into the soft curls of his chest, to bite his shoulder, to push herself against him. But instead she just stood there. Looking up at him. Silhouetted in sunshine, his eyelashes just catching the light.

'We should go for a drink,' he said, rubbing a flat hand against the exact spot on his chest that seconds earlier Hanna had been mentally burrowing her face into.

'Yeah, we should!' said Hanna.

'I mean, like, I actually finish work at six today. Just round the corner . . .' He tailed off. It wasn't quite a question, not entirely an invitation. He wasn't asking her out. But he wasn't not asking her out either. Screaming with hope, desperate to answer, Hanna forced herself to hold the silence. To make him say it. 'We could go to the Gardeners Arms? They've got a garden.' Hanna gripped the straps on her bag until her knuckles turned white. She could do it. If she could just say nothing for a few seconds more. If she could just hold this moment with her silence, she wouldn't shatter the magic. 'Do you still smoke?' he asked, his tone a little less confident. Her lack of an answer had unsettled him. Just as she'd hoped it would.

'I do all sorts of things I shouldn't,' said Hanna, before her mouth could intervene. 'But actually, I'm starting a new job tomorrow. Could you do Wednesday?' She couldn't quite believe it. Had she just rain-checked Tom Moss? Had she just played hard to get?

Tom laughed. 'Ha! Ace. Cool. A new job . . . Good luck. And cool. I'll see you at the Gardeners on Wednesday. At six?'

'Sure,' said Hanna, her thighs twitching with unreleased adrenaline. And with that he skidded his heel across the path, turned towards the road and lolloped off.

Hanna stood by her bike. Her keys felt the size of hammers in her fingers. Her feet seemed suddenly metres away from her head. She wondered if she might need to sit down. She could taste silt and salt and pollen on her lips. She had just been asked out by a topless Tom Moss after wrangling an actual horse into a field. She was going for a drink with him. This week. She felt as if a firework had just gone off inside her chest. She knew that if she started cycling now there would be a hideous moment where she'd have to cycle past Tom as he walked up Walton Well Road. She didn't trust her legs to behave. She wasn't actually sure she could pedal. So instead she sat on the bench and stared out at the meadow. A drink with Tom Moss. She couldn't believe it. A smile crept across her face. Shivers ran over her skin. And if it went well? she thought. What then? She couldn't take him back to her dad's. And she had no idea where he lived. She was still smiling. Maybe they'd have sex up against a G-clamp in his bike shop, covered in iron filings and smears of chain oil. What was she thinking? What the hell was that? She closed her eyes and remembered the hollow beneath his collarbone. Her smile widened.

Hanna sat on the bench for seven minutes, utterly unaware of the small plastic bag of dog shit just centimetres away from her open hand. She didn't hear the joggers and cyclists clank through the gate in front of her. She didn't see the woman with the buggy struggling to negotiate the metal fence. Eventually she opened her eyes and walked back to her bike. She lifted herself on to the saddle. She pulled her wet hair out from under the strap of her rucksack. She cycled back to her dad's in less than five minutes. And she completely forgot to post any of her photos to Instagram.

6
Lanyard

'Hello. My name is Hanna Markhouse.'

Why did she always do this? Hanna wondered. Give her full name to complete strangers whenever she was nervous. As though she was Melvyn Bragg, or Moira Stuart; as if the person behind the counter would suddenly flash her a look of instant recognition. *Hanna Markhouse! God, it's so exciting to meet you at last.* Who even used their surname, other than detectives in crime thrillers and serial killers? 'I'm starting today with the Audience Development team,' she added. 'As Assistant Events Manager.'

The woman behind the counter was wearing a Breton striped top and dark stretchy jeans. If you asked Hanna to describe the most mum outfit in the world, it would definitely be a Breton striped top and pair of elasticated jeans. Twinned with either Converse in a pub (pinot grigio and a big bag of crisps, please) and Clarks boots at work (ooh, I love a latte). Of course, the woman was exactly the same age as Hanna, but they would both guess the other to be at least eight years older than themselves; one because of job seniority, the other for having reproduced. Neither woman had truly come to terms with the fact that they now looked like they were in their thirties; and so neither woman could be trusted to identify their own peers.

'I'll call up and see if someone's free to come down and get you,' said the woman. 'My name is Carly Müller, by the way.'

'Thank you,' said Hanna, trying not to mention Fruit Corners.

Because the interviews had taken place in one of the museum's public meeting rooms – the very space that Hanna would be hiring out to corporate and private clients – it was only as she'd walked up the great stone steps into the museum that Hanna had realized she had absolutely no idea where she was going. When Annabel had called her late last week offering the job, it hadn't occurred to Hanna to ask her where she'd have to go. Presumably, the Audience Development team didn't just climb into the cabinet full of ostrich eggs, pull out their laptops and set up for the day. Presumably there would be some sort of office.

Eleven minutes later, just as Hanna was starting to wonder if she'd even got the job at all, Annabel arrived at her side, in a whisper of silk scarves and greying blonde hair.

'Hanna! Hello. Lovely to see you. Let's go upstairs and get you settled in,' she said, her smile not quite reaching her eyes. The two of them headed up the wide stone steps, Hanna slightly behind, trying very hard not to look at Annabel's rather flat arse. She pushed open a side door and strode into a fairly ordinary-looking office. Cream blinds pulled halfway down against the sun, two women and a man sitting at computers on large white office tables, cables running like a nest of snakes down the centre, while multi-plug adaptors lay against walls in trays like sunbathers. The desk next to the man's was clear. Strikingly clear, in fact. And the computer had no keyboard.

'This is you,' said Annabel, with that pastel-coloured smile. 'And this is Phoebe, Sanjay and Erin,' she added, pointing at each person in turn with her biro.

'Great!' said Hanna. Unsure if she should sit down or if there was more of a tour to come, she put her bag on the floor and then hovered in a semi-squat position, holding one arm of the swivel chair beside her. Annabel stood, saying nothing. The chair started to slowly rotate. Hanna said nothing.

'Well, if that's everything, I have a nine-thirty meeting,' said Annabel, turning out of the room. 'Maybe we can catch up later. See how you're settling in.' And with a tight squeeze of her face that was not a smile, she strolled out of the room.

Hanna slowly edged her buttocks on to the chair. In front of her was a computer monitor, a telephone, a pad of Oxford University headed notepaper, a desk tidy full of someone else's pens, a plastic glass with a centimetre of water at the bottom, and a small stack of

Post-its. No keyboard. No staff manual. No handover document. Feeling strangely paralysed, Hanna started to unpack her handbag on to the desk, in the hope that with enough window dressing nobody would notice that she didn't actually have a working computer or, by extension, an actual job. Water bottle. Four yellow Bic biros. Notebook. Apple. Bag of almonds. Tupperware lunchbox. Aware that her lunchbox probably smelled, she quickly dropped it back into the bag and buried it under her desk. Where she found a miniature football with a dodo embossed on one side. Hanna opened her notebook and wrote the date. Then she underlined it. Then she sat. She could hear Sanjay typing beside her. She closed the notebook. And then sat again. Every hair on her body seemed to be twitching with an almost primitive sense of threat. What was going on here? Was it a joke? Had she accidentally applied for an internship? Was that why she'd got it? Surely everybody was looking at her, wondering what the hell she was doing at this empty desk, with no job and no clue. She pulled out her phone and, pretending to look professionally engaged, typed 'technical term cat hair stand on end'. So, it was called piloerection. Good to know. Hanna opened her notebook and wrote 'piloerection' below the date. Then she closed the book again and adjusted her seat.

'Are you all right?' Sanjay had turned to face her, his hands still on his keyboard.

'Hi! Yes.' Hi? Why was she saying hi? 'Yes, fine

thanks. I just wondered – how do I log in to the system?' Hanna said, nodding at her blank-faced screen.

'Oh, right. Yes. You'll need a login,' said Sanjay. 'Rita normally deals with those.'

'Great,' said Hanna. Then, after a pause of, ooh, about four months, said, 'And where's Rita?'

'Maternity leave,' said Sanjay. How helpful.

'Ah, right.'

'But you can use mine for now, if you like,' said Sanjay, seeing the look of almost tearful desperation on Hanna's face. He wrote a long series of figures on a Post-it and then passed it over to Hanna's outstretched fingers.

'Great. Thanks. Only I . . .' Hanna motioned towards her empty desktop. 'I don't seem to actually have a keyboard.' She chuckled, as though this was the professional equivalent of being given somebody else's starter at dinner.

'Oh shit. So how are you going to log in?' said Sanjay, looking at her with something not unlike pity.

'Yes,' said Hanna. 'Yes' didn't really make sense in this sentence but it was out now. She'd had her lexical chance and she'd gone with the old trusty friend, yes.

'Maybe you could ask Carly?' said a voice from behind her computer. Pushing her chair to one side, Hanna could see the tiny head of Phoebe, leaning slightly to one side. 'She might know where we keep the spare keyboards.' *I mean, it wasn't exactly a case of a spare keyboard*, thought Hanna. *More just an actual keyboard.*

And the thought of crawling back to Stretchy-Jeans Carly just minutes after being shown to her desk made her prickle with embarrassment. But still, if that's what it took. She stood up and started to walk out of the room. Turning the handle and pushing open the door, she was faced not with the corridor, but shelves full of printer paper and boxes of toner.

'That's the stationery cupboard,' said Phoebe, as Hanna stood staring at the small cityscape of paper blocks.

'Yes, it is,' said Hanna. She really was going all in on 'yes' in this new job, she noticed.

'And you can just call Carly,' said Sanjay. *Oh, so they were all watching and listening*, thought Hanna. *Cool.*

Back at her desk, she asked Sanjay for the number. Another Post-it. No wonder they needed a whole stationery cupboard – Sanjay seemed unable to pass on any information without putting it down on a Post-it first. As she dialled, Hanna's phone started making loud clicking noises followed by a shrill grinding sound, like someone sawing through a wheelbarrow. She hung up, her heart racing. From shock, from embarrassment, from confusion. She tentatively lifted the receiver and tried again. Three digits in and the grinding started to scream out from the handset.

'You need to press four first to make an internal call,' said the disembodied voice of Phoebe from behind the computer screen. Oh good. They could hear that too. Good.

'Thank you!' said Hanna.

'So where do you live, Hanna?' asked Phoebe, still invisible behind her huge screen. 'Are you from Oxford?'

'Yes, I grew up here actually.' Hanna could hear her mouth going clicky from dehydration and panic. 'But I just moved back after breaking up with my boyfriend. In London.' Total silence. 'I'm actually looking for a room, if you hear of anything?' Total silence. 'I'm having to stay at my dad's while I look for somewhere.' The silence was so palpable Hanna could almost have used it to wash the windows.

'Doesn't your brother rent out a room, Sanjay?' Erin's voice was surprisingly deep, her Australian accent turning 'rent' into 'rint'.

'Yeah, sometimes,' mumbled Sanjay, looking straight ahead at his computer.

'Oh, really?' said Hanna, trying to sound excited rather than desperate.

'Yeah,' said Sanjay. Then he put on his headphones and started making notes on a fresh Post-it.

It took Carly forty-five minutes to locate a keyboard, during which Hanna spent a long time looking at her phone. About twenty minutes in, she'd started to wonder if there were any staff toilets and where they might be. As she didn't particularly fancy having a map drawn out for her on a Post-it by Sanjay, she decided to hold it in until either Erin or Phoebe got up, and she'd follow them. Actually, that sounded quite creepy. Maybe she'd just hold it in until lunch.

'It looks like you don't have a copy of the staff handbook,' said Carly, standing over Hanna's desk. With the keyboard in the middle, the sheer quantity of snacks Hanna had unpacked was somehow more noticeable. Carly had said this like it was Hanna's fault – as if she'd burnt her copy or used it as loo roll.

'Yes,' said Hanna. Here she was, back to the old faithful. Yes.

'Well, you'd better get one. Otherwise you won't know what's going on!' Carly had clearly meant this to sound jolly but her expression suggested that even she was aware her tone had scudded somewhere over into the long grass of pissed off. Just at that moment Hanna's phone began to ring. Hoping that it might be one of the fifteen other jobs she'd not heard back from yet, offering her an alternative to this fruit machine of bad luck, Hanna lifted her phone out of her bag. It was Iain. Before Hanna had a chance to hang up, she realized Carly had already walked off, leaving her none the wiser as to what she was doing here.

'Hello,' she answered, trying to sound professional – as though potential events clients were already ringing her personal mobile number despite the fact that she was yet to turn on her computer.

'Hello, chuck. I just wanted to call to say good luck.' Iain's voice sounded ever so slightly echoey. 'How's it all going?'

'Very well, thanks,' said Hanna, her eyes darting around to see if the others happened to be listening.

'Ah good. Well, we can celebrate tonight. I thought I might make macaroni cheese. And maybe we could watch a Western.'

'I think that's available,' said Hanna, as she wrote 'fuck this fuck this fuck this' on her pad.

'I think we're a bit low on brown sauce.' Iain's voice was strangely loud and almost metallic-sounding. 'The Co-op's on your way home, I think now, if you want to pick some up? And we could probably do with some more loo roll.'

'Yes, I'm just at my desk at the moment, but I'll take a look into it and get back to you this afternoon.'

'Oooh, gotcha,' said Iain, finally cottoning on to Hanna's tone. 'I'll leave you to it.' Just before he hung up, but while Hanna was still on the line, she heard the sound of a cistern flushing in the background. Of course he'd rung to wish her luck while doing a shit. Of course he had.

Thankfully, Sanjay's login details did work. Hanna had just managed to open a Word document, so as to have something to type into, if and when she ever found any actual work to do, when the phone on her desk started to ring. Hanna looked at it for a few seconds, like a cat being presented with a handgun. It rang again. Glancing up at Erin, nervous energy pulsing down her arm, Hanna looked back at the phone. She looked at her hand, not moving. She looked at the phone, still ringing. *Come on*, she thought. *We can do this.* She picked up the phone.

'Hello, Hanna Markhouse speaking, how can I help you?' Because when it's your first day and you have absolutely no idea what's going on, it's always a good idea to sound like a phone operator for the Hard Rock Café.

'Is that . . .' There was a pause. 'Hanna Markhouse, Events?' The voice was male, deep and ever so slightly Celtic.

'Umm, that's me,' replied Hanna, suddenly unable to locate the word 'yes' – pretty much the only word she'd been using all day.

'Hello, Hanna, this is Martin from IT. I'm sorry it's taken me so long. I'm ringing with your login details and email account. Once you're online, you'll see a Word document on your desktop called Read Me. That'll have all the information on how you get on to the system – events schedule, contacts database, that sort of thing.' Relief flooded through Hanna's stomach, thighs, buttocks and pelvis so profoundly that for a second she wondered if she was going to piss herself. At last, someone in this building had noticed it was her first day.

'I imagine Annabel – that's your line manager, isn't it?' Hanna made a non-committal grunt that sounded like someone taking the lid off a very tight jar. 'I imagine she's gone through all this?'

'Not quite,' said Hanna, feeling like one of those diplomats who has to communicate an entire dossier using just their eyebrows and pauses.

'I see. Well, hopefully there will be some useful stuff in there. And you can always ask Carly if you get stuck.'
What was it with these people and old Stretchy Jeans? Was Carly the only person in the entire building who did any work?

'OK, thanks, Martin. That's been really useful,' said Hanna, shooting a look at the side of Sanjay's head and Erin's ponytail. Feeling near-hysterical with relief and hunger, she was just about to ask him if he wanted to meet for lunch when he hung up.

By 11.17 a.m. Hanna still hadn't had a single cup of tea, or wee, or got up from her desk despite having precisely no work to do. She really, really wanted a cup of coffee. About an hour ago Phoebe had got up from her desk, cracked her fingers, walked out of the room, and come back six minutes later holding a steaming mug of tea. Hanna had missed her one chance at a hot drink. She felt too self-conscious to even ask her three new colleagues if they wanted 'anything from the outside world'. So, with her heart racing, her self-esteem subterranean, and her tongue stuck to the roof of her mouth with a combination of dehydration and caffeine withdrawal, she simply stood up and walked out of the room, making sure to follow the exit Phoebe had taken, rather than stride into the stationery cupboard again. Nobody looked up.

The door led to a small room full of filing cabinets and shelving stacks. *Shit. Not this again.* Luckily, the door at the other end was open and through it – glory be – Hanna could see one of the first-floor balconies within the main museum. OK, fine. So there was no kitchen in this shithole, or if there was one she'd never find it, but she knew that there was a café up here and she knew they had a coffee machine. Thank God she'd picked up her handbag. Walking past a glass box that housed an actual live tarantula, she felt her lanyard tap against her breasts.

There was only a short queue at the café but by the time she sat down with her coffee, it was 11.37 a.m. and Hanna was absolutely starving. The constant gnawing of adrenaline in her stomach had ripped through the porridge she'd had that morning within minutes, and suddenly, surrounded by children eating cheese sandwiches and packets of Pom-Bears, Hanna began to feel light-headed. She reached into her bag and pulled out the Tupperware. Tuna sandwich with sundried tomato, rocket and capers. She bit into one with such force that her elbow knocked the side of the table and sent a little cresting wave of coffee over the lip of her saucer and across the tabletop. She was just wondering whether to mop this up with her own sleeve when she looked up and saw, of course, Annabel walking towards her, with a Korean man at her side. Annabel did not smile. She looked down at the sandwich, at the spreading pool of brown, at Hanna's sandwich, and simply swept by, saying nothing. *Well, that ought to do it*, thought Hanna. *That's the old promotion in the bag. I'll be Director by Christmas.*

'Hanna?' A woman with thick black hair, small gold

hoops and the most incredible suede jacket was walking towards Hanna's table.

'Shazia!' Hanna bolted up and stepped away from the small puddle of coffee.

'Oh my god, you look so beautiful!' Shazia said, throwing her arms around Hanna and squeezing her with genuine force.

'Me? Oh my god, I look like a bowling bag full of alarm clocks, but look at you! You're so glamorous!'

'Ah, it's just the gold.' Shazia gestured towards her jewellery. 'And because I put on lipstick today. If you look closely, I'm all wrinkles and eyebrows.'

Shazia Akhtar had been one of Hanna's closest friends at middle school. They'd pooled their money every lunchtime to buy a packet of Quavers together and she would dole them out evenly with all the solemnity of a croupier dealing a pack of playing cards. Something about her quiet concentration, her nimble fingers, her repetitive movements had sent Hanna into a state rather like bliss. After school, the girls would often spend another two or three hours talking on their landlines. Despite spending six hours a day with each other at school, they'd manage to keep up that stream of chat – sometimes meaningful, sometimes meaningless – right up until *Home and Away* and *Neighbours*.

'What are you doing in Oxford?' Shazia asked, standing back, her hand on her hip.

'I just moved,' said Hanna. It was a white lie. Hanna had actually been back in Oxford for nearly a month.

But with Shazia standing in front of her like this, Hanna suddenly couldn't think why she hadn't got in touch with her old friend the moment she'd arrived back. Somehow, although she'd thought of her from time to time, like ice pops, hair mascara, the Red Hot Chili Peppers and Tango, Shazia existed for Hanna almost entirely in the past, in nostalgia, in a life she'd left behind. In her friend's absence, Hanna hadn't quite realized that Shazia would have been ageing right alongside her all this time. 'Actually, this is my first day. I just started working here, as an events manager.'

'Oh, wow. What a cool job!' said Shazia. 'I come here to draw sometimes. When I have a day off.'

Hanna smiled. 'How's your dad?'

'Ah, you know Mo,' Shazia laughed. 'Still eating peanuts out of a bowl without using his hands like a horse, still driving buses, still getting irate about the Labour party. He bought a new dressing gown last week. That was pretty big news.'

'Is he still . . .?' Hanna suddenly panicked over her own question. Could you ask this sort of thing about somebody's dad?

'Still single as a fork,' answered Shazia. 'He's got so eccentric in his old age I'm not sure any woman could handle the cut of his jib.' Hanna remembered with a twist of delight Mohammed Akhtar's incredible collection of tank tops. She remembered watching him practise close-up hand magic while watching the television. She smiled at the thought of hearing him bang around the kitchen making a cup of tea, while singing, at the absolute top of his lungs and in an accent apparently unchanged by twenty-five years in Britain, 'Wooooaaaah, Bodyform! Bodyform for you . . .'

'Ah, well the ladies of East Oxford don't know what they're missing,' said Hanna.

'Ha! I think they probably do,' joked Shazia. 'There can't be many sixty-two-year-old widowers who still sleep with a pillow wrapped in their wife's nightie.' Hanna winced. They had been thirteen when Shazia's mum, Najma, had died of breast cancer. Shazia and her three brothers had taken a month off school, to be at home when she died. Like a true thirteen-year-old, Hanna had swung between acute embarrassment and naive concern about her friend. Did this mean Shazia wouldn't be able to come bowling in Aylesbury next week? Did this mean Shazia would never smile again? Did this mean Shazia would be jealous of Hanna for having a mum? Who would cook Shazia dinner now? Would Shazia ever come back to school? Could they still watch *Neighbours*? Of course, Hanna had asked Julie. But as Julie had recently read *The Tibetan Book of Living and Dying*, some of her answers had been a little more philosophical than Hanna had really wanted. Julie also fiercely believed in the expression of all emotions, entirely unfiltered, at all times, so told Hanna that her friend would probably be sad for the rest of her life and cry a lot. Which made Hanna only more worried about Shazia; that she'd never pass her SATs, that she'd never get a boyfriend, that she'd be moved to a different class and wouldn't sit next to Hanna any more. In that order.

'Shazia, I still feel guilty about that,' said Hanna, the words bubbling up before she'd entirely planned what she was going to say. 'When your mum' – oh shit, was she actually going to say it? – 'died. Uh, I wasn't nearly as supportive as I should have been.' She looked down at the back of her hands. 'I'm really sorry. I don't think any of us really knew anything about grief back then. We'd only really seen *Party of Five* and you weren't actually Neve Campbell, so that didn't help much either.' Hanna looked up to see Shazia smiling. She ploughed on. 'But it must have been hard. Much harder than I can imagine. And I'm sorry, I'm really sorry.' *I should say something about Najma*, Hanna thought. *It doesn't matter how banal, I should say something.* 'I can still really remember watching your mum help you on with your rucksack when I'd call for you on the way to school,' she said. 'And the time she gave me a date cookie after Eid.' Was that it? thought Hanna. Was that really the sum total of her memories of her old best friend's dead mum? Well, yes. To be honest, she'd been thirteen and that was nearly twenty years ago; sometimes these things just slip out of reach.

'Ha! That's funny you remember the rucksack thing,' Shazia laughed. 'I used to get so embarrassed. I thought you'd think I was this little baby, still getting helped out the door by my mum, because your parents would have already left for work. I remember being so impressed when you said that you made your own breakfast and had a front door key and stuff.'

'Ha! Yeah, well I managed to get myself locked out a lot,' said Hanna. 'So, are you working?'

'Oh, I'm still painting,' answered Shazia. 'And I work at Parasol during term time – you know the play scheme in Florence Park?'

'Ah, that's amazing, Shaz,' said Hanna, trying very, very, very hard not to sound earnest and condescending. 'Are you a play worker?'

'Sort of. Although we actually call them Enablers now,' she smiled. 'I coordinate the volunteers and do a bit of the admin too.' Obviously she was basically running the place, thought Hanna. Why could her brain not catch up to the fact that she and Shazia weren't nineteen-year-olds and had, in fact, been ageing at the same speed as the rest of the planet? 'It's good because it still leaves me time for my own practice and – I don't know if this is something to do with Mum dying at that age – but I just really like spending time around young teenagers.'

'Oooh, can I see your work anywhere?' Hanna asked. Had she just accidentally swerved talking more about Najma? She hadn't meant to.

'Well, I've got loads on my phone but I'm not on social media or anything,' said Shazia, pulling out an iPhone 7 in a plastic case worn almost translucent by time and fidgeting. 'Hey, we should swap numbers too.'

'Yes! Yes, we should,' said Hanna. Then, without really thinking about why, she added, 'I've actually got to get back to work, but if I take your number then maybe we could go for a drink or something in the week.'

'Great!' said Shazia.

'Oh, wait,' said Hanna. 'Do you drink?'

'Mate, I barely do anything else,' laughed Shazia. 'Khalid, my husband, is way more strict than me. He keeps halal and prays at work and stuff. But my family were just never really like that. Well, you remember. My dad thought it was the epitome of sophistication to drink whisky while watching Sister Wendy talking about art. Anyway, here's my number.'

Hanna typed in the number and saved it as 'Shaz'. It was an act of familiarity that gave her a warm pulse of something like nostalgia and a little like sisterly love.

'So are you still in touch with anyone else from school?' asked Shazia, adjusting the strap on her handbag.

'Actually, I saw Tom Moss the other day,' said Hanna. Saying his name was like sucking a toffee; sweet and delicious and entirely distracting. 'He works at a bike shop now.' She didn't dare mention the drink, scheduled for Wednesday evening.

'Oh God, Tom Moss. The only man who could break somebody's heart and then sue for damages himself,' laughed Shazia. *What the fuck did that mean?* thought Hanna. *What does she know about Tom?* 'Is he still living in a van and pretending to be a Buddhist?' continued Shazia.

'I don't know,' replied Hanna, feeling herself flush.

'Ah, well. Right. I'd better let you go,' said Shazia, readjusting the bag on her shoulder. 'But please let's have that drink soon. I'm so happy we bumped into each other again. I'm sure we have absolutely nothing to catch up on, but we can just talk about TV and hair for an hour to kill some time.' Her smile was big and genuine and almost movie-star white.

'Yes. And our medical conditions,' said Hanna. 'That should fill some hours too.'

Walking back her desk, just a few minutes later, Hanna saw a copy of the staff handbook beside her keyboard. It hadn't been there when she'd left twenty minutes ago. Did that mean she'd been away from her desk for the one useful moment of this whole bloody day? The hydraulics in Hanna's chair sighed as she dropped into it, her handbag hitting the floor. She clicked the screen back to life. One new email.

To: <All Staff>
From: Annabel Wool
Subject: Staff breaks and café use

Staff are reminded that the café is to be used strictly for work meetings, and only outside peak times. This is by agreement with Mortons catering. Also, all staff are expected to be at their desks unless otherwise accounted for in their shared calendar.

Many thanks,
A.

Hanna dropped her head into her hands. *Fuck. This.* If ever a woman needed to cry in the office toilets, it was now. Hanna opened up the handbook and found a list of phone numbers at the back. Martin Copeland. IT. Ex. 4067. He picked up after just two rings.

'Hello, Martin speaking.'

'Hello Martin, it's Hanna here. Hanna Markhouse. The new girl. Sorry to bother you again, I just wondered – where are the ladies' toilets? My whole department are out on lunch and . . .' She couldn't quite bring herself to say either 'I need to piss like a horse' or 'I need to go and have a cry somewhere I can reapply my mascara afterwards.'

'Right you are,' said Martin, unfazed by the request. 'You're in Audience Development, right? From there, you walk through the door marked N7.01, take your first right, and the ladies' toilets are there on your left.'

'Thank you, Martin,' said Hanna, her voice almost cracking.

'No worries. Have a good one.' And with that, he rung off. *A good one.*

Slipping her mascara into her pocket, but leaving her bag under the desk just in case someone should come by and think she'd left again, Hanna headed for the heavy wooden door. First right. Then left. Like Saint Peter at the Pearly Gates, here she was, at last. The ladies' toilets. And on the wall beside them, just above the light switch, was a black-and-white A4 printout: *Don't Be A Diplodocus: Always Wipe the Seat!*

And below the text? A picture of a dinosaur. In sunglasses. Giving a thumbs up.

7
Dishwasher Tablets

I miss you today.

Hanna sent the text before her brain could intervene. Confronted by her second day at work, she felt tight, cold, nervous. One of the many casualties of breaking up with the man she had shared most of her working life with was that she now felt unconfident about her job; about her ability to do her job. It wasn't so much that Joe had helped with her career, rather that being rejected by him had made her feel inferior everywhere. The slow grinding realization that he no longer loved her had felt like being slowly, passively sacked from a job she didn't know she'd been failing at. And if it could happen with him, who's to say it wouldn't happen again, with her real job?

Do you want to chat?

It was 8.20 a.m. Hanna was more surprised that Joe was awake and able to text than that he was offering to call. She had planned to get to work early but the tug in her heart was telling her that it could wait.

Yes, please. I'm just in the park.

There was a bench beneath a willow tree, overlooking a rugby pitch. Hanna put her bag just to the left of some bird shit and sat down. It was sunny and the air was damp. Not warm, but bright. She put her phone on her knee and pulled out a box of tobacco. Hanna never smoked at work, or at home, but somehow, in these between spaces, she loved the few moments of illicit pleasure a cigarette could still give her. She'd hardly smoked for the six years she'd lived with Joe. Both his parents were serious, professional, gold-standard smokers. They lit up in bed, in the car, between dinner and pudding. As a result, Joe hated the smell of tobacco. Hated the flicking sound of lighters. Hated seeing cigarette butts on the floor. Hated even just the way people held their arm when they had a cigarette in their hand. Maybe if Joe begged her to move back she could smoke in the garden, thought Hanna. Now where did that come from? She didn't want to go back to London. Did she? This was just first-week nerves. Wasn't it? God, she was confused.

JOE GARRETT

calling . . .

Hanna found it rather funny that she still had Joe's number stored in her phone this way. Joe Garrett. As though he was a colleague, or someone who might be about to sell her insurance. Not the man who had once licked Nutella off her nipples.

'Hello.'

'Hiya. What's up?' It was strange, thought Hanna, that this greeting of Joe's had always irritated her quite so much. How she'd fumed at him for never simply asking how she was – always jumping to the potential disaster, the negative in everything, the possibility of her ruining something. And yet now, it sounded so bland.

'Oh, nothing really. I was just walking to work and feeling a bit nervous,' said Hanna, wishing at the last minute that she didn't sound quite so pathetic. Joe didn't say anything. He didn't even do that exhale that can sometimes pass for a reaction on the phone. 'My boss is an arsehole . . .' Hanna trailed off. This had been a mistake.

'Oh, right. I thought you were ill or something,' said Joe, in a strangely nasal voice. As if he was chewing the words, rather than saying them. 'But then you don't sound ill.'

Was he being deliberately deadpan? thought Hanna. Was he pissed off with her? Had he been up all night?

'No. Umm. I think I was just . . . It's really spring-like here at the moment.' Hanna paused. Nothing came back. 'There are catkins on the trees.' Sweet Jesus, was he going to say anything? At all? Ever? 'Anyway, how are you? Any good catkin anecdotes of your own?' It felt like trying to bail out a canoe with an egg cup.

'Actually, I've just bought a new dishwasher,' said Joe.

'Oh, that's good,' said Hanna, who couldn't have given less of a shit about this news if she'd been in a coma.

'Yeah, well, you'd think. But fucking Currys have

absolutely done me on the delivery charge.' Joe's tone had shifted from bored to harried. 'Came yesterday but the guy said there was a problem with the cold-water pipe. Said that most flats are now fitted with a combination pipe but ours, er' – the hesitation was agony – 'mine, is separated into cold and tank. And that the flow-away would have to be plumbed in to the waste pipe, but the kitchen waste pipe goes into the downstairs toilet . . .' Something in his tone felt accusatory. As though Hanna had personally conspired to banjax his plumbing, specifically so he couldn't enjoy his new single-man dishwasher.

'I'm sorry—'

'So he said I'd have to call an actual plumber to fit it. Apparently the Currys plumbers aren't even real plumbers – they're just appliance fitters. I mean, what the hell is an appliance fitter?' Hanna lifted the lighter to the end of her roll-up. 'But when I asked if they'd refund me the delivery charge, they said it wasn't a delivery issue—' He stopped abruptly. 'Are you . . . smoking?' He asked it as if she'd just kicked a squirrel to death.

'No.' Why was she lying? wondered Hanna, trying to breathe out as subtly as possible. Why did she care if Joe knew she was smoking? 'I'm just putting on lip balm.' She was a quick liar. And fairly creative.

'OK.' There was a beat. 'Well, anyway, I'm just worried that the plumber who did finally manage to install the dishwasher has now invalidated my guarantee because he might count as a third party. And I still don't even have any dishwasher tablets.' Hanna looked out across the treeline. At the sharp green leaves that were jostling for position behind the blossom. At the white pigeons – maybe even doves – flying in huge swooping semi-circles through the sky. She shouldn't have texted Joe. She should have sat on this bench, and smoked her cigarette, and simply held her nerves like an egg; precious, small, self-contained. She wasn't missing Joe. At least, she wasn't missing this Joe. This petty, boring, aggressive, resentful, victim-mentality Joe who never accepted any culpability for the fiascos that happened in his life. She hadn't missed slogging through his litany of grievances every evening over dinner. She hadn't missed talking about white goods and apologizing for things that weren't her fault. Instead of sitting with her feelings, she'd instead tried to manufacture a moment of intimacy with someone who hadn't expected it. How was Joe to know that she'd been walking to work, a bag of first-day-at-school nerves? How was Joe to know that, faced with the possibility of her first date since breaking up, she was feeling a bit guilty? How could he possibly guess that, in that moment, all she wanted was for someone to say that she had worth? Why did she need Joe to make her feel better?

'Next time I'm going to go with AO. I've been looking at their reviews online and they have way better guarantees and they're cheaper.' As Hanna tuned back in, Joe was still talking with that flat, exasperated tone.

'What a shitshow,' she interjected. 'I'm really sorry,

Joe. And now I'm going to have to go into work and leave you with the battle of the great waste pipe. I can see my boss going in across the car park.' More lies. More lies to someone she loved. Had loved. Loved. Whatever. She just needed to get away from this voice like a chainsaw and the unhappy plumbing of her old home.

'Cool. OK. Well, have a good day. Thanks for the message,' said Joe, sounding offended.

'No, thank you,' soothed Hanna. 'And thanks for answering. I wasn't expecting you to be up.'

'Oh, haven't you heard? I'm a new man,' said Joe, a smile in his voice. 'Set an alarm for eight o'clock these days. I quite like mornings.' *Of course he bloody does*, thought Hanna. *Now that it's of absolutely no benefit to me, or our relationship, he'll be waking up at dawn and drinking kale smoothies.* Talking to Joe had been good, she thought. Boring and irritating and guilt-inducing, of course, but she'd needed that. She needed to remember the Joe she'd broken up with; the pedantic, obsessive, irresponsible man who was always too busy with the small stuff to talk about the big picture. She needed to remember the arguments about money and holidays and dinner and the house. She needed to remember that breaking up had been a choice; the right choice. She wasn't over him yet. Not nearly. But she was absolutely over whingeing about white goods with a man who hadn't had sex with her for six months.

*

At 11.45 a.m. Hanna was sneaking corners of her sandwich out from inside a ring binder marked 'Catering'. Her phone vibrated on a jelly purple mousepad advertising Hays Recruitment that her predecessor had presumably picked up for free at a corporate event. It was Iain.

How would you feel if Mary came over for dinner tonight? read the message. *She's offered to help mash the butter and fricassee a kumquat?*

Hanna hadn't yet met Mary. Not face to face. Although she had spent an unholy amount of time looking at her Facebook profile photo since her dad had let her surname slip during one of his many tirades about the Tinder algorithm. Curly blonde hair, standing in some sort of park, looking into the sun. Her smile was broad even though her teeth were a little crooked. Probably taken by her ex, Hanna had thought. Or her secret son.

Will I have to wear a dinner jacket? Hanna typed, pushing herself from side to side in her swivel chair.

And a toupee, Iain replied.

Count me in.

Oh God, thought Hanna. *I really hope she doesn't try to give me reiki over the potatoes. Or ask to see my baby photos. Or have a dog.* In fact, she thought, what would be best was if Mary just sat silently in the corner for the entire meal, like one of those museum invigilators. Wearing a big, heavy polyester uniform. Something that made her look like a coach seat. Mary could spend the evening staring at the floor, not talking to anybody, and then go home at 8 p.m. That would be ideal.

Do you want to do pudding? Iain asked, just as Hanna had finally closed her browser window and started to enter some of the booking details for the Wowcha! Science Symposium next month.

Speckled trout in a nettle jus? Hanna replied.

My favourite, replied Iain. Credit where credit's due, Iain did not use emojis. And he had almost entirely stopped sending her photos of his completed *Guardian* quick crosswords.

'So, Sanjay.' Hanna swung her chair around like a quiz show host. 'What would you cook your dad's new girlfriend for pudding?' What had meant to sound like a friendly conversation opener had somehow come out as juvenile, flirtatious, perhaps even a little aggressive. It was as though yesterday's unrelenting sense of being out of her depth had made Hanna want to push Sanjay into his own area of discomfort. Somehow, her sense of inferiority was mutating into a weird power game.

'Uh . . .' Sanjay's eyebrows quivered in his frown like a leaf caught in a strong wind. 'Butterscotch?'

Hanna squeezed her pelvic floor. God, what was she doing?

'Butterscotch?' The question hung for seconds between them. Hanna had that totally unconvincing smile that she'd learned in Year 7 maths; the smile she used when Mr Hurrell, the newly qualified teacher, had asked her why she was going to the toilet, only for her to answer: 'To change my tampon, sir.'

'If I brought butterscotch to work, would you let me ask your brother about renting his spare room?' Sanjay could barely look her in the eye. 'I really need to find somewhere to live before I murder my father!' Her laugh was hollow, strange. She winced. How was she getting this so wrong? Why was she being so weird? All Sanjay had done was shove Post-its at her and fail to show her the office kettle.

Looking both irritated and embarrassed, Sanjay turned back to his keyboard. 'Maybe butterscotch ice cream,' he muttered under his breath, like a curse. 'I don't know.'

As soon as Hanna stepped through the front door of the flat, the hair on her arms stood on end. Alert, wary, slightly nauseous, she walked slowly down the hallway. In her bag, a bottle of red wine bumped against the carton of G&D's ice cream. A terrible temperature combination; cold wine, commute-warmed ice cream. She slipped off her shoes under the dreaded Dalí print. She paused for a second outside the bathroom and looked quickly in the mirror. Did she look smart? Intimidating? Conservative? Handsome? For some reason, she really wanted to alpha the shit out of this Mary woman. Wanted to show her that, despite the fact that, yes, she was sleeping in a single bed in her dad's flat aged thirty, she was a woman to be reckoned with. She wore a lanyard. And brushed her hair. And had been to university. And had paid a lot of council tax, once. Hanna ran her fingers under her eyes, wiping away any crumbs of mascara, trying to flatten out her eye bags.

The flat was strangely quiet. Too quiet. Which isn't to say silent. Of course, there was some Nina Simone track cooing out through the kitchen, hallway and front room speakers. But no talking. No clattering of pans or scraping of chairs. Maybe they'd run out of salt, thought Hanna. Nipped round to Azim's to buy more wine. Maybe they'd just gone for a walk? She was nervous, she admitted to herself. She'd never been in this position before – she'd sort of hoped she never would be. At the very least, if she was going to be introduced to her father's new girlfriend, she'd hoped it would happen in her own home, with a partner or friend to act as a human shield.

She walked into the kitchen, her bag cold and flat against her stomach. And then she saw it. The two-headed creature standing at the sink, panting heavily. A monstrous entanglement of her father, a chenille jumper, white bra and curly blonde hair. A hand cupped a particularly stocky C cup. Two faces seemed welded together by some cruel vacuum. The legs were strangely taut. Hanna's foot landed on a kitchen tile just as her brain caught up with what was happening. What she was looking at. For a second she just stood and watched. Kissing. Snogging. Dad. Suddenly the beast ripped apart. There was a strangled moan of panic. Hands paddled wildly at shirts, jumpers, hemlines. Two bodies threw themselves against the draining rack and countertop. Cheeks burned. Eyes darted.

'Howdy!' said Iain, blushing like a raspberry ripple.

Hanna couldn't move. Rooted to the spot, she wished dearly that she could bathe her eyes and ears in carbolic acid. She longed to undo what she had just seen, to burn clean her retinas, to wipe her brain of this Freudian nightmare. In all her life, Hanna could remember seeing her parents kiss perhaps a handful of times. Never snog. God, never snogging. Theirs had been a relationship of patted backs, held hands, forehead kisses at most. And yet here she was, a cold, dark fury spreading through her body, watching her blushing father and some woman who looked like a bag of popcorn with a wig trying to brush each other's DNA off their clothes. It was pathetic. It was disgusting. The room seemed suddenly moist, hot, damp, too peppery. Hanna dropped her bag on the chair, turned on her heel and walked straight into the bathroom. Trying to make enough noise to drown out the blood surging through her skull, she clanked the tooth mug, slammed the door of the cupboard against the wall, and started to brush her teeth like someone scrubbing a murder scene.

Revulsion, anger and disbelief foamed around her mouth. But then, behind them was something else. Something darker, stranger, more squalid. Crawling underneath her disgust at seeing her dad touching up some stranger were the woodlice of jealousy, sadness and unpleasant arousal. That had been a hot kiss.

Hanna hadn't kissed anyone like that for ages. Despite the agony of sharing a flat, sometimes even a bed with Joe, she had lain as chaste as a nun for months. Her lips, she thought, as she half spat, half gagged over the bathroom sink, were like a moth, settled on the cold, blank wall of her face. Touch them and they'd shatter immediately to dust. But this wasn't simple envy, a rage that someone had something she wanted. Under the churning mulch of resentment there was also a feeling of betrayal. That Hanna's dad had liked kissing Hanna's mum was evident by Hanna's standing here. So why was he doing this to Julie? Poor Julie, alone in her little metal box in the middle of the trees. They had loved each other once. So why was he dry-humping that hay bale with tits in the kitchen? And then, creeping under that was an even darker, damper mist. Of possession. That was her dad out there. Those arms, that back, those lips belonged to her. They'd rocked her to sleep as a baby, carried her home from nursery, read her bedtime stories. His was her body. He loved her the best. There shouldn't be room for another woman in that heart. She should be enough for him.

'Would you like a glass of Château le Thames?' Iain's voice was as bright and uncomfortable as a bare lightbulb. Hanna looked again in the mirror. *When you're going through hell*, she thought, staring at the mole on her chin, *keep going*.

'Half a pint, please.' Feeling raw, unhappy and wretched, she dried her face on an orange bath towel that had been hanging there, she knew, for at least three weeks. It would never have occurred to Iain to wash and replace the hand towels because his girlfriend was coming over. Just as it wouldn't occur to him to take out the bins, change his bedding, light some candles or take his underpants off the drying rack. It was only by some miracle of fibre consumption and timing that there wasn't a tube of Anusol resting on the edge of the bath. Hanna stood, the large, dank, slightly sour-smelling towel in her hand. She could put this in the washing basket. She could get a clean towel out of the airing cupboard right now. It was there, beside her. She could do the right thing, simply because it was the right thing. But she didn't feel like the right thing. Not here, not now. She felt like the rejected and unloved and overlooked thing. So, she thought, she could spit on this towel, hang it back on the radiator, and smile nicely at Mary's face over a bowl of sweet chilli crisps.

In the airing cupboard, above the boiler and the wooden slat shelves, hung a little marionette donkey. Iain had been given it by his friend Prakash after he'd wired up his shed. Its jointed legs and painted hooves hung in the air, unmoving. Hanna reached for a clean towel with one hand and flicked the donkey's chest with the other. It bucked and hit the hot-water pipe with a clatter. *You're an ass*, thought Hanna. *An ass*. And then she spat. On the clean towel.

'Hanna, it's so lovely to finally meet you.' Mary walked across the kitchen with a glass of white wine in her hand.

'Iain is so thrilled to have you staying. How have you found Oxford?'

'Well, we just drove along the M40 until we hit the medieval limestone,' said Hanna, attempting a smile. 'Actually, it's nice to be back. It's like moving house with absolutely none of the mental load. As in, I already know where Argos is, where to buy a pint of milk, and which number bus goes to the train station; all that logistical stuff is just washed away.' She looked over at Iain, who was standing by the cooker with his back to them, a wooden spoon conspicuously unmoving in his hand. He was listening like a hawk. 'And it's nice to be living at home again after all those years. Even if I am constantly worrying about bumping into someone from school at the supermarket.'

'How was work?' asked Iain, turning around to face them.

'Oh, fine. Sanjay confirmed we have an alcohol licence so I might start planning some events around our botanical collection.'

'Sanjay? Is he your new boyfriend?' asked Iain, a little too quickly. 'Are you sleeping with someone from work? I don't think that's a very good idea, Han. What if he pins nude photos of you up on the staff noticeboard when you have an argument?'

'I'm pretty sure he's gay,' said Hanna.

'And anyway, dear, he'd be much more likely to get his revenge online, these days,' chipped in Mary. Mary had one of the plainest faces Hanna had ever seen. Small, pale brown, soft and uninteresting. There was no proud nose, strong chin, wide smile or thick eyebrows to elevate her to beautiful. She wore no make-up, had small, even teeth, and her little silver hoop earrings were like quotation marks around a potato. How unlike Julie she was, thought Hanna. How strange to actively choose someone so unremarkable.

'And how long have *you* lived in Oxford?' Hanna asked Mary, before downing a third of her wine in one sip.

'Since 2011. I moved here with my husband, and got a job doing speech and language therapy at Iffley Mead.' A husband? Surely Iain wasn't having an affair with a married woman. Oh God, if her dad was polyamorous, Hanna was going to boil her face in a deep-fat fryer. 'He worked in film. Before he died he worked in—'

'Porn?' There was a terrible, howling silence. For her part, Hanna had absolutely no idea how or why it had happened. She'd heard the word 'film' and, like being hit on the knee with a hammer, had felt the word 'porn' just bubble up her throat like a bad reflex. She'd heard the word 'died' just at the moment the bubble reached her mouth and exploded out across her teeth. Too late. Too late. Jesus Christ. She'd just accused her dad's new girlfriend of being married to a dead porn director.

'Of course,' said Mary, her gaze as solid as a pat of butter. 'Although he made his real money from anthropology documentaries for the university.' She smiled.

'Those dirty bastards at Balliol love a bit of biocultural variation and ethnography.'

'Dirty bastards,' exhaled Hanna, reaching for a crisp.

'So Iain tells me you might be moving out soon?' said Mary, her doughy little face crimping again into something like a smile.

'Oh, well, um . . .'

'Someone at work might have a spare room? That would be neat. I mean, you don't want to be living with your dad at your age, do you?' Mary put a crisp in her mouth and started chewing in tiny little lightning-speed movements, like a squirrel. 'I wonder why you didn't look into somewhere like Abingdon or Didcot? They're much cheaper and there are pretty regular buses.'

So that's what they talk about when I'm not around, thought Hanna. *How to move me into a concrete tower block twenty miles away, overlooking Didcot Power Station, so they can have sex on the kitchen floor.* God, she needed to move out. She made a non-committal noise and picked up her phone. She opened her emails. There was a message from Sanjay at the top of her inbox. No subject line. Hanna opened it. There was just one line of text.

My brother's already found someone for his flat. Sorry. Hope you're enjoying your butterscotch.

8

Cheese Scone

'Yes, madam?' The shop assistant looked up from her tangled H-cup balconette in Evening Pink, and a cold dread passed through Hanna. Kelly Cooke. Guarding the maroon arch of the bra fitting room. She wasn't just a sales assistant in a provincial M&S. She was terror incarnate.

Suddenly, Hanna wasn't a thirty-year-old woman underwear shopping before a first date; she was eleven years old, rinsing off after Year 7 PE, while Kelly Cooke shouted to the whole changing room that Hanna was pissing in the shower.

'Madam?' Kelly Cooke's eyes drifted across Hanna's face with the hidden, milky stare of a great white shark. Hanna could feel the pinpricks of sweat erupting in her throbbing armpits. Kelly Cooke from school was now an M&S bra fitter. And Hanna was supposed to be buying a bra.

'Just . . . just these, please.' The voice that came out of Hanna's throat was like a car reversing into a bollard. Every muscle in her body was telling her to drop this handful of lycra and run straight out of the shop. She didn't need new underwear. She hated bras. This whole thing had been a silly capitalist response to her excitement about going out for a drink with Tom. He'd seen her bra already. Less than a week ago. On a bridge beside a river. Yet again she'd been suckered by a cruel twist of consumerism and low self-esteem into thinking that she needed to buy something to feel more confident. But pouring her thirty-year-old dugs into a new harness, probably hand-stitched by some bored and poorly paid mother of three in Bangladesh, wasn't going to make her feel any more prepared for an evening of awkward small talk and sexual frustration around a pub table with Tom Moss. What was she doing here? Why wasn't she walking away?

'Of course. And will you be wanting any assistance with your fitting today? Are you pregnant, maybe?'

What the actual fuck. Hanna shot a look at Cookey. Her face was as smooth and unmoving as a razor blade. It must have been an auditory hallucination. Why would she ask if she was pregnant? Did she look pregnant? Hanna had eaten an unwise quantity of dried apricots at her desk this morning so it was possible she was swelling up with a phantom baby of sulphur and methane. Kelly Cooke wouldn't be pregnant. Growing a baby in that body would be like trying to grow cress in bleach.

'You can just leave me to it,' said Hanna, the words scraping out like a spade dragged over gravel. 'I'm just going to try these on.'

'Of course.' Cookey plunged her eyes into Hanna's like a dagger. 'Just be careful of the security tags.' What the hell did that mean? Was she accusing her of shop-lifting and being pregnant?

With trembling fingers, Hanna hung the three bras on the strange little handrail in the changing room. The cubicle had a small chaise longue along one side and a maroon velvet curtain, as though Hanna were about to host a literary salon dressed in a set of new black cotton midi briefs. Why, she wondered, were bra fitting rooms always designed like this? To look like the midpoint of a brothel and an old people's home? Swirling carpets and mood lights, plush rope pulls and coffee stains. And the mirrors. Sweet Christ, those mirrors. It should be illegal to see your own body square-on from behind. The strange creases in the skin around her waist, pointing down at the edges like a pair of sad eyebrows. The moles. The pads of flesh beneath her armpits. The pink indentations of elastic across her skin that made it look like she was still wearing a bra even after it had come off. The stoop in her shoulders. The soufflé emerging above her waistband. Hanna had a lovely, healthy, strong and helpful body. It looked after her and allowed her to live her life. It worked and moved and could dance with joy. But seeing it here, from these new and unflinching angles, flooded her with self-loathing. She felt like a mozzarella ball waiting for the knife. The first bra made her breasts look like torpedo rolls. The seams somehow pushed the contents into cones, way too far apart and strangely boss-eyed from the front.

God, no. If she wore this under a shirt, it would look like she was trying to audition as an egg box. The second bra was the lingerie equivalent of draping two old teabags across your chest.

Hanna had just unhooked the fastening at the back, loosening her exhausted breasts from their disappointing cage, when the curtain behind her was abruptly torn open. There, with a tape measure over her shoulder and an almost imperceptible smile on her face, was Kelly Cooke. Staring at her. Cookey. The terror of the fourth form. The girl who had made Angela Raffier lie face down in a blocked gutter at lunchtime and had apparently lost her virginity at twelve. Standing less than forty centimetres away from Hanna's naked and freckled back, her eyes glinting.

'And how are you getting on?' she asked, her voice like honey over flint. 'It looks to me like you've underestimated your size. Have you put on a lot of weight recently?' There was the smallest hint of a pause as Cookey inhaled sharply. 'Oh sorry, no, you're the woman who's expecting a baby, aren't you? I can see now. No, none of these will be suitable.' And she grabbed the handful of hanging bras. 'A woman your size is going to need something much sturdier, I'm afraid. And while you're here, it might be an idea to get some looser trousers. I can see that you're cutting into that waistband quite badly.'

Hanna's neck flared with a hot red rash. This was unreal. She was a thirty-year-old woman, standing topless in the middle of a high-street bordello with a humous aisle, being fat-shamed by the girl who had once threatened their teacher with a brick. Hanna wasn't meant to be here. She had got away. She'd left Oxford, been to university, made it in the big city; she had clawed her way out of this claustrophobic little valley town and reinvented herself outside. She'd had a partner, a job, her own home. She wasn't meant to be broken into crumbs by a middle school bully in a windowless bra cubicle. Within seconds, Kelly Cooke was back, this time holding a flesh-coloured front-fastening bra of such monumental ugliness it looked more like something you'd find floating in the deep ocean than hook around your body. 'Now pop this on and I'll measure you properly,' said Cookey, sliding towards Hanna with her tape measure outstretched. God, no. There was no way, no fucking way, she was letting this mammary Machiavelli anywhere near her.

'I'm fine, thank you,' Hanna said, stepping swiftly to the left. Her sweat-slick flank pressed against the cold edge of the mirror, leaving a cloud of condensation across the surface. 'I don't think I'm going to bother with any of these. They're all . . . shit.'

Kelly Cooke stood firm. Neither woman had yet acknowledged that they knew each other. Names hadn't been used. School not mentioned. And yet, this was clearly an act of revenge. In her cold, vicious gaze, Cooke was absolutely the eleven-year-old who had caught Hanna pissing in the shower. She was the same girl who had helped herself to other people's lunches, boyfriends and money. She was very much still the child who had enacted her own neglect, loneliness and misery on the helpless, chewing gum bodies of her classmates. Both women stood in the airless cubicle and breathed. One heavily. One too smoothly. *How does this end?* thought Hanna. *Is she going to give me a dead leg, empty my handbag on the floor, and then go and smoke a B&H Silver in the staff toilet?* Was she going to have to shout for a manager? No. She knew what this was. And she remembered, like the crackle of electricity, how it ended.

Back in the Year 7 showers, without time to doubt, Hanna had gone immediately on the attack, shouting: 'Why are you looking at my fanny? Why would you stare at my fanny and then lie to cover it up?' And so, there in the middle of the M&S changing room, aged thirty, Hanna dropped the hopeless teabag bra to the floor, straightened her back and stared, bare-breasted, straight into Kelly Cooke's cruel blue eyes.

'Oh my god. Are you looking at my tits?' said Hanna, much too loudly, standing absolutely still. 'Why are you looking at my tits?' she shouted again. There was a rustle of curtains outside, the clanking of hangers hitting the floor. 'You're meant to be a shop assistant. Why would you stare at my tits and then lie to cover it up?' Standing, hands on hips, breasts hanging in mid-air, Hanna could feel the curiosity and horror ripple through the changing room like an electric storm. What was going on in there? Should somebody call security?

Wordlessly, Kelly Cooke turned and stepped out of the cubicle.

Exhaling, Hanna ripped her jumper back on in one fluid movement. She threw her old bra into her handbag, left the matching sets strewn across the carpet like murder victims, and walked out, her face burning, her heart racing. As she got to the maroon arch, the little folding table covered in lace knickers and suspender belts, she heard a voice behind her.

'Fat bitch.'

Hanna sailed out like a galleon. She may have been single. She may have been living with her dad. She may have been out of her depth at work. She may have had the crumpled self-esteem of a used hankie. But she'd just outsmarted Kelly Cooke. At last. She'd won.

Back at Cranham Road, Iain was pulverizing something in a pot with the stick blender. Humous? Baba ganoush? Pesto? Soup? It was hard to tell. A beige foam was circling the blades, but the countertop was so covered in oils, pulses, vegetables and herbs that Hanna couldn't easily reverse-engineer the contents of the particular concoction. Iain was a good, if methodical, cook. He didn't just follow recipes – he followed the punctuation in recipes. If something called for half a teaspoon of salt, he held the blade of a knife halfway down the spoon. People had chopped up cocaine with less precision than Iain making a flapjack. The engineer in him did, however, ensure flawless cakes, well-cooked meat and perfectly timed vegetables. Even if the process looked more like medical testing than making a family meal.

'Good evening!' Iain lifted his bottle of Badger's Tassel. 'How was work?'

'Oh, it was fine,' said Hanna, dropping her bag on to a kitchen chair. 'I finally got my own keyboard and learned how to use the printer.'

'A red letter day!' Iain tipped a teaspoon of paprika into the pot. 'I'm making wild garlic and cheese scones with soup for dinner. I found a load during my swim this morning.' There was an almost imperceptible hesitation. 'With Mary.'

'Oh, lovely,' said Hanna, swerving the mention. 'I hope you rinsed them in dog piss to bring out the flavour.' She was stalling for time. She hadn't actually thought about dinner when she'd agreed to meet Tom. Would he be expecting to eat at the pub? Or was this just drinks? Six o'clock was pretty early. Maybe he'd suggest going on for dinner afterwards? Although, perhaps that was a little fancy for a bike mechanic. Even a bike mechanic from Jericho. Shit. Hanna didn't want to get rat-arsed on an empty stomach, but then it was already 5.30 p.m. and she still needed to have a shower. There would never be time for dinner first.

'I'm actually not going to be in for dinner, I'm afraid.' Hanna's brain popped a wheelie with two fingers in the air as she tried desperately to think of an excuse. 'Sorry, I should have told you . . . Only I left so early this morning there wasn't time.'

Iain looked curious, rather than offended. Hanna had barely spent a single evening out since moving back.

'Yes, sorry. Short notice but I've got . . .' She faked a burp while furiously racking her brain for something plausible. It wasn't that Hanna was sheepish about telling Iain that she had a date. Although the superstitious part of her was reluctant to admit her plans out loud, for fear of tempting fate. It was more that she didn't want to carry the weight of his expectation along with her own nervousness.

'Come on. You can tell me. Unless it's something private?' Iain's eyebrows were pulled into an expression of concern. Which was weird. All through her adolescence Iain had hardly been what you could describe as an overprotective parent. He'd actually bought Hanna a bottle of Malibu, unprompted, the first time she stayed over at her friend Ben's house.

'Ha! Not private. No. Nothing like that.' Hanna was twisting a loose screw at the corner of the kitchen table. *Come on, brain.*

'You're not feeling sad, are you? About . . .?' Iain chose not to say the name of Hanna's ex-boyfriend. Just in case, like a block of magnesium, it might cause some unexpected reaction.

'About Joe?' Hanna was surprised. 'No. Not really. I mean, I did miss him a bit this morning.' She remembered her message to Joe from that park bench. She remembered standing at the edge of Port Meadow on May Morning, wanting to share the view with him. Out of habit. Out of affection. 'But I think that might have just been because I was feeling nervous about work.'

'OK. Well, I mean, it's probably too soon to be thinking about that sort of thing anyway.' Iain turned on the oven. 'It takes a long time to heal a broken heart.' Was he, thought Hanna, cock-blocking her? Warning her off? She hadn't even really mentioned another man and yet he seemed to be hinting at something. 'So, what's this mysterious event, dragging you away from my scones?' asked Iain, turning back to face Hanna.

'Ah no, well, actually, tonight I have . . .' Hanna stared at her knee. 'Life drawing.'

Where had that come from? Hanna – and it was hard to overstate this – could not draw. Not even a bit. Neither technically nor expressively. Her GCSE art coursework had involved a lot of collage to cover the fact that every drawing of a person she ever did ended up looking like a tuber.

'Wow! That's brilliant!' Iain's joy made Hanna feel even worse about lying. He was clearly thrilled that she was finally 'getting out there' and picking up that most miserable of all words: a 'hobby'. God, how Hanna loathed hobbies. People who had hobbies were too boring to have friends and too insecure to do nothing. Hobbies were masturbation for people who were embarrassed to get their hands sticky. Fuck hobbies. And yet now, apparently, she was the sort of woman who enjoyed not only a hobby but actually an evening class to boot. 'Where are you doing it?' Iain asked. For a horrible moment Hanna thought he was about to invite himself along.

'Um . . . the East Oxford Community Centre.' Best to say somewhere on the other side of town, just in case.

'Ah, great. Yes. You were always good at art,' said Iain, smiling. Was this man on drugs? Hanna knew that parental affection blinded people to their children's failures and weaknesses, but really. He might as well have congratulated her on being a fantastic scuba diver, or merengue dancer, or on her excellent falconry. Oh. Or he was taking the piss. That was more likely.

'Ha! Yeah. Well, anyway. It starts at six thirty and I'd like to have a shower first,' said Hanna. 'I had a nightmare in M&S.' She watched Iain tip a plastic carrier bag of stinking green plants out into a sink of cold water. 'Can you save me a scone though? They sound delicious.'

'I'll wrap it in a cabbage leaf and hide it under your pillow,' said Iain, turning to the stereo to change the album.

'Perfect.'

Back in her room, Hanna stared desperately at the regurgitating laundry bag of clothes at her feet. How exactly was she going to dress for a first date while also holding up the pretence to her father that she was heading out to her first life drawing class? She couldn't admit that she was going for a drink with Tom Moss. Iain would definitely tell Mary, and then Mary would definitely bring it up next time she came round for a glass of wine and a quick laceration of Hanna's self-esteem. *No, thank you.* She didn't need that pressure.

Hanna pulled off her jumper and stared at her breasts in the mirror. They looked like speech marks, lopsided, framing the thudding of her heart. She pulled the jumper back on. A jumper was good. She'd keep the jumper. A jumper and heels. A jumper and heels said I'm-on-a-date-that-isn't-a-date. It said grown-up sexy. It said, I'm not expecting sex but I have had plenty of it, thank you. It said spunk and polyester. She'd have to do her make-up in the street, Hanna decided, and put her perfume on in the pub toilet. Props. She needed props. Rummaging through a box marked 'stationery and office' that had been wedged beneath the windowsill, Hanna grabbed a couple of biros and a jotter pad. If she stuck the ends out of her handbag as she left, Iain might just be fooled that she was hoicking a whole bag of art supplies out with her tonight. As long as she left in a hurry and Iain didn't ask to see any pictures in the morning. As long as she didn't come home barefoot and pockmarked by love bites. If she could just get in and out of this fucking flat without raising her father's suspicion then this could be the perfect crime.

9

Biffa Bin

Resting her foot on the low wall outside number six Plantation Road, Hanna started to scrabble around in her handbag like a dog digging for bones. Freud, she knew, had argued that handbags were a manifestation of women's genitals; how women projected their anxiety, their possessiveness, their secrecy on to those handled leather sheaths. But to Hanna, handbags were far more like her missing scrotum. During her early teenage years, the bags she carried into – whisper the names – Topshop, New Look and Miss Selfridge had been small, hard, high up under her armpit. As time and life took their toll, the bags had dropped, stretched, become more potent. During the early nineties, her handbags had sprouted hair – a Friesian faux fur handbag full of hair mascara, plastic butterfly hair clips and cherry lip gloss. In her twenties, the bags had taken on a vaguely S&M flavour with metal studs, sharp metal corners and chunky brass zips.

Today, a woman in her thirties, her libido so strong it could crack nuts, her bag was large, soft, absolutely ripe with potential. In it tonight she'd stuffed the pens and notepad, a packet of oatcakes, a book, a water bottle, a selection of necklaces, red lipstick, a spare tampon in case she wanted to make a quick friend in the ladies' toilets (Hollywood had taught her that this was the most efficient way to go about it), an apple, a packet of tobacco, papers, filters, and a lighter with a picture of Leeds Castle – a place she had absolutely never visited – on the side. She had felt too self-conscious walking out of the flat in heels, after lying to Iain about the life drawing class. So she'd jackknifed a pair of pointy turquoise heels under her book while slipping out in her white plimsolls. She felt slightly self-conscious about going to the pub in heels too – a bit eager, a bit too 'I'm on a date' – but knew that the erotic charge of having a spike on her foot might be a pay-off worth trying. They'd make her open her legs just slightly wider, put her closer to eye level, arch her back a little further. The inverse sexual snobbery of her feminist upbringing, which told her that anything but a flat boot and unplucked eyebrow was a sop to misogyny, had its place. But just occasionally it was worth making a carnal foghorn of your body. And if not on a first date, then when?

On a brick, three rows up from the pavement and a metre in from the end of the garden wall of number six, there was a little Tipp-Ex heart. It had been there for twenty years, more perhaps – ever since the afternoon Hanna had locked herself out after school and sat out front, waiting for her parents to come home from work. Before mobile phones, Hanna spent a lot of time sitting on her front doorstep. As an only child and a latchkey kid, it rarely occurred to her to walk round to a friend's house to seek refuge in someone else's early afternoon TV and cupboard snacks. At nine, she had also never been to a café on her own – wouldn't have thought of it, even if she'd had the cash.

Tonight, rummaging through her handbag for the red lipstick, Hanna glanced down at the Tipp-Ex heart. The house was now lived in by another family. The parents were probably called Flora and Richard; they probably had two sons called Damien and Harry who probably liked cricket and niche pornography; they probably used an Alexa; they might even grow their own salad in the window boxes. But the house belonged to Hanna. She knew. The Tipp-Ex heart was testament to that. This was the house that Hanna could still taste, from the floorboards up. It was where she had learned to walk, cooked her first pancake, masturbated (without knowing the act even had a name), tobogganed down the stairs in a Mr. Men sleeping bag, learned to read, drunk milk straight from the bottle, and discovered her cat lying beside a gaggle of kittens in a cardboard box under the stairs. It was her house. Its hallways and banisters were the architecture of her heart. Since moving back to Oxford, Hanna had walked ostentatiously up Plantation Road four or five times, always in the hope that she would catch a glimpse of the new residents coming out of the front door. She longed for a local election, just so she could go canvassing to number six Plantation Road and catch a breath of their hallway, see what they'd knocked into her walls, see the way the sun came through her kitchen window.

NO FREE NEWSPAPERS
PLEASE

That 'please' was very Jericho, thought Hanna. Very I-don't-know-the-name-of-my-postman-but-I-always-give-him-a-bottle-of-Baileys-at-Christmas. She tried to take a look through the curtains, but the bastards had put up those half-pane wooden shutters so all she caught sight of was her own silhouette in the reflection. Diving back into the handbag, she finally pulled out a small perfume tester and her mobile phone. As she rubbed the acrid squirt of something called Symphony into her wrists and neck, she started to text Dom, her expert on all things male.

I'm going for a drink with the man who played bongos with my adolescent heart. How late should I be?

Dom and Hanna had never fancied each other, let alone slept together, which somehow gave their relationship a particular magic. Which wasn't to say Dom was ugly. Almost every single one of Hanna's friends had, at some point, propositioned him, some more successfully than others. Charmaine – a girl Hanna had met through one of those dreadful Women in Business marketing events – had made such a feverish attempt at seducing Dom through sighs, long stares, shoulder nuzzles and arm draping that he'd ended the night by suggesting she get tested for anaemia. But Hanna had just never felt the beat of that drum. She adored him, but didn't fancy him. These days Dom had a beautiful, clever and hilarious girlfriend, Marni, who he'd met at his great uncle's seventieth birthday. That Marni lived in Paris, finishing her two-year residency at a hospital, didn't seem to bother either one of them, and it allowed Hanna glorious access to Dom without worrying that she was third-wheeling his relationship.

It's 5.58 p.m., Hanna. Are you dating an 8-year-old? Dom wrote. Hanna smiled. Then typed her reply.

He works round the corner and suggested we meet after his shift.

OK. Dom's response was speedy. *So either this is an 8-year-old working in a factory or you're dating the world's earliest drinker.* There was a pause as Dom typed some more. *Speaking as your friend, I say stop playing games and go to the pub. Speaking as a man, I say give it at least ten minutes. Just long enough to make his buttocks squeak.*

Roger, replied Hanna.

Daltrey, signed off Dom.

Heeding Dom's advice, she walked straight past the pub and further along Plantation Road. It was only 5.59 p.m. He probably wasn't even there yet. The road narrowed to an alleyway, and Hanna had to step off the pavement to avoid a middle-aged woman in an electrifying combination of sun hat, thick woollen tights, orthopaedic sandals and Burberry mac as she billowed down the pavement like a windsock. Hanna heard the woman tut and, looking up from her phone, caught some mutterings about zombies and screens.

By 6.11 p.m., Hanna had completed her circuit past the brick mansions and conservatories of Leckford Road and was walking up to the Gardeners Arms. Slipping behind a parked car, she whipped out her heels and quickly changed shoes, shoving the road-dirty plimsolls into her handbag, against the apple and copy of today's newspaper. No more dicking about. She was going in. The pub had a tiny front garden, in which was standing a man roughly 360 years old. His face looked like the cracked surface of a dry riverbed. His neck hung in folds above a pale blue shirt. His few hairs danced off his head like morning mist. He was smoking a pipe and the pale blue, faintly tarry smell hung across the doorway in ribbons.

'You're new,' he said, his voice like a quarry.

'Actually, I'm old,' said Hanna. 'But I've been away.'

Inside the pub, a small group of middle-aged people in Debenhams's finest were sitting around a round table with '*Parliamo!* Italian conversation group' printed on a small piece of folded card in the centre. Hanna's entire body was, by now, vibrating with nervous energy. Her feet felt slippery in her shoes and she was altogether too aware of her knickers sliding up one side of her crotch. She didn't have the confidence to stand in the centre of the room and look around. The idea of people looking at her and knowing that she was hoping to meet someone made her flush with shame. So, flicking her eyes quickly side to side, she strode purposefully to the bar.

'Hiya,' said the bartender, his thin ponytail lying across his shoulder like a pet snake. 'What can I get you?'

'A glass of red wine, please,' said Hanna, leaning her hip against the heavy, narrow wooden bar.

'Any particular sort?' he asked.

'A delicious one,' Hanna smiled. One of the many glorious things about being a woman in her thirties – other than being able to start any sentence with the words, 'Speaking as a thirty-year-old woman' – was that Hanna no longer felt any pressure whatsoever to care about wine. At weddings, dinner parties, work events, off-licences, she had given up entirely on pretending to care. It was the middle-class drinking equivalent of taking off your bra in the lift. She'd let it go. Wine was wine was wine was wine. And anybody who really cared more than that needed bigger fish to fry.

As long as Hanna carried on staring at this man, she thought, at the dusty bottles lining the wall behind him, at her reflection in the small mirror above the sink, then she would be all right. No need to get out her phone. No need to turn around and look hopefully across the faces of the other customers, like a baby bird begging for vomit. No need to panic. Tom might be here. He might not. He might have forgotten their arrangement entirely. He might already be in the toilets spraying air freshener through his pubes. It was all entirely beyond her control.

'Would you like to see a food menu?' the man behind the bar asked.

'Sure. Thank you.' Hanna looked down at the folded yellow paper menu, but the words seemed to be jumping across the page like fleas. The combination of excitement, hunger, apprehension and lust was scrambling her concentration. Would some chips calm her heartbeat? Return some of the blood from between her legs back to her brain? Perhaps. But then again, did she really want to be the woman stood up over a bowl of cheesy chips? Wouldn't it be altogether cooler and more Dorothy Parker to sit at a table alone, poised over a glass of red wine, and pretend she was above all that corporeal shit?

'That'll be £4.85,' said the barman. Hanna still got caught out by Oxford prices. You'd think that once you'd swapped the Tube and your Oyster card for bike rides and the towpath, the price of a pint would fall accordingly. But somehow Oxford still managed to treat its drinkers as if they were working at the hard edge of Canary Wharf. Hanna tapped her card on the proffered machine and walked out to the garden. Ever since she'd discovered the joys of a cheese ploughman's and half a lemonade, Hanna had been fairly smitten with pub gardens. Wasps, noise pollution, thigh splinters and sunburn were more than a fair price to pay for a slowly warming glass of wine under an open sky. She picked a table on the small raised lawn beyond the patio and pulled out her provisions; book, tobacco, papers, lighter, phone, newspaper and lipstick. Then she put the lipstick away. It was a strange wrestling of vanity that Hanna would rather look like someone who hadn't thought to put lipstick on than someone who had made the effort of putting lipstick on. When it came to men, she always erred on the side of looking rough and unconcerned rather than pristine and conceited. She desperately wanted Tom to think she was fit while also wanting him to think that she didn't care what he thought. With the first two pages of the *G2* open in front of her, she expertly rolled a cigarette with only slightly shaking fingers. Where was he? She couldn't bear to check, but it must surely be six twenty by now. If he'd out-lated her as some weird game theory power play, he could go fuck himself. Hanna's phone scuttered across the wooden slat of the tabletop.

A new text from Dom: *Insist that he goes down on you first and try not to talk about your GCSE results.* Helpful.

Just as Hanna lit her cigarette and the nicotine spun her into a headrush so strong she wondered if the table had actually tipped over, Tom walked into the garden. He was wearing a slightly faded navy shirt, rolled at the elbows, his soft chest hair just visible below the open top button. He was carrying a pint of stout in one hand, a glass of white wine in the other, and a packet of crisps in his teeth. Hanna's vagina galloped like a stallion.

'Hannacopter, I'm so sorry you got here first. I

managed to slice my thumb on a derailleur just as we were meant to be closing up and have spent the last ten minutes trying to superglue my hand back together and cash up.' He lifted his hand to show a fairly expertly tied bandage. 'Luckily it's my left hand, so I can still . . . do stuff.'

Hanna arched her eyebrows and felt her skin tighten across her thighs. It was early for this kind of chat and she was entirely on board with it. 'Well, I'm glad to hear that a mere flesh wound can't interrupt your foreplay prowess,' said Hanna, raising the dregs of her red wine in a mock toast. Tom's face temporarily flurried with confusion. *Oh shit*, thought Hanna. He'd been talking about his job. Not sex. He'd meant bike stuff. *Oh no.*

'Well, that's a good point,' said Tom, a smile creeping across his face. 'In fact, the dressing may have given me some precious extra girth.' They both laughed, as much from relief as any actual amusement.

'Is this my wine?' asked Hanna in her best Ian Paisley voice.

'Aye,' replied Tom in kind. 'And I demand youse drink it.'

'Thank you.' As part of the strange power game we call flirtation, Hanna didn't say 'I'll get your next one.' If she acted as if Tom was buying her drinks because this was a date and he'd asked her out then perhaps, by a process of osmosis, he'd start to feel like this was a date and that he'd asked her out. She was playing her princess card. Not her natural forte but it was worth a go. 'So, how was work? Apart from the home surgery?'

'Yeah, good, thanks. I think Jeremy Paxman might have come in earlier, to buy some new treads, but it might have just been an angry horse; hard to tell.'

'Did it pay by card?'

'No, cash.'

'Oh, definitely Paxman then,' said Hanna, dragging on her cigarette. 'Horses never carry cash.' Tom's smile was like the slow creeping of a sunrise. First his jaw tensed, then his large lips cracked open to reveal white, even teeth, eventually it reached up to his eyes, and the long black lashes seemed to glisten. Sometimes even his forehead would seem to pull higher. Hanna had always loved making Tom laugh. At school she had felt each smile, each grin, each giggle as a personal victory; a touch of reassurance that yes, he liked her, and yes, she was worth having in the world.

'How about you? Did you warm up after your swim on May Morning?' Tom looked down at Hanna's nipples. She followed his gaze, then slowly looked up at him from under her eyelashes, making sure he'd seen her seeing him.

'I did, thank you. Although I did find quite a lot of horse hair on my work trousers at one point.'

'Oh mate, that was amazing.' Tom pulled his hands through his hair, opening his elbows and knees wide, like a ship rolling out its sails. 'I've never seen a woman headlock a horse before.'

'A woman?' Hanna cocked her cigarette archly.

'Yeah. I mean, sorry. Anyone.' Tom closed his legs.

'That was a stupid, sexist thing to say. I've never seen anyone lasso a horse with their own jumper before. It was immense.' Another point to Hanna. Why did flirting feel so much like fighting? A nick, a push, a wheedle, leading up to a great, thumping stab. 'So, anyway, you're back in Oxford. That's cool. Where are you living?' It was not the turn Hanna had particularly wanted the conversation to take. Not yet, at least.

'Before I tell you, I'm going to finish this and then get another glass of wine,' she said, downing the rest of her glass while standing up.

'Sure,' said Tom, unhinging his knees into a squat. There really was no good way to get on and off a pub bench. 'I can get them, though.'

'That's OK,' said Hanna. 'They actually let women order at the bar here. Which is extremely woke of them.' Tom grimaced. 'What would you like?'

'A pint of the Wells stout, please,' said Tom. 'I'll get the next ones.' *Good*, thought Hanna. *So we're staying for at least two more drinks.* That was good.

Walking back to the table, a glass of wine in one hand and a pint in the other, Hanna thought, *Just me and my husband, having a drink after our busy days at work.* These thoughts, which were of course every commitment-phobe's worst nightmare, didn't worry Hanna. She knew they weren't as psychotic as they sounded. Imagining marriage with Tom was like trying on a new coat, or walking around a potential flat. She and Tom. Mr and Mrs. Just trying on the phrase was her way of gauging her feelings towards him. Did she just want to clamber on to his large, hard body, or was there the capacity for real love in her heart here? Difficult to tell. But the idea that the small group of heavily bronzed students sitting on the patio might look at her and Tom with matrimonial envy made her almost liquid with pleasure.

'Right. Well, it's a tale as old as time,' said Hanna, sipping her wine and pulling her tobacco towards her. 'I broke up with my long-term boyfriend earlier this year and have moved back in with Iain. My dad.' Sometimes you just had to slap that dead rat on to the table in order to move on. 'Luckily, sleeping in the spare room of a geriatric ukulele-playing engineer at thirty has absolutely always been my plan, so I'm just thrilled that it's all come together so well.' She smiled. *If you act fine with things, other people are fine with things. Please, Jehovah, make it true.* 'I'd also always really hoped that both me and my dad would one day be single and living together at the same time, so I've absolutely hit the jackpot life-wise.' Bringing slightly sweaty hands to her mouth, she licked the edge of the Rizla and dragged her eyes up to meet Tom's. His expression was unreadable.

'I'm sorry about the break-up,' he said, at last. And then, like something from an instant coffee advert, he reached over and squeezed her hand. What in the name of suffering shit was this? Had she just been friend-squeezed? Was he platonic-touching her now? After it had all been going so well? Had she really gone in too hard with the single-and-living-with-your-dad stuff? Oh God. Oh *God*. 'I imagine you must have broken up with him,' said Tom, his concerned look just slightly twinkling with something else. Hanna went to speak, but he cut in. 'Because no sane man would kick you out of bed.'

It took all Hanna's strength not to jump on to the table and punch the air. *Hell. Yes.* Tom Moss wanted her in his bed. Or at least, he might. Who knew? But he hadn't left yet, anyway.

'How about you?' said Hanna, her voice ever so slightly too high. 'Where are you living? I never expected to find you back in Oxford.'

'Ah yes, well, I did leave for quite a while. After Spain I moved to Berlin and got a job with a small food-growing cooperative in Neukölln. That was really good. Then I joined an NGO creating a global seed bank and went to live in Ethiopia for a few years, working on beans. Then, when the funding for that ran out, I went to New Zealand to live with my Aunt Ruth on her homestay – my uncle had just died and so she needed someone to slash at fields of Japanese bindweed with a massive knife. I probably learned even more about food sustainability at my Aunt Ruth's than I'd learned in two years with the NGO. Anyway, when I was in NZ I got to know a group of hardcore cyclists and started going on these long rides into the hills. They offered me a part-time job as a mechanic. Like, nothing pay but I wasn't paying rent either. And so, eventually, when my mum started to miss me, I decided to come home and pick up a job in a bike shop here.'

'Don't you miss growing things?'

'Yeah, well, actually, I've taken over my mum's allotment. So I am still growing things.'

'You still haven't answered my question, though,' said Hanna, picking up her wine glass. 'Where are you living?' She was trying to imagine his bed. The duvet cover, the bookshelves, the view out of the window on a hazy, hungover morning.

Tom looked a little sheepish.

'Well, I'm actually staying at my mum's, in Wolvercote. Just at the moment.' He looked down and started running his middle finger over the bandaged thumb. 'She doesn't need twenty-four-hour care or anything, but it's just useful having me there in the mornings to get her up and stuff. And then I'm usually around after work to make dinner.' What was this? Why would Tom's mum need someone else to get her up? 'So, yeah. I know the feeling.'

'What's actually happened to your mum?' This was not, Hanna realized, the most sensitive way to ask the question. But in her family, clarity always beat sensitivity. She'd rather know what was going on than dance around the edges of something uncomfortable; better to ask a direct question than commit a string of faux pas by simply not knowing.

'Oh right, yeah. She had a stroke.'

'Ah, shit,' said Hanna. Another dazzling display of sensitivity on her part.

'Yeah. It was quite shit.' Tom was laughing.

'Sorry. That wasn't—'

He interrupted her. 'Actually, it's really nice to hear someone just say "that's shit". Because that's what it is.' Tom looked into her eyes for just a little longer than he might have done. 'People expect me to be suddenly really zen, just because my mum's got a sloppy arm. But actually it's just a bit shit.' Hanna wondered about squeezing his hand. But decided that was a bit ITV. 'More booze?' said Tom, picking up their empty glasses with a well-practised grip.

Hanna stretched, arching her back, tracing the line of Tom's shoulders and chest with her gaze.

'Yes, please. Can I have a whisky this time? Something sort of peaty? Like a Laphroaig?'

Tom went very still. He smiled. Then, looking at her mouth, he said: 'You're amazing, Hanna.'

Two hours later, the garden was dark, Hanna's mouth tasted like the ends of a bonfire, a string of lights across the decking was surrounded by moths, and Hanna's knees were clamped around Tom's thigh. They were kissing. Hanna wasn't quite sure how that first kiss had happened. Had she initiated it? She remembered that at some point she'd simply stopped talking. She had stared at Tom, her lips ever so slightly puckered, her eyes soft, and just waited. He'd get the message. She remembered pulling his shirt collar towards her. She remembered his hand on her waist. But had she kissed him? The answer was swilling around at the bottom of a barrel and, frankly, she didn't care. She was kissing Tom Moss. And it was good. Very good. So good that at one point she'd reached automatically for his belt before he whispered, 'We can't. Not here,' and she remembered that they were sitting on a wooden bench outside a pub full of white-haired academics doing a conversational Italian class.

'We should go,' whispered Hanna into his ear, squeezing his thigh ever so slightly.

'Where?' She couldn't tell if his voice was thick with lust, drink or fatigue. But there was something slightly slow about the way he'd asked it.

'Fuck. I don't know.' Hanna pressed her forehead into his shoulder. Then, rousing herself: 'We'll find somewhere.' Standing up, she got an almighty headrush. *Push through it*, she told herself. *Look busy.* And so she swept the contents of the tabletop into her handbag. Tobacco, newspaper, lipstick – when had she put that on? – maybe even the ashtray. *Oh well.* Out in the street, Hanna and Tom stood facing each other. He was so tall. There was so much of him. Like a bear. Or a tree. Or a very horny postbox. For a second, Hanna saw them from outside their own bodies. Hanna thought she looked beautiful. Hanna thought she looked happy.

'We can't go back to mine. Iain will definitely hear us,' said Hanna, lacing her fingers through Tom's as they started to stumble down the street towards Walton Street. Tom pushed her up against a lamppost, his leg between hers, his hands cupping the hair behind her ears. They kissed again.

'And we can't walk all the way to Wolvercote,' he said.

They stumbled on. Were they walking to Port Meadow? That would be somewhere. Then, without knowing how, they were outside a huge student house – the garden overhung with ivy and the sticky-sweet smell of bluebells. Hanna was pushed up against the side of a Biffa bin and Tom's hands were sliding up her back. His breathing was cracked, jagged. In that moment, she wanted him more than she had ever wanted anyone or anything in her life.

'Oi oi!' Two boys, one holding a traffic cone, the other wearing a purple nylon afro wig, were standing beside them in the front garden.

'She's getting it tonight, hey Rodge?' said the shorter boy, his limp blond hair stuck to his face with sweat.

'Most definitely, compadre,' the taller one drawled, in that particular mix of Southern Californian and Home Counties so beloved by Oxbridge students.

'Yeah, well, you can't just start fucking against our bin, mmmkay?' said the little one, snarking towards Hanna and Tom. 'You might give us all chlamydia.'

They both started laughing so hard Hanna worried one of them might puke.

And suddenly, like a lumberjack lifting a tree, Tom

pulled his hand out from Hanna's bra, picked her up by the waist, threw her over his shoulder and started to walk, purposefully, towards Port Meadow.

'Night, boys,' he called. 'We've got something to finish.'

10
Toothpaste

'Are you all right?'

There are many ways to ask someone how they are. And many more ways to tell someone that they're being annoying, in the form of a question. This was well and truly the latter. Iain came in while Hanna was doing her teeth, picked up his toothbrush and started scrubbing away at his popcorn mouth without so much as acknowledging her. Tensing her shoulders, Hanna prepared for the next bit. Within seconds, Iain was leaning over the sink, essentially shoulder-barging Hanna into the towel rail and hawking up great dripping strings of spit and foam and various other oral substances into the basin. Hanna's stomach lurched. Her last fibre of patience strained like an Alsatian on a leash. She spat into the bath.

'Could you not have waited just one more minute until I was finished?' she said, a small ring of white foam around her mouth like a set of clown lips. Iain didn't even turn around. 'I hate it when people do this,' Hanna continued. 'I hate the sound of other people brushing their teeth. Watching them spit makes me actually dry-retch. You've completely pushed me away from the sink, even though I was here first. And it's not like I've been in here ages or anything. It must have been, what, forty-five seconds, tops? Surely, surely even you can wait two minutes.' Iain stood up and turned round. And then he said it. Globules of white, minty spit flying through the air and showering her arm as he did so.

'Are you all right?'

Unbelievable.

'Look, Iain,' said Hanna, throwing her toothbrush into the bath where it pinged against the edge and ricocheted up against the white tiled walls. 'It's not hard. When someone else is in the bathroom, just leave them alone. It's not a shared room.'

'Ah, come on, I don't—'

Hanna shouted over him: 'Two days ago, you came in and did a piss while I was brushing my teeth!'

'I already said I won't do that ag—'

'I mean, what is actually wrong with you? Did you not think how it might be to have someone else's urine flying through the air less than a metre away from your open mouth?'

'I thought this was about brushing—'

'It's like the moment I take out my toothbrush, a tiny siren goes off in your head saying you have to find some way to come in here and do something disgusting,' said Hanna, her hands shaking on her hips. 'Can't I just have one room to myself, for two minutes? This is my house too.'

'Actually, it's my house.' Iain's shoulders had hardened like a cat preparing to launch. 'This is my house and if I want to brush my teeth, or do a piss, or take a shower, or apply my athlete's foot cream while singing "Lady Madonna" then, actually, I can. Because I bought it. I pay the mortgage. This room?' He jabbed a finger just centimetres from Hanna's face, at the shower. 'Is my room.'

'Oh, I see,' said Hanna, her face twisting into a bitter little snarl. 'So that's what you're doing. That's how this is going to play out. Listen, if you want me to move out, why don't you just act like a grown man, for once in your piss-up of a little life, and tell me?'

'I didn't—'

'You're an adult! Be an adult!' Hanna was really shouting now. 'Just tell me that you think it's time I left. Don't just come in every day, while I'm trying to use the bathroom, and piss and spit all over me in the hope that I'll get so revolted by you that I'll move out!'

'Are you calling me revolting?' Iain looked wounded, furious, disbelieving.

'Yep,' said Hanna, a watershed cracking at the base of her skull. 'I reckon. I think most people would agree that spitting your nuts out on to your cereal, biting your toenails, pissing next to my open mouth, shitting with the door open, scratching your bare armpits while you cook dinner, scratching your balls every time you can't remember a word, blowing your nose into your bare hand, talking with your mouth open—'

'Talking with my mouth open?'

'You know what I mean.' Hanna smacked her hand against the mirrored cabinet above the sink. 'Eating and talking at the same time, so I have to watch every meal churn around your mouth like a cement mixer.' She swung her head around in frenzied circles. 'Drinking cold tea, leaving your socks on the arm of the sofa, never washing your towel, washing up in three centimetres of cold, filthy, oily scum, clipping your toenails with a pair of kitchen scissors, farting while I'm on the phone, Febrezing the fucking curtains—'

'You wouldn't have any curtains if it weren't for me,' spat Iain, bristling with anger. 'What?' He came very close to Hanna's face, his voice low, icy, horrible. 'Would you rather I'd left you in London? To live in your sad little house with your ex? Left you to spin out your final fertile years in a poky little hole with a man who isn't your boyfriend? And who can blame him.' His neck was creeping beetroot. 'Does it count for nothing that I have basically put my life and my house into storage because you've managed to dropkick everything you had into a skip?'

Hanna was undaunted. 'Oh, please. PLEASE tell me how I'm bad at relationships,' she said, a cruel smile electrifying her face. 'And is it any wonder? After growing up with you and Mum? Two people who were so incompatible that you basically ignored each other for ten years but didn't have the backbone or emotional intelligence just to break up?'

'We stayed together for you,' cried Iain, kicking the sanitary towel bin by the loo.

'Bullshit!' shouted Hanna, with a desperate urge to push Iain's eyeballs so hard into his skull that they exploded. 'You stayed together because neither of you had the imagination or chutzpah to actually change your life. And you know what? I think you were scared.' Her voice dropped about an octave. 'I think you were so scared of being alone that you would rather live with someone who doesn't even like you than confront it.'

'I liked Julie—'

'I don't care!' interrupted Hanna. 'I don't care if you liked each other. I don't care if you "got on".' Those last two words were said through a pursed mouth, pulled down at the sides like a pantomime dame. 'My point is that for eighteen years I lived with two people who acted like fucking colleagues: nothing in common, going on holiday separately, eating at different times, arguing over what kind of milk to buy, never going out for dinner, having no mutual friends, sleeping in different rooms. That's what I thought marriage was. No wonder I can't manage a relationship – I literally have no idea what a happy marriage looks like!' Furious with herself, Hanna could feel the tears welling up behind her eyes like marbles.

'You're right there,' said Iain, his balled fist turning waxy pale. 'You judge me but you have no idea what being a parent is like. Christ, Hanna, when I was your age—'

'Don't you dare!' said Hanna, the tears spraying off her lips as she yelled it.

'I was married, living in my own house, and you were nearly six,' Iain shouted over her, punching himself in the thigh as he made each point.

'Having a baby doesn't make—'

'And I was happy!' Iain interrupted this time. 'I just want you to be happy,' he said, rubbing a dry hand across his forehead with a sound like paper being torn. 'Love isn't fifty years of first dates and wedding days, you know. It's a slog. You meet someone and you work together and, sure, time passes and you grow apart, but you make it work because—'

'Make it work? Make it work?' Hanna scraped her fingers through the front of her hair. 'Is that what you call it?' Her laugh was shrill and forced. It slammed off the tiles and back around the room. 'Wasting decades of another person's life just because you didn't want to spend the evenings on your own and weren't sure that anyone else would want you? You and Mum should have split up years ago. Years ago! You know it, I know it' – she pointed right into his face – 'and I bet Mum knows it. You didn't make each other happy. That wasn't love. It was a shared mortgage and someone to take out the bins.'

'Well, that's a damn sight more than you've got right now!' said Iain, drawing himself up as tall as he could.

'As least I've got some self-respect!' cried Hanna, stamping her foot. It was amazing how these gestures, which you assumed only happened in children's books and bad foreign-language soap operas, could suddenly explode in your own body during an argument. 'At least I can look in the mirror and tell myself that I got out when I should.'

'Me and your mum were happy.' Iain's voice wobbled. 'And we were proud of you. So proud. Having you was the best thing we ever did. I don't regret—'

'You were a terrible father,' spat Hanna. There was a horrible pop of silence. Hanna and Iain looked at each other, stunned. She could take that back. She could retreat. If she acted fast and acted now, she could defuse that bomb. And yet. And yet. She pushed on. 'You never knew any of my friends' names, never knew what subjects I was studying.' She started to count off on her fingers, staring at the knuckles so she didn't have to look her father in the eye. 'You never asked me to come with you to play football, never read my poems or framed any of my pictures.' Her voice was gurgling, her face liquid. As she paused, trying to control her voice, Iain jumped in.

'Yeah? Well, that's because you're shit at drawing!' he said, his voice quivering.

Before she could process this pathetic jibe, Hanna drove on: 'You don't have a single photograph of me up anywhere in your flat, you forgot all my birthdays when I was at university – yes, that's right; Mum told me that she'd have to ring to remind you – you never talked to me about your childhood, never vetted any of my boyfriends to check they weren't actual murderers, you have me saved in your phone as "daughter" – I've seen it – and you Febrezed my bloody bedding!' Sobs pulsed down her ribs, squeezing her lungs shut.

'You said that one already,' said Iain. The two of them were heaving and snorting like bulls caught in a pen. Hanna could see the sweat prickling on his hairline. The vein on the side of his head was throbbing like an electric eel. For her part, Hanna was doing those choking gasps that toddlers make after landing face down on a slick of gravel and finely grating off most of their skin. She dropped her head into her hands and curled up like a prawn. This was horrible. He was horrible. She'd been pretty horrible. And then, instead of taking her in his arms, kissing the top of her head and telling her he loved her, Iain did a quite remarkable thing. He started brushing his teeth. Again. Hanna looked up. Surely not. Iain was looking at her in the cabinet mirror.

'What?' he spat, spraying her image out of view with white foam. 'I'm going to brush my teeth in my bathroom, whenever I want, and if you don't like that then perhaps you should find your own place to stay.'

'Oh, don't worry. I'm moving out. I'm moving out tomorrow!'

The slam Hanna gave the front door as she flew out and down the stairs was loud enough to make a saucepan on a table in the flat downstairs fall off the kitchen counter and on to the floor. The resident, Brydie, who was eighty-four and deaf, became convinced that this was the act of a poltergeist.

God, it had felt good to slam that door. If she could, Hanna would have gone straight out and pulled apart a hay barn with her own hands. She'd tear at the wood, splinters ripping through the skin on her fingers, blood trickling down her wrists. She felt like she could take on anything. It was adrenaline, she knew. The comedown would hit tonight at some point, probably as she curled up to sleep in a bush, smelling of Papa John's, unable or unwilling to face Iain. But for now, just for a moment, she was propelled by something pneumatic. She stormed down Walton Street and into town, past couples tripping lazily down the centre of the pavement, arm in arm, too lubricated by lust and wine to unhook their bodies from each other for even a second. *Fuck them*, thought Hanna. *Fuck them.* They'd be lonely again one day. She shot through town, past the men and women burnt copper by sun and dust, drinking at the bottom of Carfax Tower. She ploughed through snake-like lines of tourists staring up at Christ Church College or hovering in front of the Meadow. And then, before her feet even seemed to have caught up with her racing mind, she was standing above the river. Looking down at the curly haired families eating chips and the hollering groups of friends drinking in the evening sun at the Head of the River. She felt like a flea-pecked pigeon. The water swirled below her feet. The bells at Christ Church started to ring.

How could Iain have been such a prick? Telling her to just be happy. To get married. To have a baby. Did he really think those things hadn't occurred to her? Did he really not imagine that she worried about running out of time? She wasn't sure she wanted children yet, but breaking up with Joe had felt both like losing the option and her only chance to decide. Every time she bled out another unfertilized egg into her pants, she knew that her chances of becoming a mum were pouring out of her body too. She knew that she didn't have for ever. But she also hadn't been willing to hang frozen in indecision because of a man who would rather spend six hours reading about fretboards on the internet than come to the park and meet their friends' new baby. It wasn't true what she'd said to Iain about having self-respect. Not really. Not yet. But she did want to meet someone wonderful. She just wanted to love and be loved in return. Being with Joe had been a double bind of an accessible boyfriend and inaccessible feelings. So yes, thank you, Iain, maybe she was worried about running out of time. Of course she was. But wasn't that why she was here? Wasn't that why she'd eventually scraped together the flapping tatters of her self-esteem to leave Joe? Wasn't this – as weird and uncomfortable as it was – her last chance?

Pulling out her phone, Hanna had that familiar twinge of fear and longing to throw it into the river. Just to make a bad situation worse; to feel something; to watch it plummet. Instead, she decided to message Tom. She knew it was silly but after the argument with Iain, she wanted Tom's attention.

Hey pal, she wrote, leaning on the stone wall of the bridge as a purple 35 bus wheezed past. *Want to fuck?* she wrote. Then deleted it. *I feel sad.* Again, as soon as the letters appeared on screen, she erased them. *Let's fall in love.* Seeing something so potentially dangerous tapped out in text gave her the same thrill as dangling her phone over the water. How easy it would be to ruin things, needlessly. She deleted the message. Then, looking around for some spurious reason to message this man, who she had slept with just once, she wrote, *Have you ever seen a baby crow? I don't think they exist.* Light. Impersonal. Vaguely enigmatic. Hanna pressed send. The ticks turned blue. It had been read. *I'm just walking down the river if you're around?* Blue ticks. Then nothing.

Hanna walked down the bridge and on to the towpath. She was slower now; the adrenaline that had loosened her knees and seared across her forehead was already starting to ebb away. She kicked a pebble into the river, only for five hungry and honking geese to start ploughing through the water towards her, mistaking the stone for food. The boats here were tatty. Bits of wood leaned up against generators and old cider bottles and saucepans full of dried-up rice. One had huge bits of cardboard resting against the side with various conspiracy theories inked across them in thick black felt tip.

But at least they weren't living with their dad, thought Hanna. At least they weren't living with her dad. Nobody had just accused them of being unlovable and out of time. God, she had to move out. And soon. She'd said it now. Maybe she could go and stay with Tom for a few days, until she could find something proper. She looked down at her phone. Still no reply to her message. It would be intense, staying in Tom's mum's house, out in the country. But it wasn't like she didn't know his mum; back when they were at school, Tom and Hanna had often hung out in each other's kitchens, eating mayonnaise sandwiches and ignoring their maths homework.

Tom's mum had given her a lift to friends' birthday parties in the back of her old Volvo. Or maybe she could beg Shazia to sleep on her sofa? They'd not seen each other since her first date with Tom last week, but they messaged a lot. Maybe that counted? The sky had faded to the last pale blue of twilight. There was a big moon, hanging heavy in the sky. God, if this was all hormones, Hanna was going to boil with shame in the morning.

On her right, a black iron gate was slightly ajar. Hanna had never seen behind here before. The thick bush that lined the towpath had always been far too tall above her head to see what happened on the other side. And so, without quite knowing why, she slipped through the gap. In front of her, as soft and smooth as velvet, lay a large playing field. It was lined on one side with horse chestnut trees, their leaves waving like huge green hands. The milky light of the moon lay across the grass, so high that she could see her own shadow. In the corner, a sprinkler was spraying water in wide arcs across the lawn. The sweat, snot, tears and toothpaste had dried into a rind of misery across Hanna's face. Her armpits smelled. Her feet were rubbed hot by unsuitable shoes pulled on without time for socks. Like a moth, Hanna was walking towards the sprinkler, unresistant. It was so quiet in that field. The rising moon was turning the whole scene monochrome. She felt like she'd somehow slipped through a gap in the leaves and come out in Narnia. She pushed her right boot off with a toe. Then pulled the left off with her sweat-damp hands. Then walked a little further. She lifted her dress off her head and walked, in a pair of knickers she'd had since she was twenty-one and a bra that didn't quite fit, into the sprinkler. This was Queen's College Recreation Ground. And she was going to spray her lady sweat all over its hallowed, ancient soil. Unable to clear her life up on her own, maybe she could just camp here until things sorted themselves out with Iain. Until Tom fell in love with her. Until someone came and rescued her from her father's castle.

11
Milk Bath

That morning, Hanna had decided to go to Modern Art Oxford as yet another way to dodge the seething resentment hanging between her and Iain in the small two-bedroom flat. She'd not bothered to check the listing on any website, nor to read any reviews of what was on. So now she was standing in front of a photograph, printed the size of a king mattress, showing a lonely female figure in a garter, a frothy veil, and what looked like some sort of rubberized face mask. Her features were obliterated, her eyes small black hollows. In another, she lay in a red bath, her legs hanging over the side, like someone about to have their cervix inspected. Across the room, there she was, almost entirely underwater, invisible but for a hand rising up like the Lady of the Lake. On her third finger, a gumball wedding ring sparkled cheaply in the bathroom lights. This felt personal. Hanna felt seen, and it was not entirely benign. This lonely figure, poised on the edge of love, loss, marriage, birth, was too close. Her cheap romance, her twilight solitude, her utter paralysis, felt too familiar.

The oily, fermenting smell of the milk bath installation in the corner of the room clung to the back of Hanna's throat. She needed to get out. Walking into the smaller exhibition space at the far end, Hanna saw a photograph of that same vacant figure, this time covered entirely with green body paint. A Gorgon in a cheap motel. A single woman. A monster. Hanna kept walking, thumping the exit doors with her shoulders and heading quickly for the stairs.

Back outside, with the fresh smell of fag smoke, doughnuts, Jo Malone and piss in her nostrils, Hanna felt a little calmer. Perspective. She wasn't curdling in a honeymoon pool of her own indecision. Not really. Yes, she was still living with her father, after returning to her hometown, single. Yes, she was still, by the laws of dinner party conversation, without a boyfriend. And yes, she had woken up this morning to a WhatsApp picture of yet another black-and-white photo of the inside of somebody's womb, with a speech bubble emerging from a cashew-nut foetus saying, 'Hello, world! Mummy's pregnant!' sent by someone from her old job. But she wasn't actually green. She might not even be envious. She might just be nothing.

It had been three days since Hanna's argument with Iain and things in the flat were tenser than the skin of a drum. The night of toothbrush-gate, Hanna had crept back in at 1 a.m., smelling damp and shivering slightly, and gone straight into her room. Iain had either been asleep or lying in bed wearing his giant noise-cancelling headphones – either way, he hadn't attempted a doorstep reconciliation. In fact, he hadn't attempted a ceasefire at all. In the morning, Hanna had woken up to Iain blowing his nose like a foghorn in the hallway outside her door. How did he make every bodily function quite so loud? Sniffing, farting, yawning, sneezing, snoring, drinking, burping – and that was before you even got to the humming, clicking, drumming and singing. She'd waited until the front door clicked with Iain's parting step before getting up and showering quickly, trying to avoid the thin grey pube clinging to the side of the bath. When she got home from work there had been a note stuck to the kitchen table: *Dinner at Mary's. Back tomorrow.* Yesterday, she'd spent the evening in her bedroom, trawling Gumtree, SpareRoom, Zoopla, Rightmove, Facebook and OpenRent, looking at unheated basements, student house-shares, windowless bedsits, and extremely formal adverts from elderly widows looking for lodgers who could also landscape their two-acre gardens. She'd eaten a cheese toastie under her Jungle Book duvet for dinner, and only come out to brush her teeth once she'd heard the television come on in the room next door and knew Iain would be out of the way. She didn't know which she was avoiding more; a continuation of the argument with her father under a set of kitchen knives or a cloying, tear-stained request for forgiveness beside fungal-smelling trainers in the hallway. Either way, she had decided to avoid him as much as possible and double her efforts to find a way of escaping his flat.

I'm five minutes away!!! Shazia's messages, Hanna had come to realize, were frequently littered with a quantity of punctuation that was almost entirely unrelated to their content. Everything!!! was a huge?????? deal!?!?!? And yet, in person, Shazia was the sort of person who would barely raise an eyebrow. Even if you admitted to, say, giving the man you were seeing a handjob in his staff room during a Tuesday lunchbreak.

I'll order us a rose tea and some baklava, Hanna replied, walking round the corner to a chain Lebanese restaurant, decorated with carved elephants and fezzes and other relatively un-Lebanese props.

Sitting at the table, Hanna scrolled through her camera roll to find the picture of Tom, early in the morning, wishing her a nice day. He'd sent it unprompted, two days after their Gardeners Arms date. Just as Hanna had been coiling herself into a solid ball of worry that he would never speak to her again, it had arrived: a picture of Tom in bed, topless, lit from a window above his head, with the caption 'Don't say I never give you anything, Hannacopter'. It was the perfect mix of arrogant and self-deprecating, funny and hot. Hanna had immediately screen-grabbed the picture and caption, so she could stare at it without being tempted to reply. Tom was a beautiful man. The sort of man who early morning dehydration and a crinkle-eyed squint into daylight rendered more attractive. Rugged. Endearing. Sexy. Since receiving that photo, Hanna had sent Tom two messages. He'd not yet replied.

'Hello, darling!' Shazia swept up to the table in a cloud of laundry powder, perfume and cocoa butter. 'I hope I'm not late.'

'Not at all!' said Hanna, leaning against the table to hug her.

'Are you all right? You look a bit . . .' Shazia glided into her seat and Hanna thudded back down on to her bum.

'Oh, fine. I just had a bit of an existential crisis at Modern Art Oxford,' smiled Hanna, trying to make a joke out of the absolute truth.

'Have you just been to see that exhibition with the green woman and the bath of milk?' Shazia asked, her hand flying up to her forehead. 'Fuck, man, that show was incredible. It made me so . . .' Shazia was searching for the right word. 'Uneasy.'

'Oh my god,' Hanna nearly shouted, the words pouring out of her like water from a fire hose. 'Shazia, I freaked out! I'm single, living with my single dad, I'm trying to get over my ex but I'm not sure what that even means, and all my friends are settling down and I keep wondering if I will ever have a baby, and suddenly I'm surrounded by mad lonely women in shell baths and pink knickers and everything smells of cheese, and Iain's got this new girlfriend who looks like a block of cheddar and they keep kissing, and fuck!' Hanna ran her hands over her face. 'It was a lot, you know?'

'A lot!' laughed Shazia. 'I tried to bring my husband but he took one look at the show online and said he'd rather go to John Lewis and look at their slow cookers.' She was so married, thought Hanna. Why was it that every time someone told her they were married, she had to physically restrain herself from asking why?

'So, how's it going, living with your dad?' asked Shazia, stirring the contents of her little silver teapot.

'Um. Well, it's temporary. Just for now. It's not big enough for two people.' Hanna was awkward; wanting to be honest but not wanting to be pitied either. 'I want to get somewhere of my own – just renting, obviously.' That nervous chuckle all thirty-somethings used when talking about housing, unsure if the person they were talking to was renting a broken shed or had been bought a house by their minted parents. 'I'm desperate to get out, to be honest. But Oxford is almost as expensive as London.'

'Preach,' said Shazia.

'I feel like I spend my life either scrolling through spare rooms or spare men on my phone.' Hanna's smile was just a little hollow.

'Well, listen. We have a room, if you're really desperate.' Shazia was looking Hanna straight in the eye, nothing coy or bashful about it. 'It's pretty small and there's only a single bed in there, but you're welcome to it until you find somewhere yourself.'

For a second, Hanna felt like a helium balloon, let go. Was Shazia genuinely offering her a spare room, away from her father?

'Oh Shaz, that's so kind but don't you think you should check with—?'

'Khalid won't mind. He's always talking about how the house feels empty with just the two of us. Seriously. You can kick in some cash for bills if you stay longer than a month, but really, the offer is there.'

Hanna's face broke open into a huge grin. 'Oh, Shazia! You're my knight in shining—!' She reached forward to hug Shazia, nearly upsetting both their cups. Her hair smelled incredible and her shirt felt like silk. 'This is a really nice top.' Hanna let her hand run down the sleeve.

'I know, right?' said Shazia, pulling the collar around her neck. 'I got it from that amazing stall in Gloucester Green on a Thursday. The guy who runs it looks like a Peperami in a shell suit, but there's a whole five-pound rail.'

'Oh God, don't tell me this,' said Hanna. 'I'm still living out of laundry bags and Iain would freak if I started buying any more clothes. Although maybe . . .' Hanna let the rest of the sentence swim through the air between them. Maybe if she moved in with Shazia, they could share their clothes, like the old days.

'Ahh, Iain. Does he still look like Phil Collins?'

'On a truly bad day,' said Hanna, smiling. 'As in, he looks like Phil Collins on the day Phil Collins divorced his wife via fax.'

'Lovely.' Shazia pushed her hair away from her forehead and picked up the menu. 'Now, let's eat some goddamn chickpeas.'

*

Back at the flat, Hanna found Iain in just a pair of boxer shorts and a fleece, unpacking the contents of a record bag on to the kitchen table. The only record in the bag, as far as Hanna could see, was a twelve-inch copy of *Songs in the Attic* – the EP Iain had written and recorded in his tiny top-floor studio the year he and Julie had finally divorced. Hanna had only listened to it once, under duress, the following Christmas. She remembered a lot of womp-womp noises and some cod Brian Eno synths. Tuning her ear to the inevitable white noise of Iain's flat, she now realized that the music coming out of his kitchen speakers was almost certainly from this EP, currently rotating on the record player next door. A wash of guitar was playing the same small chord progression while a bass plucked out an unlikely melody.

'Hello.' Hanna hovered in the kitchen doorway, holding her bag at her knees. She moved to step forward, then held back. 'Have you had an argument with Mary or something?' She nodded at the green screen-printed cover of *Songs in the Attic* on the table. It was the first time they'd spoken in more than two days, but with the prospect of Shazia's spare room on the horizon, Hanna felt able to finally break the silent deadlock between her and her father.

'Ah no, nothing like that,' said Iain, twisting an earring between his huge fingers. 'I was actually looking for something for you, as a matter of fact. I thought it might make you smile.'

On the table was a divorce certificate, a yellowing

letter to Santa, some baby teeth in an old film canister, an old council tax bill and the stump of Hanna's umbilical cord, looking like a dried cranberry in a white plastic clip. What on earth could she possibly want out of all this shit? Was this Iain's attempt at an apology? To empty a hoover bag on to the kitchen table and watch her sift through it?

'Here it is,' said Iain, pulling a long, thin strip of paper out from the pages of a 1985 diary.

Hanna crossed the threshold and stood by the table, looking at the printed figures.

Half roast chicken	63p
Fried fillet plaice	58p
Bread and butter	2p
Seasonal veg	12p
Spanish burgundy	£1.12

What was this? A receipt for somewhere called Les Soeurs? The ticket had been filled in with pencil, and the final amount in biro. Why was Iain showing her this?

'That's from my first meal out with your mum,' Iain said, nodding at the piece of paper with his eyes sparkling. 'We didn't call it a date, back then. You "went out". So she and I "went out" to a place on the King's Road. I thought it was pretty fancy. Until she came back from the loos and said there was a calling card tucked into the mirror.' Iain was smiling, a tad nervously, Hanna now thought. 'Anyway, I just thought you might like to see it.'

Hanna turned the receipt over. There, on the back, in her dad's small, draughtsmanlike writing, was a date. 5 June 1985. And then, just below it, 'And I love her.'

'Is that a Beatles quote?' Hanna asked, smiling.

'Yep. The other night, you said that me and Julie never loved each other. That we were more like colleagues—'

'Iain, listen—'

'But we did love each other. In our way. And I wanted you to see that. We weren't Romeo and Juliet, but we weren't Charles and Diana either.'

Hanna pulled out a chair across the corner of the table from her father. 'Iain, I might have found a room. I met up with Shazia Akhtar in town today. Do you remember her?' Iain made a non-committal noise, like a radiator being bled. 'Well, anyway, she and her husband live in Oxford and they have a spare room they said I can stay in until I find my own place. I thought it might be good to give you space.' *And get me away from your orchestra of bodily fluids.* 'So what do you think?'

Iain stared down at the table. He touched Hanna's shrivelled little umbilical cord with the back of his finger. Then, standing up quickly, decisively, he nearly shouted, 'Let's pack those bags!'

12
Mushroom Super Noodles

Sex against a bin? Has Oxford turned you into a racoon? Hanna was sitting on a bench outside the Isis pub, watching two dogs trying to claim ownership of a tennis ball, while bringing Dom up to speed with her dating life.

It's not easy finding love when you're flat-sharing with your father, pal, Hanna typed in reply, taking a sip of her gin and tonic. *Although he seems to be having a better time of it than me.*

Last night, Mary – Iain's new internet mail-order bride, as Hanna liked to refer to her – had turned up at the flat after work. Whether Iain hadn't warned Hanna or had not himself been warned was a point of contention – one of many. Mary had been carrying a bottle of white wine and a bag of prawn crackers – actual out-of-a-white-paper-bag-from-a-takeaway prawn crackers – and had smelled of that perfume that can double up as surgical disinfectant.

Shazia had confirmed earlier in the day that the room in her two-bed semi in Florence Park was still Hanna's, if she wanted it. Hanna had immediately started stalking the flat, trying to extract her belongings from the general humous of mess across every surface. So when Mary turned up, Hanna had half expected her and Iain to start going hell-for-leather up against the fridge, their mouths full of prawn crackers, just to celebrate her leaving. Feeling criticized by Iain's eagerness to get her moved out of the flat and resentful that her dad's dating experience seemed to be so much more straightforward than her own, Hanna had made a point of sitting between Iain and Mary at the table and lightly grilling this mozzarella ball in a Laura Ashley dress; about how much she missed her dead husband, how difficult it must be to date in your sixties, and if she regretted not having children. It was a low blow, for sure, but one born out of Hanna's feelings of inadequacy, inferiority and failure. Compared to Mary, she was a low-paid, unhoused, recently rejected ex-girlfriend who had just started sleeping with someone from school. Hardly an advert for third-wave feminism. And yet, Hanna was also genuinely interested to hear from an older, child-free woman about the shape of love in later life. For all her spikiness, she really did want Mary to reassure her somehow. And if Iain learned something about biological determinism and sexual inequality along the way, then that was a bonus. Most of all, though, Hanna had been cock-blocking. She knew it, Iain knew it, and Mary most certainly knew it. It was perhaps when Hanna had asked, sotto voce, 'Do you feel like he's still with you? Still watching you?' that even she'd had to admit she'd gone quite far.

Hanna, can I call you? wrote Dom.

Uh-oh. This was ominous. Hanna and Dom were well and truly members of the Thumb Generation. They did not make phone calls where a 7,000-word text exchange would do. Phone calls were for GUM clinics and 999. People like Dom did not ring people like Hanna. *Shit.* Was Dom's girlfriend Marni pregnant? Just like every other friend from university? Were they getting married in France and not inviting Hanna? Had they broken up?

OK. Call me now – I'm free.

Rather goes without saying, thought Hanna, kicking the tennis ball back on to the lawn.

DOMINO HARVEY

calling . . .

Hanna pressed the little green circle and remembered – in a flash – her granny's maroon push-button landline from 1998.

'What.' Hanna was not here to mess around.

Dom exhaled.

'Do I need a medic here with me? What is this? Is Jeremy Beadle about to rise from the dead and jump out of a bush dressed as my old headmaster or something?'

'Hello, old fruit. Yes. Yes, that is about to happen,' said Dom, his voice always lower than she remembered.

'Switching to voice call is quite a dramatic move. Are you all right?'

Dom exhaled again. Either he had taken up huffing glue or something big was coming down the line.

'I just heard something about Joe and wasn't sure if you'd already know, in which case I'm sorry for bearing second-hand news. But if you didn't, I thought you would probably want to be brought up to speed.' Hanna's heart went cold. So Dom wasn't becoming a father. There was no French wedding. In fact, this phone call wasn't about Dom at all. Hanna pulled her tobacco out of her back pocket.

'I see. Well, you'd better just say it.'

'OK. Well.'

'Feel free to sugar-coat it.'

'Just call me Tate & Lyle.' Dom cleared his throat. 'Right. Well. I hear that Joe has moved someone in to your old house.' Hanna's forehead twitched. Was this really the big news?

'OK.'

'Becky.'

'Becky?!' Hanna's voice sounded like metal in a microwave.

'Yes,' replied Dom.

'Becky Lewis? His ex-girlfriend Becky?' Hanna felt like someone standing on a beach, watching a tsunami coming in. A huge tide had just been sucked back, revealing the shells, broken glass, rocks and scuttling crabs of sadness she'd fought so hard to keep covered up with her denial. The pain she'd covered up with Tom and sex and work and house hunting. And here, rushing towards her like a ten-foot wall of water, it came. The truth. She didn't want to hear it. But she knew she couldn't outrun it either.

'Um, yes. Becky Lewis,' said Dom, sounding even more formal than usual.

'His ex, Becky? From university?' Hanna was not processing this easily. 'Little blonde Becky from Sheffield with that stupid fucking pout all the time?'

'Well, yes.' Dom was clearly saying as little as possible.

'Becky fucking Lewis!' The pedals of Hanna's mind were still whirring. 'Moving in to my house?!'

'Apparently—'

'*Of course* he had to do this with his shitty elf of an ex-girlfriend. It took him *two years* before he agreed to move in with me. And now he's moving his ex-girlfriend in? After less than *two months*?' Hanna's voice was cracking. 'I mean, that's pretty fucking quick, Dom. My hair is probably still in the hoover. There are probably still baked beans I bought in the cupboard.'

'I think—'

'You know what,' Hanna shouted over Dom. 'I think deep down I always knew he wasn't over Becky. Everyone said I was being stupid and paranoid, but I knew.'

'Well, I can't entirely confirm that they're back together as a couple.'

'Oh, give me some fucking credit, Dom,' said Hanna, firing her anger at the nearest available man.

‘Well, all I heard was that she’d moved out of her shared house with that girl Amy – who I know through work – and in with Joe.’ Suddenly, Hanna remembered the smell of Joe’s neck. She remembered the way the back of his trousers were worn white from his bike seat. She remembered the shape of his chest. ‘I don’t know that they’re definitely together again. Maybe he just needed someone to cover the rent.’

‘Oh God, Dom,’ said Hanna, tears pricking at her eyes. ‘I’m sorry. I didn’t mean to snap at you. I just. Ugh. I just feel so stupid. The idea of you all knowing and Joe not even bothering to tell me himself.’ But it wasn’t just that. Was it? It wasn’t just Hanna’s pride that was hurt here. It was her heart.

‘Mate. It’s fine. I’m sorry. You know I like Joe but . . .’ Dom trailed off.

‘Just the idea of him and Becky, all this time. All the time we were together. And pretending I was paranoid. But really . . .’ Hanna couldn’t say any more. A fresh wave of grief, of shame, of self-loathing pulled her voice right out of her throat. So that was it. Her old house. Her London life. Joe. Any idle hope of escaping Oxford and her dad and slipping back to her old life; it really was gone. Joe had moved on. She had moved out. And now she needed to move again.

Arriving back at the flat on Cranham Street a few hours later, Hanna walked straight into her bedroom. Her box room full of dust and boxes and nothing. She’d avoided the mirror in the hallway. Her face, she knew, looked like a partially hydrated prune. Hanna wasn't a pretty crier. And she'd cried the whole way home from the Isis. Sobbing right up the towpath, past the heavy booms of the scrapyard, the whine of the ring road, the plummy shouting of the university rowers. She cried out of shame. Shame that Joe would do that; move so easily into a new relationship. Shame that she had tried to make a life with someone who, at his core, was still hung up on the woman he'd loved at twenty. Shame that all his reluctance had been because he'd wanted to be with someone else. For years, she'd been told that one day she and Joe would get The Stuff; those grown-up things that you tick off in your thirties to prove you're a success. A proper job, a home, a wedding, a baby. But Joe's squirming resistance had pushed The Stuff further and further out of reach. And now here she was. Back here. Back in this two-bedroom flat with her dad, aged thirty, with none of The Stuff. She wasn't earning enough for a deposit, she was ambivalent about weddings, and each month her period reminded her that she only had so long on the clock. What if she never did get any of The Stuff? What if this was it? Could she really build a happy life without it? Child-free, single, renting, a job rather than a career? Did that matter to her?

Iain had The Stuff. He even had New Stuff. While Hanna sat single and unwanted, waiting days for a guy to answer her messages, Iain was eating prawn crackers with a woman who definitely wanted to be his girlfriend.

It wasn't fair. None of this was fair. Why was her dad getting together with someone new while she was still basically single and finding fresh pockets of heartbreak? Why was her dad finding this so easy while she was sobbing down her coat? He was old. He'd had his time. This was meant to be her time. And why was Joe talking to her about dishwasher tablets and electricity bills when all along he'd gone behind her back like that? How did he get to walk away from this with the same house, same friends, same sense of time never running out? Hanna started to push her head into the bedroom door. Thunk. It felt nice. That hard wooden edge felt like a tangible example of all the things that were hurting her. Thunk. She put her hand against the cool, slightly dusty wood. Smack. Then a knee. Bang. She drew her head back just a little and let it go. Whomp. Joe. Bang. Iain. Thud. She drew back a fist. Whack. Babies. Smack. Before she knew it, Hanna was pounding against the door. Throwing herself at its blank, hard face over and over again.

Suddenly the handle twisted.

'What are you—?' Iain caught her. Grabbed her fist in his big, callused hand. 'Why are you beating up my door?' The rigidity in Hanna's body collapsed like wet sand. She drew her elbows around her head and sunk her face into Iain's shoulder.

'Joe. Joe . . .' She couldn't get any further.

'What about Joe? Have you seen him?' Iain was holding her shoulder a little awkwardly, like the handle of a spade.

'He's cheated on me.'

'What?!' Iain tried to pull back but Hanna ground her face further into his shoulder. It smelled of onion and compost and sweat.

'Well, not definitely,' Hanna sniffed. 'But he's moved his ex-girlfriend in to our old house. I knew he loved her all along. And now he's in my house, with his girlfriend, and I've got nothing! What if I never get married, or have a baby or buy a . . . house?' The word 'house' came out in a kind of yelp.

'Oh, Hanna. Oh, love.' Iain put his arms around her. Properly now. He was only just taller than Hanna; less than a foot. But it was something. She started to cry again. Amazing how this stuff just kept going; how much salt the human body could carry in just the eyes. Truly, credit to the eyes; the real salt flats of the soul. After about two minutes, maybe less, Iain still hadn't said anything. They'd just stood there, the pink evening light catching on the top of the tree outside Hanna's window. Their breathing was now in sync. A great rising and falling of their shoulders, chests and stomachs, pressed against each other. Hanna was slowing down. It was out now. At least, it was out for now.

'Hanna,' Iain said at last. 'I'm really sorry. I'm sorry that Joe did that. I'm sorry if he made you feel embarrassed. I'm sorry I said all those things, you know, about running out of time. My mum was thirty when she had me.' Iain let out a sigh. 'She'd been a doctor – one of the first women to even graduate from Imperial – and hadn't wanted to give up her career before that. I'm sorry you never got to meet her. She was a strong woman.' His voice went a little softer. 'There is time. There's always time. And you deserve to be loved. Don't settle for less than that.' Hanna didn't dare look up. It felt as though Iain was under some kind of spell – his tongue loosened to magically say all the things he'd never been able to before. To actually talk about feelings. To admit emotion. 'Joe wasn't the right man for you. But that's his problem. You're right. Just as you are.' Hanna waited for a few seconds. But when she realized he wasn't going to say any more, she stood straight and wiped her face with her hands. Finally, she looked into Iain's face. He looked old. But there, in his face, was also her face. Just bits, here and there. The curves and corners that made up their DNA.

'Now, would you like a bowl of mushroom Super Noodles?' asked Iain, putting one hand on the door handle. 'With peanut butter and some grated cheese on top?' Hanna nodded. 'I'm just going to pop to the shop then. Maybe I'll get us a pudding.'

Hanna could hear Iain unlocking his bike outside her window. The clang of his D-lock as he snapped it on to the parcel shelf. She sat on the floor of her bedroom feeling damp and sponge-like. The shame of it; Joe was living with his beautiful, tiny, elfin ex-girlfriend while she ate Super Noodles with her dad and begged friends for a few weeks in their box room. How had all this happened and how was she going to crawl out of it?

A car screeched out in the street. There was a thud, followed by a crunch. A woman shouting. Doors slamming. The sound of metal being dragged across tarmac. Hanna walked over to the window. There was Iain, lying in the road, his leg folded around his bike like a tin opener. Hanna was out of the flat and running, her feet bare, the door clicking shut behind her.

13
Clipboard

'I definitely heard a crunch.' Iain was sitting on the edge of the pavement crouched over his ankle, his bike lying beside him like a bent paper clip. 'And now . . . ah . . . yeah, I don't think I can move my foot.'

'You weren't wearing reflective clothing.' The driver was standing with one manicured hand on the door of her enormous black car. It was one of those vehicles with the proportions of a lorry, the outline of a desert cruiser, but built to only ever slide along the asphalt of city streets.

'He had lights on! If you can't see the lights of another road user then you might need to question your—' Hanna was crouching in the street between the car and her dad, the damp seeping through the knees of her jeans.

'It's very dark on these little streets at night.' The woman had the snipped vowels, low heels and spherical blow dry of a female Tory prime minister. Hanna had a great urge to cut her in half with her own car door.

'Very dark? It's nine o'clock at night!' barked Hanna.

'If you can't see at night, why would you be driving that tank around my neighbourhood?' *My neighbourhood?* Hanna had no idea where that had come from.

'People on bicycles—'

Iain cut the driver off with a yelp as he tried once again to put weight on his foot. 'I think someone might need to take me to the hospital,' he said, looking up at them. 'I can't drive with this' – he gestured towards his foot – 'and my daughter's not insured.' There was a nasty silence as the woman stared down at Hanna and Iain, buckled in the gutter.

'Well, I'm afraid I can't take you,' she replied, her mouth like a Toblerone. 'I have my daughter in the back and I don't want to upset her.' Hanna glanced at the back seat to see a saucer-eyed girl in a sky-blue polo shirt staring out of the window at them. She was about five and looked like a bush frog sitting in the middle of a jumbo jet. 'I'll have to order you a taxi.'

'But that great big car is—'

The woman had pulled an almost A4-sized phone out of her pocket and was bringing it to her ear. 'Hello? Yes, I'd like to book a taxi, please. From Cranham Road to the John Radcliffe Hospital.' Hanna and Iain looked at each other, somehow silenced by the power of another person's phone call. 'Twenty-five minutes? You really don't have anything sooner than that?'

'You can't make us sit out here for twenty-five minutes!' Hanna groaned.

'OK. I see.' The driver was staring resolutely into the

middle distance, trying to prevent her gaze accidentally falling on Iain's twisted bike. 'Well, thank you anyway.' She finally turned to look at them. 'Don't you have Uber?'

'Jesus. No.' Iain once again tried to shift himself.

'Their drivers aren't allowed to unionize—' Hanna began, before Iain cut her off.

'Look, that's a huge car. You just knocked me off my bike because you weren't looking. I might have broken my ankle. You need to drive me to hospital.' Iain suddenly seemed to be speaking in his work voice. The fire engineer who could hold a meeting with the college principle to discuss evacuation units and third-storey structural evaluations had taken over and he was going to get this done. 'I'm not going to discuss compensation in front of your daughter and I'm not expecting you to drive us back. But you do need to take me to the hospital now.' Hanna was suddenly very aware that she wasn't wearing any shoes and that she had probably cried some mascara down her cheeks.

'I'll just run back in to get my coat and bag.' Hanna realized with a little pop of dread that she'd come out without her keys. 'Dad, can I borrow your keys.'

Iain tried to straighten out his leg to extract his keys from his jeans pocket, only, of course, it was the leg that had been hit and the shift in weight seemed to be causing him true agony. 'Lift me up, Han. And help me to the car.' The driver stood unmoving, her hand still gripped around the top of the car door, as Hanna pushed herself into Iain's armpit and tried to lever him up. 'Aaah, hold on. We're going to tip,' said Iain in a sharp exhalation. 'We need someone on the other side.' The driver didn't move. The daughter in the back stared. A man coming out of the Rickety Press walked over.

'You need a hand there, squire?' He was clearly shitfaced – the kind of drunk you can only get after sinking six pints entirely alone – but Hanna was relieved that someone was going to break this Mexican standoff.

'If you could just take his other arm.' Hanna had a sudden flash of what it would be like to have an elderly parent. The smell of cabbage and carpet cleaner, the low hum of a television in the day room. The doilies and locked doors and chair aerobics. To have to help them out of chairs, take them to the loo, wash them with a flannel. She was not ready for this.

'One, two, three, *allezupcha*.' Iain was up on one leg. He fished out his keys and handed them to her. 'Grab me a book – you never know how long this might take.'

Back in the flat, Hanna grabbed snacks, books, her phone, paracetamol, socks and chargers like a whirlwind. The adrenaline seemed to have smoothed her movements rather than turned her jittery. In less than two minutes she was back outside, this time in a pair of trainers, walking towards this stranger's car. The very drunk man had dragged Iain's bike over to a lamppost and was trying, valiantly, to unhook his D-lock. Hanna realized she was holding the bike key. 'I'll do it,' she said, walking into his cloud of alcohol fumes. 'Thanks so much for your help.'

'No worries. Just doing my duty.' A burp broke across Hanna's face. 'I hope your husband's leg's all right. He should sue.'

'He's my dad, actually,' Hanna said sharply.

'Ah, I thought he was a jammy bugger.' She shuddered.

Iain was propped against the car, like an old spade. The driver clearly hadn't offered to walk him round to the passenger seat and he seemed unable to take his weight on the damaged foot. As Hanna walked towards him, he pushed himself off with a hip and then stood, wobbling a little, resting all his weight on his right-hand side.

'You go in the front and I'll go in the back,' said Hanna, slipping a little into the sing-song voice she associated with nurses, nursery teachers and hairdressers. The silent, maudlin child in the back seat was now fiddling with a friendship bracelet pinned on to her seatbelt and staring straight ahead.

'Hello, I'm Hanna.'

The girl balefully looked Hanna up and down, taking in the smudged mascara, the sockless trainers, the overflowing bag of snacks and painkillers, before replying: 'Charlotte.'

'Hello, Charlotte. Did you make that?' Hanna pointed at the friendship bracelet.

'No.'

'Ah, so did one of your friends make it for you?'

'No.'

Hanna felt her conversation skills skidding through wet mud.

'Well, I like the colours.'

'You would.'

It took fourteen minutes to drive to the John Radcliffe Hospital. The entire journey was spent in a jagged silence, broken only by the sugared flint voice of the in-car satnav, guiding them to A&E. When Hanna's stomach rumbled crossing the Marston Road, she was almost certain she heard Charlotte mutter 'pleb' in a very quiet voice beside her. Pretending to mistake it for a yawn, Hanna rather pointedly turned to Charlotte and said, 'Excuse you,' with the sort of smile that could freeze butter.

'Now, there's no need to take the details of my car,' said the driver, as they pulled up outside the massive Millennium Falcon-looking hospital. 'I will give you my card, here.' She reached over and opened the glove box, in which was a little plastic pack of business cards. 'But I'm warning you – my husband is a lawyer and you should have been wearing a high-visibility jacket. You should also have been in the cycle lane, not the middle of the road.' She slammed the glove box shut. 'Goodbye.'

'Thank you' – Iain glanced down at the card – 'Georgina Mayor. I'll be in touch.'

As Iain shuffled out of his seat and on to the pavement, Hanna couldn't help herself calling out over his shoulder: 'Drive safely!' Both mother and daughter stared straight ahead, faces unmoving.

The hospital waiting room was square, bright and dotted with blue finishes. It could almost have been the entrance to a leisure centre, but for the posters about strokes, internal bleeding and Patient Advice and Liaison Services. To one side of the room was a man wearing a coat and just a towel, leaning gingerly against the wall. He looked to be in some distress, with an oily sheen to his face and hair. On a chair across from him sat a grey-haired woman holding a Tupperware filled with tissue and something pink. Someone else was sleeping across a row of chairs in a puffer jacket, despite the relatively mild night. Hanna followed a set of big blue floor signs to the reception desk.

'Hello. My father has been hit by a car,' she said. 'Not badly. Well, maybe quite badly, I don't know. He can't seem to put any weight on his foot. It wasn't his fault. I don't think.'

The receptionist had a kindly plate-face that betrayed no emotion.

'I think I might need an X-ray,' said Iain, who had shuffled his way over from the pillar where Hanna had propped him.

'Are you this woman's father?' asked the receptionist.

'Yes,' replied Iain.

'Ah nice, you do look a bit alike, actually.' The receptionist handed Hanna a clipboard with a few sheets of paper clamped to it. 'If you can just fill these out and then bring them back. A doctor will hopefully be available to see you soon.'

Hanna carried the clipboard while Iain leaned on her shoulder. A student couple walked in after them. She was wearing a tomato-red NASA jacket and he was in a nineties shell suit. She was pink-faced and sweaty, her eyes glassy, and she was twitching all over like leaves in a breeze. Hanna was irritated not to hear what the man whispered over the reception desk, but assumed it involved swallowing large amounts of washing powder and Ritalin.

'So how did you hear about Joe?' asked Iain, as they sat down on the blue, wipe-clean bench seats that were, Hanna noticed, bolted to the floor.

'Oh, Dom told me. It seems like pretty much everybody knew, except for me.'

'Ah,' Iain sniffed. It was a disgusting noise but Hanna was concentrating too hard on not staring at the man with the towel to really object. 'Does that make you feel better or worse about breaking up with him?' Strangely, while Hanna had been ready to discuss the finer weft of Joe's betrayal, the immaturity and the timing, the simplicity of Iain's question left her rather wrongfooted.

'Um. Well, I suppose it closes the door on us ever getting back together. Again,' said Hanna, biting the nail on her ring finger.

'Had you thought you might get back together?' Iain asked.

'Well, no. Yes. I suppose I hadn't quite shut it down as an option at some point.' She shuffled her feet. 'I know I've moved here and I'm trying to get my own place and all that, but I think I'd also thought that maybe, if things changed or something, if Joe changed, or I changed, or if he started to want what I want . . .'

'And what do you want?'

'I . . . I don't know,' said Hanna, feeling like a balloon sighing out its contents. 'I really don't know. Sometimes I wonder if I ever want to get married or have a baby at all. People just assume you'll do those things one day. Like, what else is there to do? But with Joe, I don't know, he never seemed ready. And because he wasn't ready, I didn't have to really think about whether I was ready.' She picked at some skin next to her thumbnail. 'This whole thing with his ex, it's like his way of showing me that we weren't right together; we probably never were right together.' Her eyes began to sting a little. A packet of Tic Tacs fell out of the pocket of the man in the puffer jacket. 'I've wasted so much time.'

'Well, if that's the case then maybe you are better off starting again here. In Oxford, I mean, not necessarily in the waiting area for A&E,' said Iain, a smile twitching at the side of his mouth.

'Yes, probably. But I do need to get my own space. That's why I'm going to stay with Shazia, while I house hunt.'

'I get you,' said Iain. 'It'll be nice for you to have a change of scene. And who knows? Maybe Shazia will have a handsome cousin you never knew about.'

'Mr Markhouse?' a short, sandy-haired man shouted across the waiting room.

'Coming!' Hanna called back, levering Iain up to standing.

'So, how did you come a cropper?' asked the man. Hanna didn't know if he was a nurse or doctor; his lanyard was twisted and she didn't speak fluent uniform.

'I got hit by a car as I was cycling to the shop,' said Iain, lifting himself up on to a hospital bed.

'Was the driver on the phone?' asked the man, sliding his hand under Iain's Achilles tendon.

'Yaaaaahh, hoooooo,' Iain gasped, as his swollen tree trunk of leg and foot was gently moved from side to side.

'I think she just wasn't concentrating,' said Hanna, wondering briefly if there was some legal ramification to their answers. It took them nearly a minute to shuffle into the triage room. The man in blue scrubs was kneeling on the floor, unlacing Iain's shoes and gently taking a grip around his rather puffy ankle.

'Does it hurt if I compress this, like this?' he asked, squeezing Iain's foot up towards his shin.

'Well, I can certainly feel it,' Iain replied, his jaw looking decidedly tense.

'That means it hurts, probably a lot,' said Hanna in a low voice. Her father's legendary stoicism – pulling masonry nails out of his knee with his teeth, breaking his fingers with a stray swing of the mallet, pulling his own rotten molar out with a pair of pliers – made him a sometimes unreliable patient.

'I'm just going to take you for a wee X-ray,' said the man. *Probably a doctor*, thought Hanna. Probably a gay, married doctor. 'Here, you can carry this.' He passed Hanna the shoe. It smelled of wet sawdust and onion. 'But I suspect you've broken your ankle. I assume this was the leg you fell on to?'

'Yes, I was hit on this side and then managed to land with it beneath my bike,' said Iain, with a 'what a wally' twitch of his eyebrows.

'Nasty.'

Iain was wheeled, much to his delight, down the corridor, past the League of Friends café to the radiology department. Hanna wasn't allowed in while the X-ray was happening, so she dawdled by a display of raisin flapjacks and cling-filmed sandwiches while surreptitiously trying to diagnose every single person who walked past. She was still holding the shoe by the laces, reluctant to put its fine residue of dog shit and foot skin in her handbag. After a few minutes, Iain was wheeled back out by a different porter who, with a large but wordless smile, started marching down the hall and past several sets of wood-effect fire doors.

'Where's your X-ray, Dad? Did they tell you anything? Are we going back to see the doctor?'

'I'm not too sure where we're going,' said Iain, more affable than panicked. 'I think I might have helped install an evacuation valve on this floor once.' Eventually, a set of double doors swung open, and Iain and Hanna were led through into a small waiting room studded with pot plants.

'The doctor will be with you in a minute to explain the X-rays,' said the porter, in the deepest voice Hanna had ever heard.

'Would you like a flapjack?' asked Hanna, turning to Iain. 'Although I'm not sure I could find them again.'

'No, you're all right,' Iain said, trying to raise himself out of the chair just long enough to scratch his balls. 'I think the shock slightly took away my appetite.'

With nothing more she could think of to say, Hanna pulled out her phone, took a photo of a 'dry riser' sign and added it to her Instagram stories with the caption 'Nice to see your boyfriend again'.

'Mr Markhouse?' This doctor – and she was definitely a doctor, Hanna thought, because she wasn't wearing any discernible uniform – was short, curly-haired and looked like she played rugby at the weekends. 'Come this way. Your daughter, too.' So they had reached the psychic level of medical professional, thought Hanna. The stage of seniority at which everything in a patient's notes was immediately and easily absorbed, without you even knowing. 'My name is Dr Blackstock. Please take a seat,' she said, without turning around or gesturing. 'I'm afraid this is quite a nasty break.' Hanna hadn't even reached her seat before Dr Blackstock was slapping X-rays on to a large white lightbox. 'If you look here,' she said, pointing to what looked to Hanna like the ghost portrait of a reindeer, 'you can see that the break is just above the lateral malleolus. You're lucky it wasn't a few centimetres lower or the whole thing may have gone.' Iain was staring, slack-jawed, at the grey picture in front of him. Hanna was tempted to lean over and snap his teeth closed, even just for the sake of appearances, but decided that now wasn't the time to be passive aggressive. 'The good news is you won't need surgery – this sort of fracture usually heals itself in a few weeks, as long as you rest it and take care not to force the ankle into any unnatural positions.' Dr Blackstock came to sit back heavily on her chair, facing them. 'The bad news is, you'll have to wear an orthopaedic boot for the next month.' She pulled a grey, Velcro-encrusted letter L out of the box beside her. 'You can take it off for airing when the foot is elevated but will need to use it whenever you are mobile and, for the sake of us all, please do wear clean socks.' She gave a brusque chuckle before handing the boot over to Hanna. 'Are you living with your father?'

'Yes, well. I was, temporarily. I'm meant to be moving out next week.'

'Is there anybody else that could come and stay with you, Mr Markhouse, while you're recovering?'

'Um . . .' Iain turned searchingly to Hanna. 'Not that I can think of. I can't ask Mary.'

'Well, for at least a week or two you are going to need significant assistance. I can write a note for your employer but I do strongly advise you have someone at home to help you out. Otherwise the break will heal slowly or may even be exacerbated.'

Hanna felt a cold rush of disappointment fall across her body.

'Would I have to wash him and stuff?' Hanna asked the doctor, trying to avoid Iain's gaze.

'Your father will struggle to get out of bed, chairs, to move around the house for a few weeks. He won't want to stand for a long time, so things like cooking and cleaning. And someone else will have to go to the supermarket and that sort of thing. Do you have many stairs in your home?'

'It's a flat,' said Hanna.

'On the third floor,' added Iain.

'Ah, yes, well in that case you might have to wait until the ankle is feeling better before you attempt the stairs.' Dr Blackstock was typing something on her computer.

'How long does a broken ankle take?'

'Well, it all depends on the severity of the break,' the doctor answered briskly. 'I am going to sign your father off any manual work for six weeks but he may feel recovered earlier than that.' Then, turning to Iain: 'You will need to use crutches for the first few weeks. I can write a note for occupational health and you can pick them up before you go home. Any more questions?'

Hanna saw her escape to Shazia's slipping away through gripped fingers. Just as she had found a way out of her dad's flat, just as she was making a break for it, he had snatched her back with a break of his own. She was trapped. Trapped with an old man wearing a space boot.

'I'll call a taxi,' said Hanna nearly an hour later, as they walked towards the exit of the hospital. Iain was swinging along on his crutches, his broken foot soaring through the air like Concorde. 'You wait here.'

Outside in the inky freshness of the night she called a minicab, then rang her boss's direct line to leave a message.

'Hello Annabel, it's Hanna here. I'm afraid my father has been involved in a car crash and I'm not going to be able to make it into work for the next few days. The doctor has told me that I have to be around in case things get worse.' This wasn't strictly true, but Hanna decided that if she was going to have to help Iain in and out of the bath, she could at least maybe slip out and try to meet Tom again, rather than sitting in her office next to Sanjay and his noise-cancelling headphones.

Then she texted Shazia. *Shaz, you're not going to believe this but Iain's broken his ankle.* Send. *I have to stay with him until it's healed.* Send. *I'm so sorry.* Send. *Can I stay with you when this is all over?* Send. Each message stayed determinedly unread until the morning.

14
Potting Shed

Hanna had woken at 6 a.m. already feeling vaguely sticky. It was only mid-June but somehow the air in Oxford always seemed just slightly damper than it had in Brockley. Her hair seemed to curl tighter, her top lip to need wiping more often. It was going to be one of those days when the underside of her breasts started to sweat before she'd even reached work. When she couldn't wear a rucksack because the weight against her shoulders would feel like a very horny dog humping her back. When she would find herself licking her wrists to blow cold air over them while holding a fairly neutral conversation with the elderly Cypriot man in the newsagent's.

'Knock, knock.' Iain always preferred to shout these words rather than actually knock on Hanna's door. Because why miss an opportunity to make loud noises?

'Yup. Yup. I'm right here.' It was weird how, despite living in this flat for weeks, despite helping him get up the first few days after the accident, despite knowing that he had once put her to bed as a baby, Hanna still cramped up at the thought of Iain seeing her in bed. Somehow the thought of him walking in and catching her there, lying under the cornflower bedsheets she'd bought herself as a present after leaking menstrual blood all over Mowgli's legs, was too intimate. She felt too old to have her dad see her in bed. It would be like having him walk in on her in the bath, or while she panic-shaved her armpits over the sink before a date.

'We're out of bread, Han.'

'OK. Right. I'll pop to Nash's before my shower.' Hanna eased herself up, her ankles popping as she stood up. When did her joints become so loud? Was it sleeping on a mattress on the floor? Or was this the beginning of middle age?

'I'm heading that way for my physio appointment,' said Iain, standing awkwardly close to the door as Hanna walked out into the corridor. How was it that Iain was so short and yet took up so much room?

'Can you help me down the stairs, or carry this?' Iain asked, holding out his little pink manila folder of medical notes. 'It's a pain with these crutches.'

'Sure,' said Hanna, regretting having not put a bra on as the corner of the folder brushed against her nipple.

Holding the door open, she glanced down at her phone. Still nothing from Tom. Last night, while hanging out another load of Iain's washing and quietly itching for a cigarette, her resolve had crumpled and she'd texted him. Or, to put it in a slightly less self-critical way, she had decided to stop playing adolescent games and just get in touch with someone she was attracted to. Like a rational, confident woman. Tom had replied almost immediately suggesting they go for a drink this evening. But when she'd asked where, he'd gone strangely silent. That had been twelve hours ago. Which, Hanna told herself determinedly, was really nothing. If a friend had done the same, she wouldn't have questioned it. If Tom were just a friend then she'd simply call him when she came out of work. She needed to stop playing games and start pretending that Tom was just a friend. Hmm.

'Do you have plans this evening?' asked Iain, as they walked slowly towards the bakery on Little Clarendon Street.

'Well, actually . . .' Should she just tell him? Go into this thing with a little more maturity? After all, if things worked out with Tom, wouldn't it be nice to just be honest about it from the start?

'Bonjour, Pierre!' Iain hooted as he opened the bakery door, far too loudly and just as Hanna was about to slide into her confession. The man behind the counter, at whom Iain was now smiling and waggling his eyebrows enthusiastically, stayed stony-faced.

'Could I get a medium wholemeal and two croissants, please?' asked Hanna, stepping up to the warm, glass front, behind which lay rows of gingerbread men, cinnamon buns, sausage rolls and chocolate cornflake cakes.

'One medium wholemeal and two croissants,' said

the man, pronouncing the word 'croissants' as if he was coughing up a furball. 'Anything else, madam?'

'Now, tread carefully with her, Pierre,' said Iain, leaning over Hanna's shoulder like a demonic parrot. 'She's just come out of a bad break-up and I don't want to see you make that any worse.' Hanna baulked. Was this actually happening? Was her peg-legged, boom-voiced, elderly father genuinely threatening retail staff in order to protect her honour?

'I'm so sorry. He's got a urinary infection and he doesn't know what he's saying,' whispered Hanna theatrically, pushing the bread into her tote bag and marching Iain and his stupid moon boot out of the shop before he could reply.

'What's the hurry?' said Iain as they tumbled on to the pavement.

'What the hell was that?!'

'I just thought, after the news about Joe—'

'Oh, please! That man wasn't coming on to me. That man couldn't come on to a Chelsea bun. Ach. Stop sniggering!' She was shouting by now. 'And for the record, his name is categorically not Pierre.'

Iain carried on smirking, utterly unashamed and unshameable. 'So, tonight. Where did you say you were going?'

'To life drawing,' said Hanna. She was buggered if she was going to open up her romantic hopes to this shuffling Neanderthal. She had actually bought a sketch from an artist on Etsy who described herself as a 'pencil mystic' already, to cover her tracks. Hanna's own attempt at drawing – using a Google image of Dappy from N-Dubz's leaked dick pic – was so bad that she knew Iain would never believe she was really pursuing this as a genuine hobby. And so Elzine Louca in Frome made £10 by selling a sketch, and Hanna was free to spend her Thursday evening out of the house without Iain asking too many awkward questions about what she was doing.

Turning away from Iain and his pathetic little cardboard folder, Hanna felt a buzz in her shorts pocket. Tom. *Meet me on the bridge by Port Meadow at 7 p.m.* Hanna's heart leaped. *I can take you for a walk.*

Going for walks was an extremely in-a-couple thing to do, Hanna thought, tripping back down the street. Going for walks was just a short step away from going to IKEA. And while Tom was kind and affectionate, he was also not yet her boyfriend. Which Hanna had to tell herself was fine. That she had no expectations. That she wasn't one of those awful women who was always trying to tie men down. Even though, as she drifted towards sleep in the evenings, alone and cold-footed, she longed to be doing so beside him.

Tom was waiting for Hanna on the bridge over the canal as she turned the corner. He was wearing a white linen shirt covered in tiny cartwheeling stick men and a pair of navy workman's shorts. His arms were brown, his curly hair shot through dirty blond. He was holding a single peony – luscious and vaguely sanguine – in one hand and a bottle of white wine in the other. As Hanna pressed against him, to kiss, she felt two glasses in his shorts pockets.

'Hello, baby,' he said, looking into her eyes with an expression that was both sweet and impish.

'Hello, sailor. This is beautiful,' Hanna said, reaching out for the flower.

'Oh, do you want that? I actually picked it for my wife, but you can borrow it,' Tom smiled. Then kissed her again.

'I thought we could walk down the river the other way. Into town,' he said, that mischievous, excited look creeping across his face again.

'Sure,' said Hanna, turning the flower in her hand and trying to look up at Tom while keeping her chin on her chest; a look she'd once heard Lauren Bacall describe on *Desert Island Discs* as something like a magic trick.

'Glass of wine?' Tom asked, flourishing his spare hand like an obsequious waiter.

'Why not?' said Hanna, pulling one of the glasses from his pocket and being sure to brush against his junk on the way out. 'It's been ages since I got an ASBO.'

They started walking towards the river. 'So, how was your day?' asked Tom, she on the pavement, he in the road.

'Oh, you know. Saved a couple of lives. Invented a cure for cancer. Read some children's books to a group of blind orphans. Sold the film rights to my life,' said Hanna. 'The usual. How about you?'

'Much the same,' said Tom, sipping his wine. 'Only I also committed the perfect murder and stole one of North Korea's chemical weapons.'

'Classic us,' said Hanna. Then felt a cold snap in her bowel. She shouldn't use words like 'us'. Men didn't like you pressuring them like that.

'Hold on, Hanna – doesn't that say your name?' Tom was pointing at an envelope hanging from one of the branches beside the railway bridge on a piece of red wool. She'd almost walked past it. In fact, she'd wondered why Tom had slowed down so much, worrying that her 'us' comment had made him decide to turn round and run home. But there, almost at head height, was the envelope, with her name on the front in blue biro. *Hanna Markhouse. X.*

'What the fuck?' Hanna slid a look over to Tom, who was beaming like a child who'd just opened the Ninja Turtles blimp on Christmas morning 1992.

Yanking the envelope down from the tree, Hanna ran a nail along the top and pulled out a small sheet of card. On it was just a single line, looking like it had been hammered out on a typewriter: *I never thought it would happen.*

'I don't . . . I don't?' She was smiling, her heart racing. Tom's mouth was pressed shut. His fist balled in his pocket. 'Did you?'

'Nothing to do with me, guv,' he said, in his

Dickensian street-sweeper voice. 'Must be one of your sugar daddies. Or oligarch husbands.'

They walked along the dirt track towards the river, Hanna's heart galloping.

There on the gate to the bridge – the very bridge she'd led the pony across on that strange, technicolour May Morning – was another envelope. With her name on it. Again, tied to the gate with red wool. She opened this one with a little more vigour.

With me and the girl from Cranham.

Hanna felt like she was lifting out of her body. He'd remembered her address. At least, he'd remembered the name of the street Iain lived on – she still wasn't sure if that actually counted as her address.

'Tom,' she said, pushing her face into his shoulder and then kissing his neck.

'What? I don't know who this creep is.' He was absolutely beaming. 'Perhaps we should call a constable. Do you want me to blow my whistle?'

On a bench further along the towpath there was another envelope, tied to one of the back slats with wool. Hanna knew, as she opened it. But still read the words: *Out on the windy common.*

And then there, above the bench, tied to an impossibly high branch, was another envelope. How on earth had he got up there? More to the point, how was she going to get up there?

'Do you need a boost?' Tom asked, his eyes twinkling

with delight, his smile pulling back to show all those shiny white teeth.

'I think I might do,' Hanna replied. 'You know, just to collect all the evidence for the police.'

He knelt at her feet. What? No. This wasn't. Surely.

'Climb on to my shoulders.' *Oh, right.* So no, this wasn't. OK.

Screaming and wobbling, Hanna felt herself lifted into the sky on Tom's huge back. She could feel his neck between her hot legs. Could he smell her? she wondered. He rubbed his head against her inner thigh. *Please God, don't fart*, she thought. *Not now.* Like a kitten in a Victorian soap advert she clawed at the string above her head, before finally yanking the envelope down. Tom lowered her on to the bench and watched her read the final card.

That night I ain't forgotten.

Hanna's breath had turned shallow; her neck was flushed. *My god.* Squeeze. How did he know? Had she said something? Their night on Port Meadow; the windy common. He'd not forgotten. And yet. And yet, she couldn't help but notice that these notes, as devastatingly romantic as they were, might just be a gesture. They didn't mention any feelings.

'Oh my god, Tom. Weren't you worried that I'd suggest walking a different way? Or want to go to the pub instead?' she said, reaching her arms up around his head and kissing that beautiful, wine-sour mouth.

'I don't do second guessing,' Tom said, after they

pulled away. Hanna laughed. Then looked down at the note. She kissed him again. Then, without checking that he was following, she started to walk down the river. If he was going to play games, then so would she. Kiss chase. She'd kiss and he could chase.

They stopped at another bench, just before a hump-back footbridge. 'I like to live in the moment, Han,' said Tom, reaching for her hand. 'You're in the moment too, with me.'

Hanna looked out across the silt-thick green river, to the allotments on the other side. A woman in a heavy blue smock and pair of lace-up work boots was sitting outside her potting shed, smoking a roll-up. Her knees had fallen open, her face was turned towards the evening sun, and a glass of red wine stood on an upturned bucket by her side. In the silence between her and Tom, Hanna could hear the strains of some Radio 4 drama – probably *The Archers* – coming from a little transistor radio balanced on the outside windowsill of the woman's potting shed. There were grey hairs at her temple, Hanna could see. Her lips were full, her thighs strong. There were wrinkles around her mouth and her eyebrows were unplucked. The woman took another drag of her cigarette and blew out a long, thin rope of smoke into the summer sky. That was the question, Hanna thought, staring at the woman's coiled rope of hair running down her back. The big question. The question that, like Medusa, Hanna could only look at through the corner of her eye, or over her shoulder in shards of broken mirror. Who was she? And what did she want? Who with? And when?

Did Hanna want a boyfriend? she wondered. Or did she just want a potting shed that smelled of compost, cigarette smoke and her own perfume? Did she want a partner? A baby? A house? Or someone to just have fun with? Was she really the marrying kind? Or was commitment just the result of childhood conditioning? Did Hanna want a mortgage? To make her own marmalade? Did she want to travel through Europe in a converted ambulance having sex with Tom? Or did she want to look down into the sleeping face of a child she'd grown from her own blood and breath? Did she want all of these things? Did she want something else? Did she really want anything?

Hanna stared into the soupy water. The woman across the river sat unmoving. Tom's breath became a blanket settling across the grass. Perhaps she should just live in the moment too, she thought. After all, wasn't the moment all anybody ever had?

'We could look for a shed or something?' said Tom, sliding his hand up her waist.

'How romantic.'

'I'm not talking about romance.' Tom pulled her against him. His body, scooped into hers, pushed like a half-moon into her thighs, her hips. He traced his thumb over her nipple which, even through a bra and shirt, was rigid. 'There will definitely be somewhere we can lie down.'

Hanna felt the yearning pulse through her. She could. Of course she could. They could go and fuck in a shed like the sixteen-year-olds that still lived inside their thirty-year-old bodies. Perhaps this was what happened when you started dating someone you once knew so well as a teenager; you reoxygenated each other's teenage selves and started drinking in parks and humping behind bins. But did she really want to be that woman? An image of Joe and Becky, kissing against her old kitchen worktop, flashed through her head. Of the lamp she'd left behind and the turmeric mark she'd made by the hob. She didn't want to lie down on an old sack and come home with leaves in her hair. Not tonight. Tom might want to live in the moment but couldn't that moment also happen on a proper mattress?

'Fuck it. Why don't we just go back to my place?' she said, her hand tracing the line of his jaw.

'But what about—'

'He'll be asleep. You can leave before he wakes up. I just want to see you. Properly. All of you.' She ran her hand down to his fly.

They stumbled back through Jericho; a broken spider of four legs, tripping over each other, locked in kisses and then scuttling on with the thought of cool sheets and bare skin pulling them forward.

'Just don't make any noise in the corridor,' said Hanna, pulling her keys out of her pocket while simultaneously grabbing Tom's belt buckle, as though she were guiding a horse.

'I hope he's a deep sleeper.'

Her key clicked in the lock. She could feel Tom pressing against her bum. Silence. They crept down the hall, past Iain's room. There was no time for a pee, thought Hanna. No time to even take off their shoes. Her hand was clasped in Tom's; a gesture that was both romantic and excited. Like a couple in love but also like two hyped-up children queuing for a rollercoaster. Her door opened with just the tiniest scrape against the floorboards on the other side. Hanna slid in and Tom instantly had her up against the wall. His big, slightly callused hands were undoing her buttons, his thigh between her legs. They were kissing. She smiled as his trousers dropped to the floor. Too scared to turn on even her bedside lamp, she moved around so she could see him in the moonlight through the window. God, he was beautiful.

'You look amazing,' she said.

Tom smiled. 'I'm going to make you feel amazing.'

Hanna woke up to the sound of giggling. It was bright. Too bright. Tom's hand was curled around her stomach, his leg thrown over the top of the duvet. In the split second it took her to notice the way the hairs on his thigh burnt copper in the sunlight, she heard the giggling again. They'd overslept. The plan to sneak Tom out before dawn had washed away on a wave of adrenaline, lust and last night's wine. Maybe he could dash out while Iain was having a shower? Or, God forbid, his early morning shit. Maybe Tom could stay in bed until Iain left for work? Calling in sick to work would only arouse Iain's suspicion more. Maybe she could create a disturbance in the kitchen while Tom ran out? Set fire to a tea towel?

Giggling.

Hold on. Who was giggling? Was that a woman's giggle? Hanna could hear a shoe scraping against the floor in the room next to her. The nudge of a chair. Someone was shushing.

'Tom.'

'Mmm?'

'Can you hear giggling?' Tom's face cracked open like a pasty. Golden, slightly oily, but tempting. 'I'm sure I heard a woman giggling,' whispered Hanna. Held together, their skin not just against each other but almost grafted together, they listened.

'I can't hear anything—'

'Sssshhhh! They'll hear you!'

'Sorry,' Tom whispered, still too loud. 'But I can't hear—'

And there it was again. Giggling. Hanna heard Iain's door open and the sound of feet on floorboards. How many feet? Not just his. Definitely. And Iain never did anything quietly. If he were just leaving his room, he'd be whistling and farting and clearing his throat.

'Oh my god! He's brought that woman back!' hissed Hanna, collapsing back into the mattress, suddenly aware of an apparently spare arm caught between her and Tom. Where was this meant to go? Under him? Across her chest? Round her head? Tom reached over and kissed the hand of the spare arm. 'We'd said no overnight guests!' said Hanna, turning to face Tom's broad, sleep-crinkled face.

'Well, I think we've spooned that one, pal.' His erection was now visible under the duvet.

'But he promised!' Hanna went rigid again as a tap turned on in the bathroom. 'Maybe if they're in the bathroom you should . . .' Tom kissed her. She pulled away. 'Seriously. I cannot have you and potato-face Mary having morning coffee in my dad's kitchen. This isn't a fucking commune.' Although the tap was still running, Hanna could hear the Velcro rip of Iain's moon boot straps from the room next door. *Shit.* If Iain was getting dressed then she might be able to sneak Tom out in the next seventy seconds. But what if Mary came out of the bathroom while they were attempting their escape? 'Oh God, what if she's naked!' Tom's face was cracking into a grin. 'This isn't funny! Imagine if it was your mum.'

'But it's not my mum. Or your mum. Come on, Hanna-copter.' His hand was travelling down over her belly. 'If we really are trapped in here . . .'

'Tom.'

'You know you—'

'Tom, I can't!' Hanna could feel the panic creeping across her shoulders. Should she confront Iain in the hallway? Bollock him and Mary for breaching their agreement while Tom hid in a laundry bag behind her door? She heard the bathroom door open. There was a barely audible slip of foot into shoe outside Hanna's door. Oh shit, had Tom left his shoes in the hallway? No, there they were, under her bookshelf. The front door creaked open. There were a few seconds of furtive rustling and then it closed. By now, Tom's head was between Hanna's thighs. He might as well be doing a Sudoku across her freckles for all the attention she was paying. More footsteps. Then Iain's bed creaked against the adjoining wall. Hanna glanced down at her phone, partially hidden by one of Tom's socks. 5.07 a.m. The sneaky little shit. He'd gone back to bed. Maybe Iain would even go back to sleep, if they just waited long enough. Trying to sound as much like a single person rolling over in her sleep as possible, Hanna manoeuvred Tom up to kiss her. As their hips met, she prayed he would be quick. Quick and very quiet.

After half an hour, hearing nothing more from Iain's room but the occasional snort and rasping snore, Hanna tiptoed out of her room, opened the front door and watched Tom, his hair like fresh straw, the smell of her still on his hands, walk out into the corridor. As he reached the landing on the floor below, he looked back up at her. Hanna was leaning over the banister in just a T-shirt and knickers. Tom smiled and put his hands over his heart. Reflexively, she did the same. Hands crossed across her heart, palms flat, their eyes locked. Her foot poked through a gap in the railing. Her hair fell around her ears. Hearing the block's front door shut, she stepped back. Feeling something under her big toe, Hanna lifted her foot. A used condom dropped to the concrete floor.

15

Stamped Addressed Envelope

The envelope landed with a smug slap. Since moving to Oxford and back in with her later-life lothario father, Hanna had received precisely seven items of post: three bank statements, a letter inviting her in for a smear test, a credit card application, a DBS certificate and this. It was soft, heavy. It had the swelling of an expensive loaf, a hotel duvet, a cinema erection. Hanna picked it up and was surprised to see her own name on the front, apparently hand-printed in dark turquoise on cream paper. Who knew she was here? She was hardly on the run, but telling everyone your home address was a bit like giving out your landline number or sending people your Myspace profile; people just didn't bother any more. Did they? Turning the envelope over, Hanna saw an address in Walthamstow printed across the back. Well, that hardly narrowed it down. Since about 2015 it seemed like pretty much everyone Hanna knew was moving to a Warner flat in Walthamstow and growing their own tomatoes.

She took the letter into the kitchen and sat down at the table. It felt like that morning over a decade ago when she'd stood in the hallway of Plantation Road holding an unconditional offer letter from Sheffield University to study geography. Back when she thought she'd be the one to halt climate change and drink beer out of a shoe all at the same time. Today, Hanna's phone was still gripped, claw-like, in her hand from when she'd been sitting on the toilet, scrolling through photos of a heroes-themed house party to which she had not been invited. And to which, it seemed, Joe had turned up dressed as David Foster Wallace. Joe hated fancy dress. At least, the Joe she'd known had hated fancy dress. So much so that when they'd been invited to their friends' cowboy-themed party for their four-year-old child last year, Joe had stood at the door and actually argued with the birthday boy about putting on a hat. In the end, Joe had crouched down, held the child by the shoulders and said, 'Look, man, I'm a cowboy builder. I'll make all your kitchen units wonky and I'll leave the valves in your underfloor heating open so it leaks. Now, do you want this present or shall I just go home?' And yet here he was, wearing a bandana, a baggy shirt, a pair of wire-rimmed glasses, and laughing with a pixie-haired blonde woman in somebody's kitchen. He had a glass of wine in one hand and a copy of *Infinite Jest* in the other. Hanna had sat, pyjama bottoms around her ankles, her breath shallow, studying the pictures on the toilet like a conspiracy theorist inspecting footage of the moon landings.

The flap of the envelope came away easily, and as Hanna pulled out the folded paper she wondered, for a microsecond, if this was finally it. If this was the letter she'd been half hoping for, half dreading since breaking up with Joe. A five-page odyssey of self-reflection and regret from him. A desperate apology and plea for Hanna to reconsider their future. A promise to grow up, get a real job, start hanging up his own towel. A few short lines within it, explaining why he had made a mistake with Becky, how she was a living nightmare, that he wanted to make it better; and to have Hanna in his life for ever. In that moment, Hanna wasn't even sure how she'd reply to such self-flagellation. In her bones and brain and blood she felt entirely uninterested in a future with Joe. Time had cut away so many of the strings that had wound them together; their absence had flattened him into boredom and betrayal. But still, she wanted him to want her. Or at least to recognize and regret that he'd lost her.

Then from the central fold of the letter there fell a small square bingo card. Not the kind of multicoloured, shiny slip you get at the real bingo, but a very tasteful, cream and turquoise card, printed like something from a 1920s summer fair. In the top left-hand corner was a monogram: a P intertwined with a V. Hanna's heart sank. She knew a P and V. And this was just the sort of shit they'd pull.

'We've struck lucky!' the invitation read.

Vicky O'Connor and Phil Omola
are becoming the O'Comolas
and we want you to help us celebrate with a full house

For the love of God, what fresh hell was this.

Please mark your card and let us know if you can join us as we hit the jackpot

Oh, please.

On 27 May
At Stoke Newington Town Hall

Of course. Of course Vicky and Phil had made novelty invitations to their bingo-themed wedding in the twee capital of London on the Spring Bank Holiday. Of course they were creating a composite surname. They were blotting their number on this frail travelling co-incidence we call life and publicly pretending that love would last for ever. May. That was ten months away. Who, in their right and feeble mind, had any idea what they were doing on a single Sunday in ten months' time? That was the point, of course. To tie down all the single, free and uncommitted people nearly a year in advance. To wind her in with the ropes of social duty and ritual-istic guilt, so she couldn't take on an extra shift at work or visit her auntie on the day they decided to have a party. Sure, Phil and Vicky had been together for ten years, lived together for eight; they'd bought a house, got a cat, had a shared bank account, had had sex 1,087 times, and had spent every Christmas together for a decade. But Hanna still needed to agree nearly a year in advance to devoting a whole day to them and their relationship.

There were instructions on how to fill in the bingo card which now, on further inspection, Hanna saw was actually a sort of RSVP checklist. And, of course, it came with its very own self-addressed and prepaid envelope to send back to Vicky and Phil's flat on Leucha Road. There it would be posted through their tasteful green door beside their beautiful handmade macramé hanging basket and their extremely subtle CCTV camera. That anyone her age could have the wherewithal, the energy and the money to send out maybe two hundred prepaid, self-addressed envelopes gave Hanna a feeling like vertigo. This was the very same Vicky who only a year before meeting Phil had been caught by a delivery driver having sex inside a large metal crate full of Kingsmill bread outside the Co-op. How had she got so sorted? On the card were little boxes in which to write the details of your dietary requirements, parking allocation, accommodation and, Lord have mercy, plus one.

There it was. The stone that broke your teeth within every wedding. The plus one. Sitting at the kitchen table in a pair of her father's yak wool socks, some greying pyjama bottoms and a free T-shirt from a half-marathon she'd run in 2012, Hanna was expected to be able to write down the name of someone she'd be intimately involved with – wedding-guest involved with – in nearly a year's time. Plus ones had been easy before Dom had met Marni. For years, Hanna and Dom had been each other's plus ones at Christmas parties, work parties, engagement parties, birthday parties, book launches, film screenings, weddings and two funerals. Because he had an actual adult job, Dom owned four suits and the emotional maturity to match. The latent question – why was Hanna taking her old university friend to an engagement party while her actual boyfriend practised bass lines in the back room of an old shoe factory in Penge with his terrible band? – usually remained unasked. Dom liked parties and Hanna liked being at parties with Dom. He would remember to bring flowers, to print out maps, to sign cards, to download QR codes, and to say the name of the host as they shook hands. He would hold Hanna's hand unselfconsciously as they walked past a table of flamingo-like women standing at the sidelines muttering about who had and hadn't had a baby yet. Dom could be relied upon to talk to anybody's aunt, boss or new partner and still have a nice time.

Hello slapbass, have you been invited to Vicky and Phil's 'I've bingo-ing crazy' wedding?

As she waited for Dom to answer, Hanna went over to the kitchen worktop and ate a handful of Brazil nuts. What was it about these that made them taste vaguely like pork? And what was it that selenium did to sperm? And did that also mean they shrivelled ovaries but nobody had bothered to check? Also, why did some nuts have the consistency of soap while others were like biting into concrete?

Oh yes. I think it'll be fun. There was a pause as Dom typed more. *Marni says she's going to dress as Dale Winton and pull National Lottery balls out through her flies every time they make a toast.* This was swiftly followed by a GIF of Dale Winton snapping his fingers on *Supermarket Sweep*.

So he was taking his girlfriend. Of course. His beautiful, funny girlfriend would take the train from Paris and they'd spend the weekend together talking about marriage and kissing on the dance floor. Hanna sighed. Not out of jealousy or self-pity. Or at least, not only because of those. She felt disoriented. How had she drifted so far out to sea? Was she going to be the only single person at the wedding? Would they sit her at the kids' table and expect her to eat jelly and talk about Pokémon with Phil's fourteen-year-old nephew? Would she be put on a side table near the toilets with all the elderly female relatives – the grandmothers and warty aunts and Salvation Army second cousins – and be expected to make small talk about window boxes for three hours? Or would she be put next to the one single man at the whole party, who wears a festival wristband in November and does celebrity impressions and calls women 'chicks' and is perpetually trying but failing to grow a moustache? And, oh God, who was she going to take?

She scrolled through her phone for an old, flattering photo to send Tom. Finding none, she decided to try being in the moment and just send him a message.

I'm alone in the flat. Come over. We could eat watermelon and have sex in the shower. She waited a few seconds, then put the phone face down on the table, as though she could fool the universe into thinking she didn't care. The phone buzzed. Hanna scrabbled so quickly to get it back into her hand that she managed to bend the nail on her ring finger the wrong way. Hoping for a message from Tom, she sucked the air through her teeth in pain and turned the screen to face her.

Marni says maybe you can dress as Shane Richie.

Tom's message hadn't been read.

Tearing a corner off the thick card of the invitation, Hanna put the phone in the cutlery drawer. She rolled the chunk of wedding invite into a little spiral, placed it at the left end of a Rizla and helped herself to a pinch of Iain's tobacco, from the drawer in the kitchen table. *Well, if you can't beat them, smoke them.*

Dom arrived into Oxford train station at 10 a.m. the next day. Growing up in a tourist town, Hanna had got pretty used to traipsing around the same old highlights when guests arrived. The Radcliffe Camera, the Covered Market, Magdalen Bridge, maybe a trip up the tower of St Mary the Virgin to have a look out over the golden rooftops, blah blah blah. Inspector Morse, Harry Potter, Philip Pullman and on and on. Hanna had done it many times before. She could do it lying on the kitchen floor with her eyes closed. But Dom was different. Dom was coming to visit the city that

Hanna actually lived in. The city that had built her and shaped her.

'Rude dog! How are you, darling?' asked Dom, as he stepped through the barriers and bent almost double to give Hanna a light hug.

'Thank you so much for coming!' gasped Hanna. 'It's so exciting to have a visitor.' When she'd first left London, Hanna had received a flurry of people wanting to go on a punt, eat a pub lunch and stroll around some medieval shit, especially on the Bank Holidays. But since the novelty of having a friend outside Zone 4 had worn off, Hanna had noticed a distinct drop-off in people willing to spend fifty-five minutes on a train to come and see her.

'Well, you know, I just really wanted to sit knee to knee with an oily haired stranger talking loudly to his wife about real ales on a train, and this was the best excuse I could find at short notice.' Dom smiled, and his ears seemed to twitch into his auburn hair like a dog waiting to be scratched.

'I thought we could take a stroll down the Cowley Road, visit all my favourite underage drinking spots, maybe swing by the Goldfish Bowl to tickle the piranha and then walk home along the river?'

'I'm entirely at your mercy,' said Dom, holding his hands up like an extra in a cowboy film.

Walking through town, Hanna found herself pointing out increasingly mundane and torrid sites of interest, as she and Dom shuffled through packs of tourists, all wearing matching fluorescent rucksacks or following a guide carrying a huge flag.

'That's where I had my first Saturday job,' Hanna said, gesturing towards a shop selling bras big enough to bathe a baby in. 'Back then it was a haberdasher's, and one day I managed to cash up so badly that I ended up putting £7.87 of my own money into the till to cover it up.

'This is where I got off with Connie Beale's boyfriend on New Year's Eve,' she said, pointing at an alcove on the outside of Queen's College where a queue of people were waiting for the number five bus. Dom walked quickly on.

'This is where I tried to take up smoking a pipe, after watching that BBC adaptation of *Moll Flanders* where she smokes a glass one in the back of a hansom carriage while fucking an old man.' Hanna stopped with her foot on the step outside Havana House. 'Do you need anything?'

'I'm good for pipes, thank you,' said Dom. 'I like to seduce my old men the old-fashioned way – with chewing tobacco and a spittoon.'

As they passed the Private Shop on Cowley Road, Hanna explained how every time a tourist had asked for directions, she and her friend Jack would faithfully guide them here. Sometimes they even drew maps. Opposite the Jamaican Eating House she pointed at the building where David Cameron had apparently lived as a student, and the music shop where Iain had once played such a perfect rendition of Jimi Hendrix's solo from 'All Along the Watchtower' that three boys waiting outside the barber's next door had started clapping.

'Would you actually like to see some tropical fish or were you just joking?' asked Hanna, stepping around a dog tied up outside the Helen & Douglas House charity shop by a tartan wool scarf.

'Honestly, it sounds like fun,' said Dom.

'There's a pub across the road from the Goldfish Bowl that we used to call the Evil Tavern,' said Hanna. 'But it's been done up now and is all homemade pizzas and craft beer. We could go there for lunch? It's meant to be quite good on Sundays.'

'And who can ask for more than "quite good" at our age,' said Dom, slipping an arm through the gap at Hanna's elbow. 'Take me to your finest guppies and don't spare the mustard.'

'Deal. Now, can we talk turkey for just a second?' Hanna asked, quickening her step to keep up with Dom's six-foot stride. 'Who the fuck am I going to take to Vicky and Phil's wedding?' A quick tang of anxiety flashed through her. She glanced up at him quickly. He seemed unperturbed. 'I was wondering about Tom,' she said, her cheeks slightly flushing, both from concern she'd offended Dom and the delight in saying Tom's name out loud. 'Although it might be a bit soon. We've only really been seeing each other a few months and it's still super casual.'

'Super casual' was the self-protective way of saying 'mildly confusing'. Since Tom's great bush letter stunt on the way to Port Meadow and his early morning flit from Iain's flat the next day, Hanna had only heard from him a couple of times.

'Oh yes, how's that all going?' asked Dom, peering into the lounge windows of the small Victorian houses on their left.

'Well, we've both been quite busy,' said Hanna. 'We went for a lunchtime drink, which was lovely, but the rest of the time it's usually just messages.'

'Hm . . .' Dom was, as ever, impossible to read.

'He says he likes to just live in the moment. Which I really like.' Hanna cleared her throat. 'So he makes these lovely spontaneous plans.' Dom still said nothing. 'But he is also a bit crap at replying sometimes.'

'How long does he leave it?'

'Usually just a few hours. But my last message, it was more like a day and a half.'

'And you say he looks after his mum?' asked Dom, pinching a sprig of rosemary out of someone's front garden.

'Yes. So we have to keep things quite casual.' Hanna tried to sound light-hearted. 'Although I do sometimes wonder if I have the energy for casual. I mean, I think I'd actually quite like some non-casual sex, soon. I'd quite like some meaningful, maybe even official sex.' Hanna blushed. Not out of prudishness but a sense of vulnerability. Dom could always do this with her; give away so little that she ended up splurging her guts out. 'But then again, it doesn't actually feel casual with Tom.

Like, he'll hold my hand in public.' She glanced up at him. 'He uses all these old nicknames from when we were kids, and he says such lovely things.' She slowed down as the road came to a junction. 'I know it makes me a terrible feminist, Dom, but sometimes I just really want him to say, "I belong to you and you belong to me." ' She laughed nervously.

'Do you actually have to bring anyone to this wedding?' asked Dom, stepping off the kerb and into the road. 'You can stay at ours if you're coming up from Oxford and I'm sure Vicky and Phil would be happy either way. They probably just want to know numbers for catering and stuff.'

Just at the corner of Magdalen Road and Hurst Street, Dom stopped. They were outside Silvester's – a tiny green hardware shop that had been in East Oxford for longer than Hanna had been alive. As a child, she'd walked there with Iain a hundred times to buy rawlplugs, Polyfilla, tea strainers, compost, lightbulbs and twine. She could clearly remember the tinkle of the bell as they'd stepped into the small, dusty shop, with its shelves full of plates and plant pots and plaster of Paris piled up to the ceiling. She remembered the thin, white-haired man in his navy blue overalls who would stand at the counter, nodding, as Iain took out his paper list. She remembered the peach-cheeked woman in a flowery blouse and a navy apron, who would help Hanna pick out a small packet of seeds from the racks by the door. And now she was standing beside her best friend as he stared at three oven gloves, laid out in the window like a flower, beside a small Calor gas canister, a patch of AstroTurf and a row of wooden clothes pegs.

'Are you all right, pal?' Hanna asked, looking up into Dom's face. His expression was unreadable and unfamiliar.

'Yes. Yes, sorry.' Dom cleared his throat. 'Marni has that oven glove. I think she inherited it from her granny after she died. It's just weird seeing it here.' He looked up at the green painted sign, faded and cracked by the sun. 'I never expected to see my girlfriend's dead grandmother's oven glove in a hardware shop in Oxford.'

'Oh, we have everything here,' said Hanna, leaning into Dom's shoulder. 'I hear we're getting Ceefax next month.'

Dom smiled. 'You know what I mean,' he said.

'Yes, of course,' said Hanna. 'Sorry. Do you miss her a lot?'

'Only every day,' he replied. 'Sorry. I know it's not like you and Joe. I'm really lucky. It's just that sometimes it feels like I've made my life unnecessarily complicated.' Hanna nodded, but resisted the urge to chip in. For once. 'Vicky and Phil, Ben and Eve; they're doing what I sort of assumed I'd be doing one day. Naff as all that matching tattoos and Instagram shit is. But instead, I've been with my girlfriend for three years and over that whole time probably only ever spent about a month together. There's so much we just haven't . . .' He sighed.

Hanna waited. A man on a bicycle cycled past them, a sleeping toddler slumped in its seat behind him like a little old drunk in dungarees. Dom still said nothing. A seagull, lost miles inland, soared over the quiet street. A small, lime-coloured leaf skittered along the pavement at her feet. Hanna pulled away from Dom and looked up into his short, pale, not-unhandsome face.

'Is this your way of telling me you're still a virgin, Dom?'

His face exploded into a huge grin.

'Ripe and ready to pluck,' he said, pinching the inside corners of his eyes with thumb and forefinger. 'Ha.' He sniffed. 'By the way – and obviously you didn't hear this from me, and I'd rather it didn't go any further . . .' There was an agonizing second while he waited for Hanna to catch on and nod her assent. 'But I heard that Vicky and Phil nearly broke up at the beginning of the year because he'd become addicted to robot porn.'

'Excuse me?' Hanna interjected.

'Yeah. Like CGI videos of women being spit-roasted by cyborgs and stuff. All very . . .' Dom paused as though he was trying to describe a wine. 'Niche. Anyway, he was caught watching it at work. Nearly got fired. And so this whole wedding is sort of Vicky's way of trying to draw a line under it all.'

Hanna let out a long, low whistle. 'Wowzer.' And

then, somehow, there was nothing more to be said. She looked up at Dom. He looked down at her. A car turned into the road behind them.

'Nice try distracting me from the old virginity situation, by the way,' she smiled, stepping into the road and towards a red-brick building covered in pictures of tropical fish. 'But don't worry – there's a sucker fish at this place that really knows its way around the male form.'

'Well, thank God for that,' said Dom, following.

Maybe not everybody is that sorted, thought Hanna as she walked across the tarmac. *Maybe some of it's just Polyfilla and self-addressed envelopes.*

The following Saturday, Hanna and Shazia had decided to meet in Summertown to raid the charity shops. Hanna was early, as usual, despite walking the long way round through the North Parade street market. She'd texted Tom a photo of a salami, lumpy with walnuts, with the caption 'Thinking of you'. The perfect blend, she thought, of flirty, funny and affectionate, with a honking great subtext: 'please reply'.

'Are you looking for something specific or are you just browsing?' asked Shazia, as they ambled up towards Oxfam. She was wearing soft, oatmeal-coloured trousers that gathered at the ankle in a cuff, and brown sandals.

'Well, next week I've got this big climate event at the museum and I want to look smart,' replied Hanna. 'But obviously, if anyone compliments me on what I'm wearing, I have to be able to prove that it was ethically sourced.'

'And you're skint,' said Shazia, the corner of her mouth and eyebrow curling up in unison.

'Yes, there is also that,' replied Hanna. 'Seriously, Shaz, how can you even wear beige trousers? Don't you ever sit in bird shit? Or worry you'll get your period? Or drop mustard down your leg?'

'I carry baby wipes.'

In Oxfam, Hanna found herself stroking a large, royal-blue chenille jumper.

'I wouldn't call that smart, love,' said Shazia. 'More, Tory-wife-on-the-campaign-trail-at-a-coffee-morning.'

'Oh. No. I wasn't actually looking at it. I just—'

'I know. Sometimes you just have to stroke the jumpers,' said Shazia. 'I'm the same with anything silk.'

'Exactly. Just a question of texture.' They headed over the road to Scope.

'How are things going with Tom, then?' asked Shazia, who had clearly been hoping Hanna would bring it up herself.

'Oh, good. Yeah, fine,' said Hanna, looking down at a pile of jigsaw puzzles rather than facing Shazia's inquisitive gaze. 'There's something really nice about being with someone who knew you years ago. Do you know what I mean? Like, there's a shared history or like, a shorthand.'

'How often do you see each other?'

'Um . . .' Hanna didn't want to admit to Shazia how

little she saw Tom. She didn't actually want to work it out like that; in days per week. Shazia was married; Shazia owned a flat and a shed and her own car. She didn't understand what dating was like. She just didn't get it.

'Maybe once a week?' Hanna fudged. 'It depends on how busy we are.'

'And have you told Iain?'

'Oh God, no. He'd be unbearable. I can't say any men's names without him going off the deep end. The first time I mentioned Sanjay from work, Iain made this big thing about how dangerous office romances can be to your career.'

Shazia gave Hanna a sly smile. 'Would you like to date Sanjay from work?'

'Ha! No. He's lovely but he is so meek. What I like about Tom is that he's properly my equal. Being with him is genuinely thrilling. Like, I never know where we're going to end up.' Hanna turned a vase over in her hands. 'Actually, I snuck him back to the flat the other night.'

'No way!'

'I didn't want to keep shagging in alleyways, Shazia! But it's worse: in the morning, we could hear Iain sneaking Mary out.'

'NO WAY.'

'I know. Iain totally broke the no-overnight-visitors rule.'

'Well—'

'Yes, I know. You don't need to say it,' Hanna laughed.

‘But I don’t get it,’ said Shazia, holding a long beige mac up to her chin and glancing in the mirror. ‘Why don’t you just go back to Tom’s? Surely his mum would be cool about it? She loved you at school.’

‘Well, it’s complicated,’ said Hanna, although just at that moment she couldn’t quite remember why. ‘Oh, look,’ she said, holding up a navy jumpsuit with a shirt collar and small gold buttons on the cuff. ‘This is quite smart. Quite events-y.’

‘Yes,’ said Shazia. ‘You could solve climate change and climb a ladder and get naked every time you go for a pee.’

Hanna’s phone buzzed as she was standing in the changing room. In just her bra and pants, she pulled the phone from her jacket pocket. It was a message from Tom. He must have known they were talking about him.

Don’t eat me all at once. And a smiling, winky-face emoji.

16
Ukulele

As was so often the case as she approached her front door, Hanna desperately needed the toilet. Ever since she'd been a child and had looked up halfway through her business to see Marianne Steeple leaning over the top of her primary school cubicle, smiling like a gargoyle, Hanna had been a little reluctant to defecate outside her own home. Overnight work trips were a nightmare, mini-breaks not much better, as her sphincter resolutely barred the way until Hanna was back on her own lino, the other side of her own letterbox.

Stepping into the hallway, the urgency pressing at her trousers carried Hanna down the hall, ignoring the new coat hanging there, deaf to the sounds coming from the kitchen. She lightly touched the switch on the wall. The late summer sun had fallen behind the roofs outside, staining this whole side of the flat dark by 7.30 p.m. It would soon be the season of baked potatoes and bonfires, conkers and carrot soup. Sitting on the toilet, Hanna opened up a promotional email from Alton Towers, inviting her to book a £34 August Splashtacular. She'd organized a hen do at Alton Towers a few years ago and been getting promotional emails ever since. Somehow, the memory of seventeen secretly drunk women dressed as penguins queuing up for Nemesis, while Gemma snorted cocaine off a house key, had stopped her unsubscribing.

Hanna eventually stood up, flushed and opened the bathroom window. A rush of cold air, smelling slightly of woodsmoke and river water, passed across her face, and hopefully neutralized the evidence of what she'd just done. As she washed her hands, she checked her face for new hairs. These long black strands, more like eyelashes, seemed to spring out from her skin overnight. More than once, Hanna had had to walk out of work meetings after discovering a three-centimetre whisker sprouting from her cheek, which absolutely had not been there an hour earlier. For reasons best known to itself, her body appeared to be preparing for middle age by cracking out a full beard, and keeping on top of it took daily vigilance. Obviously, Hanna had always hoped that by this point she would have become one of those strident, self-possessed women who refuses to bow to patriarchal notions of gender conformity and lets her body express itself as hairily as it sees fit. But then, she'd also always hoped that by this point in her life she would be in a happy, long-term relationship with someone who loved her precisely as she was. Having sex with enigmatic men against bins while living in her dad's spare room hadn't, necessarily, been part of the long-term plan. In the last few weeks Hanna hadn't heard much from Tom. Cycling through self-doubt, frustration, shame, lust and disappointment, she'd told herself not to chase him, that in order to keep him she had to be more casual, more in the moment, less demanding. And yet, she couldn't help but remember this feeling from being with Joe; of being in limbo, of putting his feelings above her own, of always being the one to compromise. When they'd broken up, Hanna had promised herself not to make the same mistakes.

She clicked off the light and walked down to the kitchen. There were, she now realized, two guitars playing in there. She'd grown immune to the jangly, when-I'm-cleaning-windows sound of Iain's ukulele when she got in. But this was different. Someone in there was playing a guitar bigger than a toaster.

'Hello, love.' Iain looked up as she walked into the room, his moon boot stuck out like a peg leg. 'You remember Oscar.'

Oh, yes she did. Oscar's loose afro was a little greyer than when she'd last seen him, the lines around his eyes a little deeper, but he was still recognizably her dad's handsome friend.

'Oscar! Hello.' Something in their body language pinged through the air. Oscar did not stand up to hug her. She did not bend down to kiss him. Instead, like two wary animals, they held each other's gaze, feet planted, unmoving. To be fair, Oscar had never been one of those men who gave you piggyback rides or let you climb up their leg to do a flip. Maybe because he'd never had children, maybe because he'd spent so much time on stage, his energy had always been slightly removed, observant, hands off. And yet, Hanna noticed, he was looking at her more intently than any man had done for a while.

'Hello, Hanna,' he said, unsmiling. 'You're big.' In somebody else's mouth those two words may have sounded clumsy, accusatory, even creepy. But somehow Oscar managed to drop them into the room without breaking any definite social code.

'Yes. Enormous. How are you, Oscar?' Why was she saying his name so much? she wondered. Was this mock formality or simply mocking?

'I'm very well, thank you.' He still hadn't taken his eyes off her, and was now sliding his left hand up and down the fretboard of his guitar.

'Would you like a drink, love?' Iain levered himself up and limped towards the fridge. While his ankle was significantly better, he was still wearing his orthopaedic boot around the house and Hanna was still doing the majority of the cleaning. Iain had started going back in to work three days a week and Hanna had started to see the light at the end of the tunnel. In a week or two he'd be signed off by the doctor and she could, finally, move in with Shazia. Or, perhaps by then she'd have miraculously saved up enough for a rental deposit on a one-bedroom flat, while things were quiet in the city, before the students came back.

'Sure,' said Hanna, who was actually desperate for a

cup of tea but somehow didn't want to admit that in front of Oscar. The door of the fridge clunked slightly as Iain pulled it open.

'Hmm, we're running a bit low – I could pop to Azim's. I wanted to get a look at the evening paper and I've been cooped up in the house all day.'

With Iain now shuffling down the hallway, patting his pockets and grabbing one of Hanna's small canvas shopping bags from the hook, Hanna sat down in the seat facing Oscar and took a sip from Iain's drink.

'Do you . . . play?' asked Oscar, stroking the palm of his right hand round the curved arse of the guitar.

'Not the guitar, no,' Hanna replied, letting her legs fall open in a gesture that was both faux masculine and, she knew, provocative. She thought of Tom. His last message had been all about shift patterns and a plan to cycle around Europe with one of his bike friends. No mention of their relationship. 'Much to Iain's disappointment, my musical achievements pretty much began and ended with a year's worth of piano lessons with his mate Jerry.'

'Ah, Jerry Hapsburg?' said Oscar, his face splitting in two around a huge smile. 'Big house on Polstead Road? Silk waistcoats and a lion tattoo on his forearm?'

'That's him.'

'I know Jerry. I stole a girlfriend off him once, in 1982. I had to give him my import copy of *Catch a Fire* to make up for it.' This account of women as tradeable goods would, in normal circumstances, have Hanna spitting into Oscar's glass. But somehow, like so much about Oscar, it seemed merely anachronistic; seedy in that slightly glamorous way that things that happened nearly forty years ago could be.

'Are you still playing?' This was one of those questions, Hanna knew, that simultaneously scythed down Oscar's ego and gave him the opportunity to show off.

'Yes. I still play with Burning Spear and Rhygin.' *Here it comes*, thought Hanna. 'We just played Glastonbury and a load of festivals out in Europe.' *Of course*. Was he trying to impress her? But then again, thought Hanna, weren't we all trying to impress each other, all the time?

'And is that all you do for fun?' Even Hanna was slightly surprised by the directness of her own flirtation. Did she really fancy Oscar? Or was she just missing Tom? Trying to make Tom jealous? She pulled her hair back, arching her spine. Her nipples were hard, visibly so, and Oscar was definitely looking.

'Not just that.' Oscar left a heavy pause. The fridge hummed behind Hanna. Oscar puckered his mouth thoughtfully and stared deep into her eyes. For a second, she forgot all about Tom and Joe and the potting shed and her heart and work and the fact that she was trapped inside her hobbling father's house. She didn't think about weddings and backpacking and baby showers and careers and affairs and mortgages. She was just there, in the moment. Like she'd been trying so hard to be. Then Oscar plucked a couple of notes, absentmindedly, on the guitar in his lap. 'I actually have an allotment now, by Burgess Field.' He sat back. 'I've got these pumpkins that look like sea anemones. It's like having a little rockpool in the middle of the city. Only instead of water they're surrounded by flowers.' Only a man like Oscar could flit between such sexual intensity and this kind of whimsy. 'You should come and see it sometime.' And just like that, his leg was sliding up the inside of her knee. It felt big, hot, hard. 'I can just imagine you . . .' Another agonizing pause. 'Pulling up weeds.' *Wow*, thought Hanna. This was on. He might be twenty-five years older than her. He might be her dad's mate. But this was on. She bit her bottom lip and pushed back against Oscar's leg. Did she feel guilty about doing this? Guilty about Tom? Absolutely not. You couldn't be unfaithful to someone who had shown no commitment. Did she feel guilty for Joe? It had been so long since they broke up, but had she really lanced him from her heart so completely? Perhaps. Right now, she was alone, uncommitted and feeling dangerous. Oscar was handsome. He was untouchable.

'Well, that does sound fun—' Hanna's voice was slightly cracked and drowned out by the sound of a key in the front door.

'I got Guinness, Nigerian import, and some cashew nuts,' said Iain, panting down the hall like a Jack Russell. Hanna and Oscar immediately sat back, their legs pulling apart. Hanna finished the dregs of Iain's beer and tried not to think of the particles of her father's spit and regurgitated food she'd just swallowed. Oscar crossed his legs.

'And you can't have a jam without a little sugar!' Iain laughed, coming into the room and throwing a large bag of chocolate buttons on to the table. Hanna and Oscar said nothing.

The whole museum was taken over the next day by a conference on climate change organized by the university's environmental sciences department, the Oxford Climate Action Group and local council representatives. It was, for Hanna, the culmination of three months' work and – aside from some rather awkward questions about the museum's commitment to carbon divestment – had gone well. Hanna had finally been able to use the merest iota of her degree in her work life, having got in touch with one of her old climate science tutors from Sheffield and invited her along to do a talk. More importantly, everybody had found the toilets, meeting rooms, water refill stations and recycling points, and everybody who needed to had received their travel reimbursements on the day. In Hanna's job, that counted as success. To celebrate, she and Tom were going out for a meal at the Punter. It would be their first date in three weeks.

We should go and drink gin and eat chips in a garden and toast you as the sun goes down over the canal, was what he'd texted her. He was always so incredibly romantic in texts.

At 5.54 p.m., Hanna was stacking the last row of chairs in the seminar room when she heard a rattle like sheep hooves on tarmac behind her. Annabel, bedecked in enough wooden jewellery to build a rowboat, had stepped into the room and was swiping theatrically at an iPad.

'Hello, Annabel,' said Hanna at last, pushing the stacked chairs against the wall under the window. There was a stuffed leopard under the smartboard (which Hanna had considered moving when the room was initially booked by the Green Party in order to discuss Low Traffic Neighbourhoods) and a collection of bone-coloured rocks beside the radiator.

'Oh, so here you are,' said Annabel without looking up from her screen, as though Hanna were a puppy who had just pissed in the washing machine.

'Yes, I was just deconstructing the conference set-up,' said Hanna, hating herself for using the stupid events team jargon even though she knew doing so would please Annabel.

'Well,' said Annabel, clonking a mahogany-coloured bangle against her glasses as she swept some hair off her face. 'I just wanted to say well done.' This was said in precisely the same tone with which you would inform a patient that their renal exam had exposed some sort of fistula and that surgery was now considered essential. 'I've just been looking at some of the online feedback from the attendees today and you've scored . . .' She peered at the iPad as though trying to decipher the

Rosetta Stone. 'Surprisingly highly on the satisfaction survey.'

Despite herself, Hanna beamed.

'Oh, well I'm just glad that it reflected well on the team,' she said, trying to keep her modesty the right side of snide. While Hanna had been chaperoning delegates, setting up guest profiles on the server, handing out marketing literature and chasing catering orders, Annabel had spent much of the afternoon walking up and down the mezzanine smiling at anyone wearing a lanyard.

'Yes. And we've had five new enquiries into room hire already. You should consider today a success,' said Annabel, finally looking up at Hanna with a pinched smile. 'It was a shame that one of our banners got pushed behind a pillar for the Vice Chancellor's address but, still' – she thwacked the iPad against one of her large, beaded necklaces – 'at least I managed to fix it before the photographer left.' With that, Annabel and her remarkably flat arse swept out of the room.

Hanna quickly flicked off the lights and ran to the office to grab her bag and jacket. She was still smiling as she darted past the cockroaches and tarantula tank. As she entered the room she noticed, there on her desk, a little packet of butterscotch Werther's Originals. They had a green Post-it stuck to them with 'Well done' written in Sanjay's small, neat capitals. And someone else had washed up her mug.

*

Walking into the pub, Hanna saw Tom already in the garden, smoking a cigarette and reading a book. Good God, but he was handsome. If Hanna had been asked to describe the ideal man she could be meeting in a pub tonight, it would come very close to Tom. Tall, handsome, wearing a nice jumper, reading a book, outdoorsy, kind, smelling of bonfires, unconcerned about money, attentive, quick-witted, articulate, political, funny, and a really lovely penis. Standing at the bar, watching him turn a page with his large, still-tanned thumb, she knew she was being stupid. She'd overthought this. Her fear of rejection was holding her back from the possibility of real happiness. She liked Tom, really liked him. She'd known him – sort of – since they were nine. Her friends would like him, he could drive, he could talk to strangers. She should just invite him to Vicky and Phil's wedding. Ask him to be her plus one and stop trying to second-guess and guard against the future. They were in their thirties, they'd been sleeping together for a few months; it wasn't beyond the realms of possibility that she should invite him to her friends' wedding. Was it?

'Hey baby, you look nice.' The door to the beer garden banged behind Hanna as she received the compliment with all the grace she could muster, while also holding a double gin and tonic plus a large packet of ready salted crisps.

'Thank you. I thought I'd make the effort, now I've solved climate change.'

'Seriously, it's really good you did that,' said Tom,

putting his book back in his rucksack just slowly enough for Hanna to read the cover: *Wheels Within Wheels* by Dervla Murphy. 'Because I really wanted to cycle to Spain this year and simply don't have time for any droughts or forest fires in my schedule.' He stood up and kissed her on the mouth. He tasted of beer and tobacco and smelled of Nivea. His beard was just long enough to feel soft against her skin but not so long to hide his frankly architectural jawline.

'Yeah, well, I thought now we're well into the new tax year I might as well do something to make this quarter really sing,' she replied, sitting down on a heavy wooden chair. 'I just got off the phone to the head of the UN. He says I can take next Tuesday afternoon off as time off in lieu for, you know, saving the planet and everything.'

'Well, you know what they say about António Guterres.' Of course he knew the name of the head of the UN off by heart. 'He's never been one to fuck with HR.' Did Tom think she worked in HR? Hanna wondered. Or was this just another joke?

'How are you?' she asked. 'How's your mum?' It felt daring to be this intimate, to play the mum card this boldly, so early in the night. But maybe Hanna was feeling bold.

'My mum?' Tom looked at his watch. 'Just sitting down to *Emmerdale*, I imagine, with a plate of Ritz crackers covered in that pâté that looks like toothpaste made of meat.' It was pure deflection, but Hanna let it go. She had bigger fish to fry here tonight. 'How is *your* mum?'

'Oh, probably sitting down to listen to *The Archers* while drinking a gin and cider and doing some tarot cards. You know the sort of thing.' It wasn't a joke but Tom smiled anyway. 'I was wondering . . .' Despite herself, Hanna swallowed a little nervously. *Here goes nothing.* 'Do you have any plans in May?'

'As in the month?' asked Tom, looking ever so slightly like a fox that's just heard the call of a bugle.

'No, as in James May, the former presenter of *Top Gear*,' replied Hanna. 'I was just wondering what plans you had inside his rectum.' Tom laughed, although his shoulders didn't entirely relax. 'Yes, May the twenty-seventh, to be precise. What Larkin called Whitsun.' Was she gabbling? She may have been gabbling. 'Only . . .' She waited for just a beat, to try and guess what he was thinking. 'Only, my friends Vicky and Phil are getting married in London, and I have a plus one and it'll be free booze, and we can get the train and maybe stay in some fetid little hotel room for the night and have sex up against a broken wardrobe, and loads of my uni friends will be there and they're really nice and you won't have to wear a suit and, oh, it's bingo themed so you might even win some . . . money?' That had definitely been gabbling. Hanna forced her lips against her clenched fingers, her elbows shaking slightly on the table. And waited.

'Did you just invite me to be your plus one at a

wedding next *year?*' The inflection on 'year' sliced through Hanna's heart like an ice skate through a toddler's hand. *Oh God.* What had she just done? 'Baby. I'm. Uh . . .' Tom raked his fingers through his hair and tipped his head up to look at the sky, now streaked with orange and indigo and blue. 'I'm sorry but I just can't . . .' He took a deep breath. 'I'm just not that guy.'

Hanna winced.

'I don't do plans,' he continued. 'I told you that.'

'Yes, I know.' Blood was flushing up Hanna's neck, streaming across her cheeks and down her chest, staining her skin bright, dark pink. She thought of his friend and their plan to cycle to Spain. 'I just thought. Well. We've been, you know. And. Well, I just thought you might . . .' Hanna felt like a pair of bagpipes kicked down a communal stairwell. Her honking, wheezing attempt at an explanation was worse than no explanation at all.

'Hannacopter.' That nickname, God. It was like inhaling 2003 every time. 'I think you're amazing.' Hanna's chest twisted. This was never good. She knew a shit sandwich when it was heading towards her on a plate. And Tom was most definitely about to deliver her a shit sandwich. 'But you should know. I just don't believe in monogamy. One man, one woman, for ever – all that bullshit.' It was as if a hundred tiny knives were suddenly piercing Hanna's eyes, throat, chest, womb. *All that bullshit?* Did she agree? Did she think love, two people, a lifetime, was bullshit? Apart from her grandparents and maybe Dom's parents, she couldn't actually think of anyone who'd successfully achieved it, right now. Her own parents certainly seemed to think monogamy was bullshit. But did she? Hanna swallowed the pine cone seemingly lodged in her throat. 'I like being with you, like this, right now. But I can't say that I'll want that for ever,' said Tom. 'Or that I won't sometimes be attracted to other people.' The adrenaline that had been released when she'd asked the question had suddenly turned to something more like fear. Here it was. 'And I can't sit at somebody's wedding and pretend that I believe in what they're saying. I think those promises and vows are bullshit – lies we tell ourselves so we don't have to face the truth: that the future is chaos and we are alone.'

'Right,' Hanna said, so quietly it was almost just the unsticking of her lips.

'Did you honestly think I'd want to come to a wedding with you?' Tom's lip had curled slightly. 'Next year? Come on, Hanna.' The light from the pub behind her was bouncing off his eyes. 'You must have known it was pretty unlikely.'

Tom let out a bark of something a little like laughter but entirely without humour anywhere through it.

'Sorry,' Hanna mumbled.

'And with your uni friends, too.' He said it like she'd suggested going to the wedding of a dog with mange. 'Everybody talking about their cars and how much they got as a Christmas bonus last year.' Was this a money thing? wondered Hanna briefly. *Is he just chippy about not going to university?* Was it class? 'There will probably be some guy in a kilt even though he's only been to Scotland once.' Hanna looked down at her knees and tried to breathe. 'And the father of the bride will make a load of awful jokes.' His hand was splayed across his thigh, as though he was trying to rub something from his palm. 'And everybody will be all twitchy about who's next.' Tom giggled, perhaps nervously, perhaps pleased with his little speech. Hanna felt tears weighing against the back of her eyelids. She couldn't speak.

'Oh, sorry, baby. Look, listen, I didn't mean anything about your friends.' Tom reached for her hand but Hanna pulled it under the table. 'I just. You know, I don't like all that stuff,' he continued, speaking more quietly. 'You and me, we're great but we'll never be that. I live in the moment. I love you in the moment.' Hanna felt something deep in her body rise up and then writhe in on itself like a snake touched by a hot iron. 'I want to be with you in the moment. But I don't ever want to be somebody's plus one. Even the term – it's so offensive. Like you're not even a real person, just an appendage to somebody else's digit.' Tom folded his hands loosely together on top of the table and looked down at them as he carried on talking. 'I don't ever want to be somebody's boyfriend, honey. I don't ever want a girlfriend, or a wife, or any of that shit. I'm just me. And I'm here. Now. You get that, don't you? I thought you got that?' His voice was soft now, more wheedling. 'You were always cool.

Laid back. Not like that. We understand each other, right?'

And just like that, the puttering flame of hope that had been warming Hanna's heart for months went out. Cold. Dead. She said nothing. Because there was nothing to be said.

Two hours later, she deleted Tom's number from her phone. Four hours later, she sent an email to someone on SpareRoom about a studio flat in Marston. Nine hours later, she deleted every single photo of Tom from her camera roll. The next morning she walked a different way to work. A week later she got an STI check. All clear.

17
Flat White

'And this is the wet room,' said the estate agent, the lapel of his jacket catching, just slightly, on the Swarovski tie pin jutting out from his chest.

A wet room, Hanna realized, was a room so small that instead of fitting a separate shower, you simply tiled the entire floor and half the walls, installed the shower above the sink, and sprayed water across your toilet roll, towel and slippers every time you got clean.

'It's great,' Hanna trilled, taking in the thumb-sized extractor fan and frosted window looking out on to an exterior wall. That would be cold in January.

'Yeah, I like a wet room, actually,' said Abdul. 'Much more modern.' He seemed to be searching for something else, some closing phrase or punchline. 'And hygienic.' Hanna looked at the black blooms of mould crawling across the grout in the corners of the room.

'Definitely,' she smiled, another thick slap of Abdul's aftershave hitting her face as he lifted his arm to the shower head.

'That's a power shower, I reckon.' He looked over his

shoulder at Hanna. 'Mad pressure you get from these things.'

'Oh, crazy.' She felt her face pinch into something not unlike a smile.

Now that Iain was back on both feet and Hanna had finally managed to save up some money for a rental deposit, the hunt for a flat, room, even just a bed somewhere other than her dad's, had stepped up a gear. One spare room in Summertown had turned out to be a sofa bed in the living room of a couple in their twenties, who had been bought the flat by his parents and clearly saw Hanna as a handy way to help cover the mortgage. She had stood silently in the kitchen as they talked her through the cherry-red appliances, murmured something about having too much furniture, and erased their contact the minute she reached the front door. She was desperate, but she wasn't an actual pet.

Since her break-up with Tom – she flinched a little at the word, knowing that a few months of sex and longing hardly counted as an adult relationship – Hanna was now determined to end the year living somewhere that didn't smell of Febreze, boiled potatoes and old man's farts. She was frantic to get away from the sound of Iain and Mary kissing in the hallway, to no longer have to pluck her eyebrows beside his drying underwear, to stop waking up to the sound of him blowing his nose into his own hand. Oscar hadn't been back to the flat and Hanna was starting to feel a bit queasy about the way she'd flirted with her dad's friend so easily. Was all this time living with a middle-aged man turning her middle-aged herself? Last night she and Iain had watched *The Good, the Bad and the Ugly* while eating vegetarian hotdogs, coleslaw and mashed potato, sitting on either end of the sofa. She hadn't been on a single date for weeks, and had started baking flapjacks and brownies to take into the office every Thursday to try and win round her colleagues before the weekly staff meeting. It was only a matter of time, she suspected, before she was wearing a pair of glasses on a gold chain, visiting National Trust properties and listening to *You and Yours*.

'Can you just remind me, how much is the rent?' Hanna asked, as they shuffled back into the small, square, windowless hall.

'It's, ah . . .' Abdul started flicking at his iPad, rather flamboyantly, Hanna noticed. As if he were performing a great piano concerto. 'The rent is . . .' Why could estate agents never just say 'I don't know'? thought Hanna. Why this compulsion to act like the answer to everything was just at the tip of their very busy tongue?

'I think the advert said £995 a month,' said Hanna, knowing it was £1,200.

'Right, yeah, it's, um . . . one second.' Hanna tried to peer over his large, dancing fingers to see if he was having to panic-close Tinder. Or maybe it would be Grindr. 'Right, yeah, it's twelve hundred a month but that does include council tax. And your utility bills here would be really low, thanks to the insulation, especially if you're living on your own.'

One thousand two hundred pounds a month, to live in a flat roughly half the size of Iain's, thought Hanna. After tax, that would leave her about £550 a month to live on – bills, food, travel, clothes, dates, everything. Was that manageable? Just. Barely. Certainly. Hopefully. But did she really want to spend nearly 70 per cent of her salary on a flat that was a half-hour bike ride from work, miles from the station, nowhere near Shazia, with no outdoor space? Had she really left London just to rent a London-sized flat at a London-sized rent? But then again, did she actually have a choice?

She had been sleeping in Iain's spare room for nearly half a year. No partner, no mortgage, no baby, no wedding invitations, no Monzo card, no car, no holiday plans, no garden shed. She hadn't even been able to find her proper coat in the storage container and so had bought a black, shiny puffer jacket for £20 instead. Meaning she looked like an overgrown teenager now, as well as felt like one. She spent so much time on her phone, scouring the internet for dateable men, affordable housing and gossip from her friends, that unless you looked very closely at her first few grey hairs, she could probably pass as an extremely dehydrated seventeen-year-old. At least, that's how she felt. She needed to get out of that flat. She needed to catch up with her friends. Hanna didn't want to be the conspicuous one; turning up to weddings alone, turning up to birthday parties smelling of her father's cooking, turning up to christenings with thick, scrawled-on eyebrows and a haunted look in her eye. She just wanted to be a grown-up. A grown-up woman with a grown-up life; not to hang in the suspended animation of a heartbroken daughter without her own kettle.

'Great, thanks, Abdul,' said Hanna, turning to reach for the door handle, only to realize it was hanging off from a large, loose bolt. 'Well, I'll let you know by the end of the day.'

Abdul let out a noise like an extra-large packet of crisps opening on a plane. 'Between you and me, I wouldn't leave it that long,' he said conspiratorially. 'I've got a lot of viewings for this place today – it's always been a very popular property.' Hanna stepped on to the thin, grey carpet of the hallway.

'Really?'

'Yeah. It'll go in a day, this one. One day.'

Hanna pulled a smile across her lips. 'Well, thank you for the warning. I'll see.'

As Abdul stepped into his aubergine-coloured Mini Cooper, Hanna started to walk down towards South Parade.

Hey, Shaz. Are you about? she texted. *I just viewed a flat and need to debrief. I'll buy the cake?* This faux adoration of cake was normally the sort of thing that would make Hanna sneer; grown women pretending to be as thrilled by baking as a seven-year-old at a birthday party. But she also knew that cake was a sort of universal shorthand; an emotional currency. It said, 'I will psychologically regurgitate all over you but will sweeten the deal with something sugary and bready.'

Shazia replied while Hanna was looking at ankle boots in Oxfam.

Sure thing. I'm just in town. Shall we meet at the Handle Bar at 11? After ten years of living in London, where every journey took an hour and anyone living within a forty-five-minute walk was considered a neighbour, Hanna still couldn't believe that it was possible to make plans and meet someone all within half an hour in this little city.

Great! Thank you.

The Handle Bar was down a street where Hanna had once accidentally singed all the lashes off her left eye after trying to light a cigarette using a stranger's Zippo. Luckily, over the intervening decades, the smell of burnt hair had finally dissipated, and as she walked up the spiral staircase to the café's large loft, Hanna was struck again by just how beautiful Shazia was. Sitting at the table on her own, not looking at her phone or checking her make-up in the back of a spoon or trying to hoick up the sagging gusset of a pair of old tights, she was the picture of poise and effortless symmetry. Her thick, black eyebrows, so animated in conversation, were now soft curves below an unwrinkled brow. Her lips were large, shapely, and with none of the gloss or swollen look so beloved of social media tutorials. Her nose, too, was big; defined, long, with strong nostrils that quivered when she laughed. In their teens, Shazia had been frequently approached about being a model – she was tall for her family and often joked about being the South Asian Erin O'Connor. But she had been too sensible, too self-effacing and too determined to do righteous work to ever be pulled in by the glamour of something as morally compromised as modelling.

'Hello! Hello, hi, hello,' said Hanna, walking towards the table and trying out her portfolio of accents. 'Thank you for coming to meet me.'

'Not at all. I was in town anyway. I wanted to go to Holland & Barrett to buy some of that hippy shit that's supposed to make you less tired,' said Shazia, smiling. 'Whatever it is, like nettles and iron filings and bits of moss. I don't know.' She pulled a leg-sized bottle of Floradix out of her bag. 'If nothing else, I can always use it to feed my houseplants.'

The waiter approached. 'Can I get you ladies anything to drink?

'I'll have an oat milk latte and a large glass of water, please,' said Hanna, feeling – as she always did – a mix of pride and shame that she could rattle off her coffee order so professionally.

'Do you have any decaf tea?' asked Shazia, tilting her face up to the waiter, unselfconsciously but devastatingly.

'Yes, madam. Normal decaf, redbush and decaf Earl Grey.'

'Ah yes, decaf Earl Grey please, but with lots of milk,' Shazia replied before turning to Hanna. 'Lemon in tea can go fuck itself.'

'I thought you said you were tired?' said Hanna. 'Why are you having decaf?'

'Oh, just something I read,' Shazia smiled. 'That actually cutting out caffeine can sometimes make you less tired than having spikes and troughs.' Hanna resisted the urge to snort. 'Anyway, tell me about this penthouse apartment you've found.'

'Oh God, I don't know, Shaz,' said Hanna, picking up a fork and pushing it gently into the gap between her knuckles. 'It was basically fine – a pretty small one-bedroom flat in Summertown—'

'Oooh!' said Shazia, in that half-camp, half-siren wail with which British people greet the mention of anything or anywhere 'fancy'.

'Yeah, but I do mean small,' Hanna interjected, smiling. 'Like, I'm not sure I would be able to fit a sofa and a dining table in there. And there isn't much light. And some of the fittings seemed a bit shonky.'

'How much is it?' asked Shazia, without hesitation. Directness, Hanna realized, was one of her favourite characteristics in a friend.

'Twelve hundred a month.'

'*A month?!*'

'Yeah.' Hanna looked down at the table.

'Shit, Hanna, that's like double our mortgage.' Shazia's nostrils were going full pelt. 'That's so much money.' The waiter arrived with the drinks, placing them down with a certain degree of theatricality.

'I know. It's the same as I was paying in London.'

Hanna's smile had turned a little grim. 'But at least I had a garden there.'

'And a fairly crappy ex-boyfriend,' said Shazia. Having never met Joe, Shazia could get away with this sort of comment, while other friends were still trying to walk a fairly diplomatic line between the two exes. 'Are you really that desperate to get your own place?'

'Well, yes. Sort of. I'm pretty desperate to move out of my dad's now and have saved enough to put down a few months' rent as a deposit.'

'That's good,' said Shazia.

'But I don't know if that flat would be all that sustainable long term. And they want me to sign a lease for a year. It would be nearly three quarters of my income going straight on rent.' While this wasn't numerically true, it felt, in the moment, emotionally true to Hanna.

'Hm.' Shazia's reply was encouraging but non-committal.

'Basically, I know I sort of buggered it up last time, when Iain broke his ankle, but I wondered . . .' Hanna hesitated, pushing the fork into the pad of her thumb. 'If, um, well. If your spare room offer still stands?' Forcing her eyes up to meet Shazia's, Hanna tried to keep her face friendly but neutral.

'Ah, babe. I'm . . .' Shazia swept her hair behind her shoulder. 'Well, let me just check with Khalid again, but I'm sure if it was just a really short stay, while you're house hunting . . .' The lack of enthusiasm in this response felt a bit like drying yourself with a damp towel, but Hanna checked her disappointment. After all, she was asking a favour. Not everyone wants to share a bathroom three ways after the age of twenty-five.

'That would be amazing, thank you.'

'Now, what are you doing for Christmas?'

Hanna let out a noise not unlike a cow being pushed through a chain-link fence. 'Christmas? Shazia, it's only September!'

'Yeah well, tell that to the window display at Boots,' said Shazia, her eyebrow cocked. 'It's already full of tinsel and gold and little birds in woolly hats. I swear, Christmas preparation basically starts at Ramadan. I got an email about Christmas crafting ideas in August this year.'

'Christ Almighty.'

'Yeah. Blame that guy. I swear.'

Hanna stirred her coffee.

'So what are you going to do?' Shazia asked.

'About the flat?'

'Well, yes. And Christmas. And your life, babe.'

Hanna snorted. 'Well, I hope that I won't still be living at Iain's by then,' she said, resting the warm bowl of the teaspoon against her cheek. 'I mean, a lot can happen in three months.' Shazia blushed and looked at the floor. Was she still feeling awkward about the spare room thing? 'As for Christmas, I don't massively want to have to schlep to a caravan in the middle of nowhere to listen to my mum doing Saturnalian chanting,' Hanna smiled, happy to change the subject. 'But then the idea of spending it just me and Iain in that same damp little flat – or worse, with my dad and his playdough girlfriend – is even worse.'

'This is when being a motherless Muslim really comes into its own.' Shazia was smiling but Hanna felt flooded with guilt.

'Oh shit, sorry, Shazia. I'm so sorry. That was insensitive.'

'Don't worry. It happens all the time. I know you didn't mean it.'

'Obviously I'm really lucky to have both parents I could spend Christmas with.' Hanna's neck was turning red. 'It's just a weird choice, this year.'

'Well, do you have to choose?' Shazia was squeezing the teabag with her fingers, as steam curled up around her knuckles. 'What if you invited Julie to Oxford? She might like to see where you're living now.' The idea hadn't even occurred to Hanna. Both of her parents? In one place? At Christmas? When she'd been with Joe, they'd usually spent Christmas with his parents, passive smoking and watching increasingly shiny televisions. Somehow, having two parents still together always trumped Hanna's choices. But today, the thought of it sent a quiver of irritation down her body. Why had she wasted so much time melting away her youth on Joe's parents' sofa? Why had she slogged her way through so much of that relationship when it clearly hadn't been right? Sitting here, in her old hometown, opposite her old hometown friend, the whole thing seemed so clearly flawed. She had been so right to leave Joe. Eventually.

'I suppose we could invite Mum.' Hanna was processing the idea out loud. 'It's not like she and Dad are really that acrimonious. In fact, they never really argued, even when they were living together.'

'It would be nice for Julie to spend it with her family,' said Shazia.

'Yeah. I mean, I suppose we are her family.' Hanna's voice was slightly slow, as though each word did not quite follow the other.

'Han, I have watched enough Netflix Christmas films and supermarket adverts to know that Christmas is all about family,' Shazia smiled. 'That and hideous knitwear, spray-on snow and something called eggnog.'

'Yeah, what the fuck is eggnog?' said Hanna, just a little too loudly. The waiter looked over as she and Shazia laughed like two old seagulls on a bin.

By the time they left, Shazia was yawning and looking decidedly less fresh than usual.

'Are you all right, Shaz?' Hanna asked, taking her friend's arm in an uncharacteristic gesture.

'Yes. I'm just tired.' Hanna wondered if Shazia was still pissed off with her about the mum comment. In fact, now she thought about it, the last few times she and Shazia had met up, Shazia had seemed a bit quieter, a bit less fun, a bit pissed off. Maybe the initial heat of the rekindled friendship had started to burn out? Maybe Shazia found Hanna's chaotic life childish and stressful? Maybe Hanna had forgotten Shazia's birthday or her mum's anniversary?

'It's not something . . .' Hanna swallowed. 'It's not something I've done, is it, Shazia? I'm really sorry if I've been out of line or something. I suppose I got sort of obsessed with work and Tom and all that.'

'No, it's nothing to do with you,' said Shazia. There was something a little astringent in her voice. Or was that just Hanna projecting again? They walked on past a couple of shops and empty window boxes. Shazia was slowing down. Hanna held on to her elbow and tried to keep pace. Suddenly, Shazia pulled her arm free and raced to the side of the pavement. She vomited, choking only slightly, into the gap between a Toyota Yaris and a Ford Focus.

'Oh lovey, are you OK? Do you think you ate something weird?' Hanna rummaged through her handbag for a tissue and her bottle of water. 'Are you feeling sick?'

Shazia stood up. 'Not any more!' she said, with an unconvincing smile and tears in her eyes. 'Hanna, I've not been sure how to tell you this, but I'm—' And in that split second between the two words, Hanna suddenly realized. What an idiot she had been. How blind and boorish and in denial. 'Pregnant.'

But what about me?

Before Hanna had time to chastise her thoughts into

something more palatable, more sisterly, more kind, there it was: what about her? What about her plan to move in with Shazia? What about that spare room? What about her getting left behind? What about her losing out? What about all those nights of wine and singing and slagging off old school friends Shazia had promised her? What about next summer? What about Hanna's lonely heart and empty bed? What about finally breaking out of Iain's flat?

'Oh, Shazia.' Hanna felt like she was trying to swim up to the surface of a deep sea. Her lungs were burning, her head swimming. She wanted to say something but could think of nothing beyond this immediate sense of loss just beyond her skin. 'Congratulations.'

'Thank you.' Shazia smiled, looking into Hanna's face intently. 'And I'm sorry. I know, well, I know what it's like. I'm basically the last one out of all my cousins to get pregnant, so I know. And I'm sorry about the spare room.'

And just like that, Hanna started crying. Tears broke the watershed of her eyes – trickles flowed across the wrinkled channels around her eyes and dropped on to her coat. This was awful. This was appalling. Her friend, her wonderful, kind friend, was having a baby and Hanna couldn't stop crying. Was it jealousy? Frustration? The shock curdling with a stomach full of coffee? Was it irritation that yet another one of her friends had stepped on to such a bloody obvious, conventional path? Was it anger at having her plans of escape ruined once again? Was it panic? Pain? Hurt pride? In that moment, Hanna simply couldn't tell. Whatever the cause, something was pushing all the air out of her lungs. Shazia would never forgive her for this. She would never forgive herself for this. This was supposed to be one of the happiest moments of her friend's life and she was ruining it.

'Shazia, I'm so sorry,' Hanna choked out, pulling her hands across her eyes as though she was trying to slap away the tears. 'It's amazing. You're amazing. You're going to be the most incredible mum and Khalid must be so happy. And Mo . . .' *Oh God.* That last word was more of a yowl than a name. The thought of Shazia's lonely, lovelorn father suddenly having this new life to pour his affection into was more than Hanna could bear. Maybe Hanna should try vomiting too. Maybe that would help.

'Look, Hanna, it's fine,' said Shazia, rubbing Hanna's back. 'I know. I'm really happy. Me and Khalid, we're thrilled. Fucking terrified, but thrilled.'

'I'm so sorry for keeping you out so late and not ordering any proper snacks,' said Hanna, holding her forehead in her hands.

'I do feel like dog shit but that's nothing new,' Shazia smiled.

'How pregnant are you?'

'Twelve weeks. I'm sorry – I didn't want to tell anyone before. We just had our scan on Tuesday. It's mad, man, there's this tiny dancer hurling around inside my womb and I literally can't feel anything.' Hanna nodded. Twelve weeks? For twelve weeks Shazia had been carrying around this secret, this prize, and Hanna hadn't guessed. She felt like a dolt. And, despite herself, she also felt hurt. She wanted to say something kind but right now all she could think was that this was unfair. That she was losing her friend. They'd just found each other again and now Shazia was about to become the entire property of motherhood. Poof. Gone. She may never come back. And here was Hanna. Back where she'd grown up. Back where she'd picked up her mum's family allowance every Thursday. Back where she'd bought her dolls and ridden her bike and scraped her knees. With nothing. No partner, no home, no burning ambition, nothing growing in her body but cholesterol and probably some lung shit she doesn't want to think about. No family. No allowance. Just a bloodstream full of caffeine and a face wet with tears.

'Shazia, it's amazing,' said Hanna, meaning it. She was happy for her friend. Really. Somewhere under her panic and bewilderment and sadness, Hanna really was excited at the thought of Shazia becoming a mum. 'I'm really sorry,' she added. 'I should let you go home. I'll call you this week. I'm really . . .' Hanna struggled against the thorns in her throat. 'I'm just really shocked, I think. But you're amazing.' She took Shazia's hand and laced her fingers between hers. 'And your baby is very lucky.'

Her baby. A mother. The mother of a baby. As

Hanna crossed Walton Street and walked into the top of her road, a great slick of tar poured through her body. Squatting on the edge of the pavement, her head in her hands, Hanna's face broke into a silent scream. Of self-pity, embarrassment, anger, envy, astonishment, grief, she couldn't say. But underneath it, because it's always underneath it, was the agony of hope.

18
Plaster

As Hanna came out of the Boots on Cornmarket a few days later, she spotted Mary, staggering under the weight of a giant box. The sight of her was laughable; this dumpy, beige-haired turnip of a woman, pushing towards groups of students and tourists almost blinded by the size of the parcel in her arms. And yet, before she knew it, Hanna was heading towards her.

'Hello, Mary,' Hanna said, falling into step with the woman she had so dreaded bumping into every morning outside her dad's bathroom. Mary swivelled round, nearly colliding with a bench as she did so.

'Oh, Hanna, hello.' The two women smiled tightly at each other.

'Are you in the process of kidnapping a child?' Hanna asked, before her brain had had a chance to self-edit.

'Yes, a little ugly one to clean under my furniture.' Hanna may have been haunted by the idea of this woman having sex with her father, but she had to admit that Mary was quite quick off the mark.

'Good idea. Do you need a hand or are you going to cut them some leg holes?'

'Well, it's a bit embarrassing.' Mary's arms were shaking slightly under the weight of her giant box. 'I ordered this online and it's turned out to be much bigger than I expected.' She tried, unsuccessfully, to flick away a stray hair that was dangling in front of her eye. 'And now I've got to carry it all the way home.'

'You could get a taxi?'

'Oh, taxis aren't really my style.' The warmth of Mary's smile heated up a few degrees. 'And anyway, it's only round the corner. Also, now I think about it, I don't think I know any taxi numbers.'

Hanna looked down at the cuffs of Mary's beige coat, juddering under the effort of this enormous square package.

'Why don't I take one side?' Without Iain there, trying to push his genitals into Mary's sturdy flesh, Hanna felt less prickly than usual. 'Where are you walking to?'

'St John Street.' Mary did not offer this answer with the inflection of a question, Hanna was pleased to notice, although she had no idea where St John Street was. It was amazing to her, after decades of living in this extremely compact city, how frequently she discovered these gaps in her geography. It must have shown in her face because Mary followed it up with, 'Just off Beaumont Street, near the Ashmolean.'

'Oh, right,' said Hanna. 'You mean the nicest street in town?'

'That's the one.' Mary was not going to apologize, nor blush, nor look away. And somehow, this subdued Hanna's thirst to wealth-shame her.

Rounding the corner by the Randolph – one of those grand hotels that now looked more like a residential home for the elderly – Mary and Hanna nearly garrotted a student dressed in tweeds, smoking a pipe. 'Look where you're going, you silly little cliché,' Mary tutted, much to Hanna's delight. 'Is there anything more embarrassing than people treating university like a three-year fancy dress party on the theme of "posh"?' She was peering round the edge of the box at Hanna. 'When I was a student here, we all pretended to be from the North Country and to have grown up starving. Now they're all buying second-hand signet rings and pretending to love hunting. It's pathetic.'

The box wasn't rattling, Hanna noticed. But there was definitely something heavy sliding about inside. As they crossed Beaumont Street, Hanna felt the weight of it tip over entirely on her side. What had this woman ordered? Hanna couldn't see a label on the outside and the box had clearly been too big to fit in any carrier bag.

'Here we are,' said Mary, turning to face a large, thin, golden-brown three-storey townhouse with a bottle-green door. There were two stone steps leading up to it and, as the doorway wasn't big enough for them to walk through abreast, Hanna let the box slide down to her knee and then on to the doorstep, while Mary took out her keys.

'I've always wondered who lives on this street,' said Hanna, trying not to sound too beguiled.

'Oh, it's all ancient old academics and Russian property developers,' said Mary, opening the door to reveal a large, honey-coloured front room. *No hallways here*, thought Hanna. *No wet coats to push past or boots scattered all over the floor.* 'Are you going to come in?' It was somewhere between a question and an invitation, but Hanna found herself pushing the box over the threshold and her feet following on after.

The room was filled with huge plants, with fronds wandering over bookcases, picture frames, lamps and window ledges. There were also books, hundreds of books, lining most of one wall and stacked up against another. The walls were bare plaster, warm and almost dusty-looking. Without thinking, Hanna reached a hand up to stroke the finish.

'Yes, Remy and I never did get round to painting this room,' said Mary, watching her. 'We meant to, but then I decided I rather liked the plaster.' Hanna rather liked the plaster too, though she wasn't going to say so. 'What would you like: tea? Wine? Coffee? A whisky?'

'Coffee, I think,' said Hanna, who was already awash with tea but felt that sitting down for a glass of wine with her dad's girlfriend was just too weird. 'I can't drink whisky any more since I found out it was what Margaret Thatcher drank.'

'May she writhe in peace,' said Mary. 'Well, how about a gin and tonic then? The sun is over the yardarm, after all. I mean, it's November; the sun barely makes it above the horizon at the moment.'

'OK,' Hanna replied. 'If you're having one.'

'The nice thing about living on your own is that you can drink whatever you like, whenever you like,' said Mary, gesturing for Hanna to follow her into the kitchen. 'For men, that often leads to alcoholism and brown teeth. But I found, after my husband died, that actually I drank less, but more expensively.' The kitchen was phenomenal. Like something from a 1940s French farmhouse, with a huge oak table, mismatched wooden cupboards, a large ceramic sink, copper pans, enamel mugs, and shelves of pottery, dried herbs and pickling jars. Everything was slightly worn but clean and bright. Mary opened a cupboard and took out two thick green glasses, added ice from the freezer and sliced the lemon straight on to her hand, without a board.

'I'd love a kitchen like this, one day,' Hanna said, running her palm along the worktop which, unlike Iain's flat, was uncluttered, without any wires trailing across the butter dish or old socks tucked into the cupboard handles.

'Well, the nice thing about not having children is that you can put all your money into furniture without it getting ruined by felt tips, teething babies or stray footballs,' said Mary. Hanna had the sense that this was a line Mary used often; pre-empting pity with self-assurance. 'It also means you have more money, of course. And only yourself to spend it on.' Mary handed a glass to Hanna and clinked her own against its rim. 'I knew I never wanted to be a housewife. Back in the 1970s a woman wasn't even allowed to buy a fridge without her husband's signature. I remember I went into John Lewis, or whatever it was then, and insisted that I speak to the manager. I showed him two years' worth of my payslips and bank statements and then, when he wouldn't budge, I told him that my husband had left me; that I was pregnant and that if he didn't change his policy, I would likely starve,' she laughed. A deeper, less mousy laugh than Hanna had heard from her before. 'It was all rubbish, of course. But it was the principle that I found so objectionable. I was a university graduate with my own income, paying towards my own mortgage. The very least I could do with my money was buy a bloody fridge.' Mary gestured Hanna towards one of the kitchen chairs; solid, simple wooden 1930s chairs with curved backs and no armrests.

'I knew you couldn't get a bank account without your husband's signature but I didn't know it extended to white goods,' said Hanna, a citrus burst of gin filling her mouth.

'God yes, the seventies were awful. I was lucky; I joined the women's liberation movement when I was just a teenager and then had a sympathetic husband. But for a lot of women, it was like being stuck in the 1950s; washing nappies, the lowliest of admin jobs, crap television, constant housework, the expectation that the sum total of your ambition was to be a mother.'

'Did you not want children?' Hanna couldn't believe

the question had come out of her mouth. The Question. The very question she loathed being asked herself and that she'd sworn she wouldn't ever turn on another woman. But Mary looked unfazed.

'I was never particularly sure either way. But then I found out that my tubes were stuck and Remy's sperm wasn't up to much, and so quite quickly I realized it wasn't ever going to happen.' Hanna had been calling Mary's dead husband Lord Remington Steele in her head ever since she'd first learned the name, during that awkward prawn cracker dinner at the flat back in April. 'I was never one of those women who clucked around nieces and nephews or stood outside school gates looking longingly.' Mary brushed her knuckles lightly against the side of her glass. 'I was very much in love with my husband, I didn't want to give up my job and, as I say, it meant I had the freedom to do things that a lot of my peers missed out on. Like living abroad and buying a house quite young, and never having to fit my life around school holidays or wipe other people's bums or get mastitis.' Perhaps sensing that she was protesting just a tad too much, Mary added: 'I have no doubt that the maternal experience is exceptional and meaningful and gives women a great sense of purpose. But I think a happy relationship is far more important, in the long run, than having a baby.'

Hanna thought of Joe and his awful band, the way he would sulk whenever her friends came round, his petulance, the way he never took holidays, his determination to stay young and free but also to be looked after, paid for, cleaned up after. Then she thought of Tom. How had she so nearly made the very same mistake again? Falling for a man who could not commit to her, who believed that 'living in the moment' was more important than sharing your life, who wanted to play the role of a loving partner only when it suited him, and not to take on any of the sacrifices or responsibilities that relationships really involve. Then she thought of the woman outside the potting shed. The woman who sat smoking in the evening sun, hard-thighed, self-assured, quiet and alone. The woman who could listen to the radio and harvest her own tomatoes and grow lines on her face without worrying that one day she would be left behind.

'How about you? Do you want a baby?' Mary was fishing out a piece of lemon with her pearly pink nails.

'Yes,' said Hanna, like dropping a bowl on a granite floor. Her words smashed through the denial, the hope, the principles and the independence she'd worked so hard for over the last few months, since coming to Oxford and starting again. 'I think so.' She paused. 'I think I've always wanted a baby. Only now I'm thirty and single and so probably have to make peace with the idea that it might never happen.' Somehow, Hanna had never quite said these things out loud. Not to her friends, not even to herself.

'Thirty isn't so very old, Hanna,' said Mary. 'I didn't even try to get pregnant until I was thirty, despite getting married when I was twenty-three. There were too many other things I wanted to do first.'

'And do you regret that?' Hanna didn't know if it was the gin talking or being in Mary's house or perhaps her hormones, but somehow her antagonism towards Mary seemed to have dissolved like an aspirin, leaving a strange clarity between them. Hanna felt she could ask Mary anything in that moment. 'Do you regret leaving it so long?'

'I have never once regretted not having children,' Mary replied, looking at her steadily. 'But you are not me. You might want to be a mother more than you want to be a wife, or have your own office, or whatever it is that propels people through this strange little life. Either way, we need to get you out of that flat. Your life cannot move forward while you're living with your father.' Mary did not squeeze Hanna's hand, or stroke her hair, or try to hug her. She just stood there, facing her down. This small, childless woman with a big house and no regrets. 'Unless you're hoping for a virgin birth, I suppose.'

Hanna's voice came out rather sticky, like something rattling up from a blocked drain. 'Well, Mary, it is nearly Christmas.'

19
Carrots

Standing at the kitchen window, wearing a jumper knitted in the pattern of the carpet from *The Shining*, Hanna poured half a pint of Baileys over a bowl of Crunchy Nut Corn Flakes and looked out at the frost. The car windscreens down below were scored with ice and the edges of the bin bags were twinkling white. Hanna touched the window with an already pale fingertip and felt the sticky dryness of early morning cold on the other side. Well, this was festive.

The front door banged and Hanna could hear shuffling, puffing, blowing and stamping in the hallway. It sounded like a steam train grinding to a halt over gravel. Like arm-to-arm combat in a stationery cupboard. It was Iain, taking his shoes off after an early morning swim. Perhaps he was actually going deaf, thought Hanna, in a forgiving mood. As well as his perpetual need for noise and attention and for people to be aware of him, maybe he actually didn't realize how loud he was. But then a rasping raised-leg fart like someone dragging a bench across the floor ripped through the flat and Hanna remembered that no, Iain really was just a very loud toddler in an adult suit.

'Yo ho ho!' As he stepped into the room, Hanna noticed a trail of snot smeared across Iain's cheek. It had probably been there for most of the morning. 'Broke the ice this morning! Not on the river – just a couple of puddles – but it felt kind of wild.' Hanna smiled. 'What time is Julie getting in?' Iain asked, walking over to the kettle and flicking it on. 'Getting in' made her sound like a cross-Channel ferry, thought Hanna. Not a barely employed yoga teacher from Essex with a Zipcar account.

'I think she said she'd try to be here by ten-ish,' said Hanna, wishing he'd wipe his face. 'So she can listen to the Christmas Day service on the radio on the way.' The sweetness of the cornflakes was making the Baileys taste a bit like nail varnish remover, but she was going to persevere. She wanted to be on a small breakfast buzz by the time her mum arrived, and eating a bowl of Irish liqueur felt somehow less degraded than doing vodka shots in the shower.

'Has she found God?' asked Iain, pouring boiling water into his one-cup cafetière.

'Mum has found more gods than you've found parking spaces,' said Hanna. 'But I think she particularly likes hearing the singing on Christmas morning. She's an annual Radio 4 Christian, I suppose.'

For perhaps the eighty-seventh time, Hanna wondered quite how this had happened. Why she had listened to

Shazia and suggested to Iain that they invite Julie for Christmas. Why she was spending the day in a small flat with two people who barely knew each other any more, three minutes from the house in which they'd all grown up. Or grown apart. Or just grown tired of each other. And Julie wasn't just coming for the day. Oh, no. Iain had proudly offered up the sofa bed to his ex-wife so they could all spend the night baking like three little sausage rolls in an oven of family reunion and claustrophobia. Hanna was nervous. The cooking, the crackers, the presents, the toasts, the small talk, the interrogation, the salt, the stress. The inevitable questions about her love life, the unwanted details about Iain's love life, the curious and sometimes painful secrecy of her mother's love life. She was wary of slipping back in to her old role of mediator; the glue between these two apparently incompatible people. She was also disappointed to still be living with her dad. The student house-shares, the studio viewings, Shazia's spare room; they'd all come to nothing. Every flat she'd found had been either too expensive or just too awful. Nobody at work knew of anyone looking for a flatmate or lodger. And so, with the year nearly at an end, she still hadn't managed to get out of Iain's flat or find herself a home of her own.

'And you're sure she'll be happy with just the veg? She won't want any of our pie?'

'She said that she would bring some sort of chickpea situation and the pudding,' said Hanna, tipping the bowl to her mouth and drinking the last grey pool in one go.

In an act of Christmas compromise, Hanna, Iain and Julie had planned a meal of roast potatoes, vegetarian stuffing, cauliflower cheese, roasted root vegetables, Brussels sprouts with pine nuts, a red onion and goat's cheese pie, red cabbage, pigs in blankets and mashed swede. In short, a pig-only vegetarian Christmas dinner partly driven down the M40 in the back of a rented Ford Fiesta. Hanna remembered her grandmother's Christmas dinners, cooked on an Aga in her big Herefordshire kitchen. A turkey – ordered from a local farm and delivered by a sixteen-stone man in a transit van who her granny still called 'the grocery lad' – would spend the day sweating peacefully in the bottom oven. Granny Ethel – Julie's mother – had given not a single toss for her daughter's vegetarianism, and Hanna had been secretly thrilled with this imposed day of meat every year.

'I'm wondering about going for a run,' Hanna said to Iain, putting her bowl in the sink but not actually washing it up. It would be quiet at 8.30 a.m. on Christmas Day, meaning fewer people than ever would get to see her electric-blue front wedgie as she jogged across the grass in a pair of sports leggings given to her by Shazia. The leggings had been an ill-advised pre-pregnancy buy and nicknamed 'The Flying Camel'. They alone made up a quarter of Hanna's entire sports wardrobe, alongside a pair of trainers, a specialist bra she'd bought for

£6 from a stall in Wood Street Market with Julie, and a bumbag.

'You certainly could,' said Iain. 'I'm happy to crack on with the veggies this morning, if you want to make some room for the coming feast.' Hanna rubbed her toe across the floor. 'I was going to watch a bit of *The Wizard of Oz* – it's on at ten this morning – while peeling the potatoes. But that's not necessarily a two-man job.' Now he'd got her. There were two films that Hanna found almost impossible to pass up: *The Wizard of Oz* and *Mary Poppins*. She had no interest in fantasy whatsoever. Trolls and orcs wandering through pseudo-medieval battlefields or bits of goo left her cold. But something about the magic of a real world transformed got her right in the sucker. Mary Poppins's carpet bag, the Tin Man's rust; the beauty in the prosaic in these films made her feel more festive than any quantity of tinsel, brandy, gifted hand cream or spray-on snow ever could.

'Maybe I'll just nip out for a short one and be back for the film,' said Hanna.

'Right you are. I'm going to put a tot of this Baileys in my coffee.' *Bugger.* Hiding in plain sight, Hanna's allocated kitchen cupboard had become a repository for condoms, tobacco, bottles of gin, forwarded bills, corned beef, and even a few dirty mugs on mornings when she couldn't be bothered to wash up before work. Somehow she'd forgotten to put her half-full bottle of Baileys in there alongside the rest of the rogues gallery before Iain came in. But hey, if he knew that she was getting mildly bashed over her breakfast cereal then so be it. At least she had bought it herself.

Hanna had just laced up her trainers, downloaded an old episode of *Desert Island Discs* and was heading out of the door when she heard the buzzer go. It was only 9 a.m. Was Mary paying them a visit at 9 a.m. on Christmas Day? Hanna leaned over to the handset and picked it up.

'—can never understand these things. Hello? Darling? Can you hear me? Stupid bloody things, why can't they just—' And lo, it came to pass. Her mother was early.

'I woke up at five a.m. and it was just so beautiful – with the frost on the trees and the pink moon – that I thought I'd make a nice early start.' Her mother was stomping up the communal stairwell carrying an enormous woven straw bag, a poinsettia, what looked like a roll of carpet, a wheelie suitcase, a tray of something covered in tin foil, and a little fibre-optic Christmas tree the height of a kettle.

'Mum, let me help you with your—'

'Thanks, darling, the rest is in the car. I've left it open.'

Stepping towards her, Hanna caught the smell of frankincense, sesame oil, Chandrika soap and just a hint of damp.

'You look jazzy,' said Julie, looking Hanna up and down with the speed and ferocity of Zorro's sword.

'Although, darling, you know I can see your entire vulva in those leggings.'

'Yes, sorry, I know. I was going to go for a run and they're the only—'

'A run? When I've just got here? Don't be silly.' Julie pushed past her. Hanna heard footsteps in the flat opposite and knew that Mr Weatherall would be ogling them eagerly through the keyhole. 'Is it this one?' Julie boomed, as she marched towards Iain's open door.

Stepping out into the cold, Hanna stopped for a second and breathed in the dank, chilled air. It wasn't nearly cold enough for snow, but the tang of coal fires in the air did make it feel a little bit Christmassy. Pouring out of Julie's car boot were carrier bags full of presents, coats, a bag of oranges, a spare duvet, books, a candelabra, a whole box of cherries, silver boots, a bunch of lilies and, sitting proudly on top of a gold plastic plate, a cabbage. Never one to underprepare, Julie had outdone herself this time.

'She told me to help you bring up the bedding—' Iain was standing at Hanna's side, chewing lightly at the inside of his mouth. 'I suppose this is how Joseph felt when the Three Wise Men turned up with all that myrrh.'

By the time they got back into the flat, Julie was leaning on the kitchen counter, drinking a glass of something orange and singing along loudly to a hymn blasting out of her phone speaker. She clearly hadn't been able to figure out Iain's crackpot hi-fi, and so had simply turned her own volume up as high as possible and chosen to drown out the Ella Fitzgerald coming from the speakers.

'How are you, Iain? You always did look like a thirteen-year-old girl when you shaved. And still insisting on shorts, I see.' Her tone was friendly, even if the words were snide.

'Yep. Well, with legs like these, it seems a crime to keep them under wraps,' Iain replied, doing a tiny soft-shoe shuffle on the kitchen floor. Hanna wondered how long this jocularity would last.

'You weren't really going out for a run, were you, Poots?' asked Julie, turning to Hanna. 'Not on Christmas Day. Oh God, have you got all thin now you're single again? Addicted to exercise and dating apps and cocaine? I was worried this would happen.'

'What? No!' said Hanna. 'I've actually put on weight, I think. And I'm not on any dating apps. I can't be in case I bump into my own father on there.' She hadn't meant to say this. In fact, she'd vowed not to be the one to bring up Iain's sordid love life.

'Oh, for God's sake,' said Julie. 'You're not still chasing after women at your age, are you?'

'What do you mean, my age?!' cried Iain.

Even if Mary wasn't, in herself, the worst person in the world, Hanna was quite pleased to see Iain's libido coming under fire in this way. She'd have been unlikely to admit it, but Hanna had found the way her father's priorities had been redirected away from her and towards Mary a bit hurtful.

'You're hardly a rutting young stag,' continued Julie, her bangles rattling against the sink. 'I've started tantric meditation and—'

'Please God, no,' wailed Hanna. Now this she really didn't need. The Baileys seemed to be curdling inside her head and her stomach was roiling like a ship in high seas. Wasn't this sort of oversharing supposed to stop when your parents divorced? Or actually, wasn't this meant never to happen at all, ever?

Iain was scratching his chest absentmindedly and staring somewhere above the fridge. 'I suppose I've still got the same old urges . . .'

'Please can we stop talking about this,' said Hanna sharply. 'Isn't there something we should be doing instead? Like decorating a tree or, like, putting out presents or something?'

'Oh yeah, I've been meaning to talk to you about presents,' said Iain, pushing a hand into his shorts pocket and rubbing at a knot in the floorboard with his big toe. 'Now, this year, well, I think you'll agree.' Hanna waited. 'I've decided to give donations to charity rather than exchange presents.' Julie and Hanna shot each other a look. Which of them was going to say it?

'No presents?' said Hanna, running the back of her hand across her forehead. 'Did you just say you're not doing presents? And you've only just thought to mention it now, today, in a house full of presents?'

'Well . . . I . . .'

'This is worse than when you gave me a broom,' said

Julie. 'At least I could use that to accidentally smash that hideous bowl your mother brought us back from Lebanon.'

Hanna tried to scrape together some fragments of dignity. 'It's not that I mind not getting stuff,' she said, her jaw only slightly too tight around her words. 'In fact, I'd love to take the consumerism out of Christmas. It's just that it would have been nice to know that that's what we were doing before I wasted two hours and forty quid in the M&S men's department looking at indistinguishable black leather accessories.'

'Ah, did you get me a new belt?' Iain's face was suddenly like the boy on the Tunnock's caramel bar, alight with joy.

'Well, I bought *a* new belt. But I think I'll take it back and give the money to WaterAid now, actually,' said Hanna, picking up a walnut from one of the seventeen different Tupperwares Julie had started unloading on to the small kitchen table. 'It just would have been good to know that was the plan,' she added, rattling through the cutlery drawer for a nutcracker.

'Yes. I wouldn't have bothered trawling eBay for that live recording of Salif Keita from 1987,' said Julie, pulling a nutcracker out of her burgundy leather handbag and passing it to Hanna.

'Ah,' said Iain. 'Well, maybe I—Ha. Hm . . .' He shrugged, and rubbed his left hand across the back of his neck. 'Sorry about that.' There was an icy pause. 'Does anybody want to watch *The Wizard of Oz* and wash the carrots?'

'I'd rather you showed me where I was going to sleep so I can unpack,' said Julie.

'Unpack?' said Iain, a little too surprised.

'Yes, Iain,' said Julie. 'Some of us prefer not to sleep in our clothes under a horse blanket. Some of us even choose to wash our feet.'

By the time the potatoes were ready, Julie's 'chickpea fillet' had turned a fairly volcanic shade of black. Hanna stood at the hob, trying to mash a swede that, despite being boiled for two hours, retained the texture of flint. She could hear Julie and Iain in the next room muttering occasionally. Somehow the murmur of radio, music and television, the whirring of the oven, the thumping of upstairs's furniture and the car stereo outside only heightened the tense silence within the flat. Hanna could remember this cold, dough-like silence. It had lain down her back and over the dinner table for years during her childhood. The chilled, lumpen disinterest between her parents had turned so many meals to ash in her mouth, so many evenings into lead, so many afternoons flat. No wonder she'd gone to such insane efforts to mark time with Joe; her paper chains, trick-or-treats, fancy dress, window paintings, Valentine's Day minibreaks. No wonder she had been drawn to Tom's big gestures and romantic messages. All had been a desperate attempt, she realized, to create noise, colour, connection with someone. She had grown up knowing only quiet, distance and pale, withered fatigue. Her parents had coexisted, sure, but all their activity had been individual, separate and unshared. Hanna had been overcompensating for this her entire life. With Joe, with Tom, with her friends, she'd been trying to whip up constant forward momentum, for fear of lapsing into their particular kind of paralysis.

'It's such a shame you don't wear lipstick,' said Julie, coming into the kitchen with a glass of white wine in her hand. 'It can make such a difference.'

'Thanks, Mum,' said Hanna.

'No, come on,' said Julie, shaking her fringe out of her eyes. 'You're beautiful. You know that. Everyone says you're beautiful. But there's no shame in enjoying make-up. I didn't sacrifice my feminist principles just because I dyed my hair and wore lipstick.'

'As I remember, you wore lipstick so I couldn't ever kiss you before you left the house,' said Iain, standing in the doorway holding a bowl of peanuts.

'Can we please not talk about this again,' said Hanna.

'No, OK. Why don't we talk about Plantation Road?' said Julie. 'I drove past number six on the way in. It looked like it had a different family in there. I can't believe the Aitkens would sell it on so quickly. Do you think they were just trying to turn it for profit?'

'I think they split up,' said Iain, little chunks of peanut flying out of his mouth. 'Something about gambling. At least that's what somebody said.' Hanna had no idea her dad had kept such close tabs on the people who'd bought their old house. She'd just presumed that, like her, he'd consigned the place to history.

'She was such a sharp little rat of a woman, do you

remember, Iain?' said Julie, screwing her face up like a tissue. 'And he was all cowboy boots and dyed hair. I bet they're living in Hemel Hempstead or something now. Paying off their gambling debts with our capital.'

'I think Sandra, the wife, moved to Bournemouth,' said Iain.

'Please don't tell me how you know that,' said Hanna, pouring the gravy into a large blue jug. 'Anyway, I think all the food is ready. If anyone wants to eat any of it.'

'Well, lovey, it looks like an absolute feast,' said Julie. And just for that moment, as they pulled out their chairs and picked up their cutlery, Hanna felt a strange rush of pride. This would never have happened a year ago; she, Julie and Iain all sitting down to a meal together. When she was with Joe, she'd been so occupied with trying to keep her relationship roadworthy that she'd let her parents fall by the wayside. Her mum and dad had become peripheral, her sense of family shaky. But now here they were, around the table she'd been sharing with her dad for months, together. Maybe it was the Baileys talking, but Hanna felt proud to have got this far. Maybe what Mary had said was right; perhaps thirty wasn't too old to start again.

'After dinner I wondered if maybe we could go for a walk on Port Meadow,' said Hanna, as they all clanked the serving spoons and rearranged the cutlery.

'Are these carrots organic, darling?' asked Julie.

'They're from Bonners,' answered Iain. 'I bought them myself.'

'But are they organic?'

'The man said that each one had been rolled along the thighs of a wild, corn-fed badger and watered only with spring rain,' said Iain. If it had been intended as a joke, it fell well wide of the mark. Julie looked hurt; Iain flushed. 'Sorry. No. I don't remember if they're organic.'

'Well, I wish you could,' said Julie. 'Because carrots are an absolute sponge for toxins, you know. You might as well eat a stick of polystyrene for all the poisons and plastics and other pesticides in them.' Hanna could feel the conversation veering into Mum Science and was keen to climb out of it.

'Did you bring any games or anything, Mum,' Hanna cut in. 'Trivial Pursuit or anything?'

'I'd hoped we could warm mercury in the fire and then throw it in a bucket of cold water and use the resulting shapes to predict our future year,' said Julie, absolutely meaning every single word of this. 'But it looks like Iain doesn't have a fire.' She sniffed. As though this were some sort of personal oversight on his part, not an entirely expected outcome of living in a 1960s council flat. 'Luckily I brought Monopoly too, just in case.' *Monopoly?* Was the woman completely insane? Hanna had never experienced a single game of Monopoly that didn't end with at least one person storming out of the house. Usually more than one. Decades-long friendships could be brought to rubble by just one round of Monopoly. This was the board game equivalent of bringing petrol to a primary school bonfire.

'Maybe we should play the dictionary game instead,' said Iain. 'You know, use it to predict our future but with slightly less chance of spilling molten metal across the living room carpet.' The dictionary game had been invented one summer during a very long, very wet and very boring holiday in the west of Scotland. Somehow the three of them had failed to pack nearly enough books, and the television in the cottage where they'd been staying had blinked out on the first night, leaving them with nothing but Ian Botham's autobiography (called, inspiringly, *Botham: My Autobiography*), one Ian Rankin novel (which they took turns to read over the course of four days) and a *Concise English Dictionary*. One night, after listening to curlews out on the front field, Hanna and Iain had come in and started picking pages and words at random, with their eyes closed, trying to use the resulting phrase to tell their fortune. Iain had even wrapped one of Julie's organza scarves around his head, while divining the meaning of the words. His fortune teller routine was pure am-dram but, somehow, it worked. For that evening, and for every evening that followed, the three of them had sat around and howled with laughter at the strange conjunctions that came out of the yellow and mildewed pages.

Mortify. Erotica. Bwana. That was one of Julie's.

Agree. Drill. Woodlouse. A favourite of Iain's. And at

the end of the evening, Hanna had somehow managed to pull from the ether: Smasher. Haddock. Gynaecology.

It had been one of their best holidays. A golden wonder, snatched from the jaws of defeat. Despite the rain and the gnats and the muddy beach, they had made each other happy on that trip. No wonder Iain had suggested the dictionary game. All three of them were probably remembering that holiday, thought Hanna. As they sat in this too-small flat, smelling of onion and sandalwood and burnt potatoes and toilet cleaner, perhaps they were all trying to remember how it felt to be a happy family.

And then Hanna realized. Sitting underneath all the dread and stress she'd had about Christmas this year was something else: hope. Hope and all the sadness that only hope can bring. Because, despite her best efforts over the last seven years, and all the tangible evidence to the contrary, there was still a tiny corner of Hanna's heart that hoped she could have a happy family. Much as she'd tried to bury it with work and friendship and travel and fury, there was still an inextinguishable desire in Hanna to be part of a functional, nice, cheerful family. One of her own making or the one she'd been born into. The sort of family that could play board games, hug easily, sing carols, decorate a tree, pull crackers and watch telly. Much as she fought it off at every corner, she still sometimes looked at the families on biscuit tins, or in supermarket adverts, and wished they could be her family. She knew they couldn't – that was why they hadn't spent Christmas together for eight years. That was why she'd just accidentally given her mother a wok for the second time in three years. That was why Julie had spent an hour in Hanna's bedroom speaking French on the phone in a low voice, without explaining or apologizing for her absence. That was why Iain had scratched his balls right at eye height before carving the cheese and onion pie. They were not and would never be the kind of family that sells gravy granules. And maybe that was why Hanna felt so conflicted about getting married and having a baby herself. Maybe that was why she found it so hard to really know what she wanted. But, deep down, she still hoped to be part of a happy family. However it looked.

20
Condoms

'Good morning,' said Iain, standing at Hanna's door in just a towel. There was an embarrassed little face across his loose and sagging torso. The nipples looked like eyes. The fluff across his chest was a worried, grey unibrow. The strip of hair that drooped between his fleshy pecs and down to his navel formed the line of a nose. His belly button became a little puckered mouth; the rounded, unelasticated stomach beneath it a chin. Hanna retreated slightly into her bedroom doorway. 'Hey, can I ask you something?' Her heart sank. Was Iain going to ask again what her plans were for moving out?

'Have you, ah. Have you ever done one of these home testing kits?' By the strange expression on Iain's face, and the fact that he was naked but for a towel, Hanna knew immediately that this wasn't blood pressure they were talking about. 'I've, ah, got this kind of swab thing – like a big earbud – but I'm not actually sure where I . . . you know, swab it.' If euthanasia were legal in this country, thought Hanna, this would absolutely be the time for a lethal injection. Her, Iain, it didn't really matter which of them got juiced. As long as it put an end to this conversation.

'Sorry, are you asking me . . .?' Hanna struggled to wrap her brain around this loop-de-loop of horror. 'Are you asking me how to do a swab?'

'Yeah,' said Iain, his eyebrows shooting up his forehead.

'Well, don't you just run it round the back of your throat?' Sometimes, thought Hanna, if you wanted something enough, the universe would provide. Maybe Iain had suddenly decided to find out if he was 4 per cent Belarusian and had sent away for one of those DNA kits. Maybe he was wondering if he was allergic to gluten. Maybe this was all a dream and Hanna would wake up in a minute to the sound of birdsong on her phone.

'Oh no. It's not for my mouth. At least, I don't think so. It's for this . . . Well, I've got a strange rash.' Hanna actually yelped. She leaped back from the doorway like someone who'd trod on a snake. In her mind, she saw herself slamming the door in Iain's face and jumping out of the bedroom window, becoming a dropped Cornetto across the pavement outside. But instead she merely stood there, one leg bent, her nerves jangling right to the tips of her fingers.

'Sorry. Only, I can't read the instructions without my glasses and I assume you've probably done this before.' Surely, thought Hanna, he could see this was not the time, place, or – more importantly – person with whom to have this little chat. 'The lady I spoke to on 111 told me I could do a home test for chlamydia if I didn't fancy going to the doctor.' The words 'lady' and 'fancy' here somehow stuck out for Hanna like stones in a mouthful of spinach. More so, strangely, than the word 'chlamydia'. 'So I went to the pharmacy and bought one, but I'm not sure I bought the right one.'

'Are you seriously asking me to talk you through a do-it-yourself chlamydia test at seven twenty-one in the morning?' asked Hanna, her face unable to settle on a single expression.

'No. Well. Not quite that. I just. I'm really not sure.' Iain didn't look apologetic. In fact, he looked put out that Hanna was making such a big deal about this. Surely it wasn't too much to ask your only daughter to do a quick swab of your bellend before breakfast? It wasn't like she'd never seen it before. Part of her – lest we all forget – came out of it.

'Look. From what I know, the male test is just a urine sample,' said Hanna, her voice going slightly froggy as she tried to settle on a suitable emotional pitch. 'I think you bought the wrong one – the female one. Please don't try to swap it now you've opened it. Just take the £2.50 hit or whatever and go back and buy a new one. For men.' It was typical of Iain, thought Hanna, that he would do all that research and then not just talk to the person in the shop. 'I'm sure lots of people make the same mistake.'

'Oh.' Finally, Iain looked sheepish. Age had pushed down on him for so long that he was now the same height as Hanna. Standing in the hallway, his mildew-smelling towel hanging dank around his flaccid waist, he seemed a little pathetic. Out of his depth. Suddenly Hanna realized that it may have been more than thirty years since Iain had actually slept with someone new. He'd mentioned some kissing, some 'fondling' in the time since he'd divorced Julie. But the last time he'd been in this position, actually had full sex with someone new, might have been back when he was a twenty-something hooking up with her mum. And, although she'd begged to be spared the details, Hanna had heard enough to know that even back then Julie had been far more sexually experienced than Iain. That had also been before the AIDS crisis had really become understood in the UK. Contraception, STIs, GUM clinics; these things were probably all new and confusing for Iain. Especially as, like so many men his age, his entire sexual education had come in the form of some Triumph bra catalogues hidden under his mattress and traded with friends for money and cigarettes. No wonder he'd bought the wrong test. And no wonder he didn't have anybody else to ask.

The first time she'd done a chlamydia test, standing in the bath in her old student house, Hanna had texted photos of the kit to all four of her housemates with the caption, 'Just call me Marie Curie'. The first time she'd done a pregnancy test, squatting over a disposable plastic cup in her sixth-form disabled toilet, she'd sent a picture of the stick, stained blue and with just one line across its end, to three of her friends, to make sure she'd done it right. But as a middle-aged man with no brother and few friends, who could Iain really turn to? *Google would be a nice starting point*, thought Hanna ruefully. But as so often happened with Iain, her embarrassment was now slowly sliding into pity. The very fact that she was in this flat, had spent so much of the last year heartbroken and touchy, that she felt usurped by her dad's love life and jealous of his romantic success, had made it difficult for Iain to have anything like a proper relationship with Mary. She felt a stab of guilt. He had, after all, given her a home for the best part of a year, given her space, asked for just a peppercorn rent, made her some dinners and eventually been sympathetic about Joe. She hadn't always made this easy for him. Especially where Mary was concerned.

The amount of work done in offices between 3.45 p.m. and 5.30 p.m. is equivalent to about three Post-its and a phone call. On a good day. Hanna sat at her desk staring at her inbox, feeling each second grind past like a lawnmower over bricks. There was a report to be written about the bookings revenue in the final quarter of last year, that nobody had yet asked for but was nevertheless a month overdue. There were emails to be replied to. Payments to be chased and invoices to be generated. But somehow, just at this moment, when her lunch had been digested but the end-of-day panic hadn't set in, Hanna could muster precisely no energy to do any of it. And so she picked up her phone and started to scroll. Which was how she saw it. A photo of Joe and Becky; him standing behind her with his hand resting protectively on her stomach; her looking into the camera, her hand on top of his. The pose jarred immediately. It looked like a mock-up of one of those royal engagement photos put on cake tins and decorative plates. Their shoulders were sitting too high. Their hands looked like flat fish. And why was he standing so close to her? In the base of Hanna's brain, the response that makes you duck when a large bird flies overhead had been triggered. Something was wrong. Before she even knew it, she knew it.

Looks like it's going to be a busy summer!

Joe had reposted the picture and caption from Becky. What did it mean? Hanna's brain crawled over the words like lice. A busy summer? A busy summer. The hand. The stomach. Was this a band thing? It didn't seem like a band thing.

Before she could stop herself, Hanna started to scroll through the comments. There were eighty-seven of them. That seemed like a lot.

OMG you guys! Congratulations!

Such exciting news. You're through the worst bit now. NOT.

Holy shit, for real?!?!

Something was flickering on in Hanna. Something was starting to pull together into a full thought.

Yippeee! We're just two months ahead of you.

Hold on.

Woah missy, is that a BUMP?

Hold on.

Such lovely news. Congratulations you two. Can't wait to meet the little guy (or girl?).

No, wait.

You guys are going to make such great parents.

No.

Hanna felt the phone tumble from her fingers and land across her keyboard. No. Not this. No.

And yet, why not? Why wouldn't she find out that her ex-boyfriend was having a baby with his ex-girlfriend via social media? Why would anyone think to tell her? It wasn't like she and Joe spoke much these days. Ever since that false start with Tom last summer, she'd felt the space between her and Joe get wider and thicker. And Joe had never been good with confrontation. Obviously he hadn't said anything. Instead of telling Hanna that he didn't want to be together, he'd waited for her to leave and then quickly moved in his ex. His ex-girlfriend. Who was now his girlfriend? And they were having a baby? But Joe didn't want babies. Or just didn't want her babies? But now he was having a baby? The thoughts were coming out of Hanna's brain like the little white spaghetti strings of sebum when you squeeze your blackheads. Separate, revolting, some thin, some thick, and yet all from the same oily source. Joe, her ex-boyfriend, was having a baby. With his ex-girlfriend. Sweat pricked on Hanna's hands. She felt her head go light, while something in her bowels turned to lead. She was single, living with her father in a small town, round the corner from her primary school, and her ex-boyfriend was having his ex-girlfriend's baby. Fumbling the phone back into her hand, Hanna took a breath and, praying to the gods that she wouldn't tap something by mistake, took a screenshot.

Dom. Send. After fifteen seconds the phone vibrated in her hand.

Oh, Hanna. I didn't know. I'm really sorry.

And now everybody knew. It was 4.15 p.m. on a Tuesday and everybody knew. Hanna was loveless, childless, homeless; she'd lost the game. Hanna looked again at the photo. It had been posted just an hour ago. Becky was wearing a faded black T-shirt, black jeans, and some sort of weird suit jacket. She looked like a twelve-year-old applying for a Saturday job as a waitress. Joe's face was weird too. No, wait, it wasn't his face. His neck was weird. Too wide. Heavy-set. It went down into his collar like a fleshy tube. It was the same width as his face. God, it looked like the neck of a dad. When had Joe got a dad neck? His hair seemed thinner too. And the hand he was laying so limply across that black cotton belly was wrong. Ugly. His fingers looked like radishes. What had happened in the last year, that Joe had got so unattractive and so committed all at once? Hanna felt like she was looking at someone in a bad Joe fancy dress costume. It felt like a prank. The well of sadness within her seemed somehow deeper than she had expected. She could feel the echoes, but couldn't quite see the water. She felt weird. But not yet actually sad. And then she did it: possibly the strangest act of bravado she had committed in her entire life. Rubbing her thumb down her thigh, gripping the phone in the other hand, she brought her finger towards the screen. Tap. Tap. And just like that, she'd liked the photo. Her. Hanna. Joe's Hanna. The Hanna half of Joe and Hanna that for seven years had been his. Had liked a photo of him and his new, pregnant ex-girlfriend.

'Hello, love. I'm making baked potatoes. Do you want yours rubbed in oil or just dry?'

The flat was warm. Steam coated the kitchen windows and Hanna felt her shoulders unwrap.

'Um . . . I don't mind,' she replied. 'Whatever's going.' She sank down into a chair in the kitchen. A chair that had, without anybody even noticing, become her chair.

'Are you all right?' Iain pulled open the oven and a jet of heat spread across Hanna's legs. 'If this is about this morning then—'

'No. It's nothing to do with that,' Hanna interrupted. 'I. Um. I saw today that Joe is. Well. He's having a baby.' She paused. Not meaning to add dramatic tension to this announcement but merely to try and wrestle her sliding mouth back into place. 'With Becky. His girlfriend before me. I think they must have got back together when . . .' Actually, when had they got back together? That night of the argument? Before Hanna left? Did that mean that for those four months when Hanna and Joe had been sharing a bed, lonely, adrift, suddenly embarrassed of each other, he had also been sleeping with Becky? Had they been together this whole time? Was that how Joe had filled the room so quickly? Did they sit on the sofa Hanna had picked out from the IKEA sale? Did they have sex on the mattress her Auntie Molly had given them? Suddenly all the questions Hanna had never dared to ask Joe about his life roared up to the surface. When did people announce a pregnancy though? Three months? Six months? *It's going to be a busy summer.* It was January. Summer was five, six months away. So they were only a bit pregnant? But had been fucking all this time? Or just got back together?

'Oh, honey.' And there was Iain. Kneeling on the floor. Beside her. His hand was rubbing her back. Like she was in labour. 'That's really hard. That's . . .' He gave up as Hanna burst into tears. Great choking, snotty sobs. She'd finally fallen down the well. At last she'd reached the water.

'A fiery horse with the speed of light,' Iain was shouting. 'A cloud of dust and a hearty' – now Hanna joined in – 'Hi-yo, Silver! It's the Lone Ranger!' The two of them were sitting on the sofa, square black plates of baked potatoes, beans, cheese and broccoli on their laps. A man in a clingy pale blue suit – now Hanna really looked at it, it was more like a Babygro with a gun holster round the middle – was riding a beautiful white horse across a desert. About three centimetres of his face was hidden by a little black mask and, once again, this had blinded everyone around him to the man's true identity. Everyone, that was, apart from his trusty and long-haired sidekick Tonto. Tonto was actually quite fit, Hanna thought. The actor had probably been the victim of terrible Hollywood racism back in the day. He was definitely the more handsome of the two.

Once she'd finally stopped crying, Hanna had realized quite how hungry she was. How pranged out she'd been. The adrenaline of seeing Joe's message, the sheer lunacy of liking the post, had eaten through her guts like ice. And so when Iain had suggested eating dinner in front of the television, she'd sunk into the creaking seat with exhausted relief. That some small and distant cable channel was showing reruns of the original *Lone Ranger* seemed like fate. In the nineties, Channel 4 had started showing the series during the otherwise joyless stretch of scheduling time between the end of school and dinner. If Iain was back early, he'd often join Hanna in the front room of Plantation Road and watch a couple of episodes, whistling at the gun tricks and calling out the continuity bloopers. On walks at Granny Ethel's house, they would sometimes run across fields, or hide behind bushes, pretending to be the Lone Ranger and Tonto, catching bad guys. It had been one of their few shared cultural touchstones. And so now, tear-weary and sunken-hearted, Hanna let the black-and-white equine high jinks play out around her as she forked potato into her mouth.

She and Joe wouldn't have made good parents. She had been right to end it. They'd never have made each other really happy. Her need for security, intimacy and commitment had made him resist ever growing up. The more she'd pushed him towards grown-up life – jobs, homes, vows, babies – the harder he had resisted. He had dug himself into a hole of perpetual adolescence and she'd been unable to pull him out. Had she wanted those things because she really wanted them, or because she thought Joe didn't? Did she want them because her friends had started to have them? Did she want them because ever since playing in the home corner of her nursery, she'd been told that she wanted them? Who knew. How could you ever pull apart the threads of that net? But she did want them. Ever since Mary had asked the question, Hanna had known that. She did want a baby. And a partner. And a happy family. That's what she'd realized at Christmas; that in her very modern and feminist heart she still carried around an old-fashioned desire to be part of a family. But any which way, she didn't have one. Not yet, anyway. And she was still here. Still alive. Still had enough time. If she could just get out of her dad's flat and start living independently again.

Hanna looked at the screenshot of the photo again – not daring to open up the original post to see if anybody had replied to her like. She didn't want that man's baby. Not that version of Joe, anyway. Imagine if they had done it? If she had taken out her coil and he'd gone along with it? He'd probably have wanted to call their child something like Silas or Lockwood or Bo. He would have made such a colossal fuss about doing night feeds – spending the entire next day in bed, complaining about a headache, snapping at her, not-entirely-accidentally dropping cups – that she would have ended up doing it all on her own. And he would have resented having the baby in their room so he couldn't read at night. And he would have wanted Hanna to go to baby raves where 6 Music fans in pirate costumes would have drunk lukewarm cider and danced to the house music of their youth and pretended that it was for their kids' benefit, without actually engaging with their kids at all. And the more he'd have retreated from his own fathering, the further she would have swollen over to fill the gap. Until, at last, he'd have left. And she'd have been a single mum. And she'd probably have had to move back in with Iain. Just like now. Only this time she'd have had a baby and stretch marks and no pelvic floor, and insomnia and the constant worry of keeping somebody else alive.

'Do you remember the day I was born?' Hanna asked Iain, turning her head to look at him.

'I do,' he replied, still looking at the television. Hanna waited to see if there was more. Iain exhaled. And then looked down at his hands. 'I think I can remember that day better than anything else in my life.' He got up and walked over to one of the bookshelves.

'I actually wrote it all down. Just the next day. I wanted to tell my mum all about it. I knew she wouldn't ask and probably wouldn't come to visit for a while, so I wanted to get it down in case I forgot any of it.' He drew down a large hardback book called *Life on the Arabian Peninsula* and, from its pages, pulled out a photocopy of a letter, handwritten. 'Would you like to read it?' For a second, Hanna was unsure. Perhaps her particular mix of grief and longing and envy today would render her too raw, too flayed open, too tender for this. And yet, she did want to know. She wanted to know about every second that had brought her into this world. She wanted to hear about her parents' early relationship and their immediate unconditional love for her like a marathon runner wants to drink water. Since seeing that receipt, tucked away for decades by Iain, she had come to believe for the first time in her life that perhaps her father and mother had once actually loved each other. And loved her. She wanted to read that love again, hear it in Iain's words, catch it in his handwriting.

'Yes, please.'

And so Hanna read it.

I have never seen another person go through anything like that, Mum. It was like watching her burst into flames. Julie was a Titaness. Pure strength. I don't think I've ever loved another living thing as much as I loved my wife that moment, as she curled over, clenched her fists and just let rip.

What came out looked like a dolphin: she was all slippery and blue. Little Hanna's eyes were so squashed that I could barely see them. (Yes, we're calling her Hanna, after one of Julie's Danish family. Short for Johanna – a pretty name, don't you think?) Julie just seemed to deflate when they finally put this tiny creature on her front, after wiping off all the cream cheese gunk. You know, I now believe that women are the wonder of the world. I can hear Dad laughing at that, as I write it. But it's true.

Hanna felt the tears dropping from her chin before she realized she was crying. Her mother – to be so brave, so strong, so focused. And for Iain to have admired her. Hanna felt something slip, ever so slightly. Like when you pull on a shirt and a bone in your chest clicks, or you bend down and your hips seem to thunk back into the right alignment. That was it. Reading this letter had made her feel aligned. At last.

'It's an amazing letter, Iain,' said Hanna. 'Dad.'

Iain looked over at her from the sofa. She was standing by the bookshelf, her hand shaking ever so slightly. 'It was an amazing thing to watch,' he replied. 'Julie was formidable, she really was.'

'If I'm ever in that position—' Hanna's voice caught in her throat. She put her hand to her neck. Breathed out. 'I mean, that seems unlikely at the moment, but you never know.' Iain smiled at her, then looked down at the floor. 'If I ever do it, I promise to write you a letter, too.'

'Ah, an email would be fine,' said Iain, standing up in a rattle of knee clicks and sighs. They both smiled. 'Shall I put this back or do you want to keep it?' he asked, pointing at the letter, still in Hanna's hand.

'Oh, you look after it,' said Hanna, passing it back into his meaty, callused paw. 'I'd only lose it.'

Just before she went to bed, after hearing Iain brush his teeth, take a piss right in the middle of the toilet bowl and get into his creaking bed, Hanna slipped into the kitchen. On top of the bread bin, beside Iain's selfish little one-cup cafetière and his lanyard and his house keys, she put a box of condoms. It was a peace offering. A thank you. An apology. A licence.

21
Poppadum

'Would madam like to see the menu?'

Hanna wondered just how many people didn't bother. How many Hi-Tec-trainer, chambray-shirt, ill-fitting-belt, Blue-Harbour-aftershave, packet-of-Dunhills-and-a-copy-of-the-*Telegraph* men came in here and ordered the same thing every single week, without ever reading the menu. How many Elizabeth-Arden-perfume, pearl-earrings, Next-trousers, pink-lipstick-and-a-layered-bob women ordered a chicken korma, boiled rice, plain naan and a gin and tonic without once looking to see what else was on offer. Once she might have sneered at these people; cut her eyes at such small-town insularity, sighed with pity at their drab, unquestioned lives. But today, Hanna felt something a little more like envy. To know the edges of your life with such clarity – would it be so bad? There was a kind of comfort in certainty, a pleasure in restriction.

'Yes, please,' said Hanna, trying to be as ingratiating as possible without actually cringing.

Shazia had suggested the restaurant. It was managed

by a cousin on her dad's side. While that meant Shazia might have to spend three minutes at the beginning of the meal talking through the various health conditions of their mutual family, it did also mean they were seated at a nice table with plenty of room. Which was just as well; at seven months, Shazia now looked like a snake that had swallowed a hoover.

'I think I'm going to have a dopiaza,' said Iain. 'I like tomato curries.'

'I'm going to have biryani,' said Shazia. 'Biryani is one of those things my dad just never got a handle on, no matter how many times he was shown.' She laughed. 'And I've never met a carbohydrate I didn't like.'

As usual, Hanna wanted four different side dishes and no main; a habit that sometimes meant she got to eat her entire meal twenty minutes before her friends' food arrived. Despite the fact that she couldn't see it, Hanna could somehow sense Mary's thigh pressing up against Iain's under the table. The idea barely registered. In the last few months, Hanna had made a conscious effort to stop resisting the thought that Iain and Mary were sleeping together. She had tried to start thinking of their relationship like weather – there, on her doorstep, in her face, but nothing she could change. And, like the weather, there were good bits as well as bad. Nothing – not even the sound of your dad kissing in the corridor – could last for ever. And without Hanna's disapproval to make him feel illicit, Iain seemed to have calmed down a bit on the groping front too. Maybe it had just been nerves, after all.

'How is Mo?' asked Hanna, suddenly impaled by guilt. 'Shit – sorry, Shaz, you should have invited him along too. It would have been really nice to see him.'

'On a Saturday? Are you joking? When there's a new series of *Maigret* on BBC Four? We'd have had to bring him here in a wheelbarrow,' Shazia laughed. Her affection for her father was so clear, so honest, so immediate, Hanna felt the need to reciprocate. She smiled over at Iain but he was too busy reading the wine list to notice.

'Shazia, do you know, is a korai very spicy?' Mary asked. Hanna was just about to jump in and ask why the hell Shazia should know, before remembering that actually, Shazia probably did know; her family worked here and she'd been eating out in Oxford for all those missing years when Hanna was in London. 'I love strong flavours but chilli just makes me cough,' Mary continued. 'Maybe it's age but I just don't seem to be able to stomach much heat any more.'

'You can always ask them to use less chilli,' said Shazia. 'Or we could ask for a table fan.' And this, thought Hanna, was why Shazia had been her best friend. That kindness, twinned with a sharp sense of humour. What a woman. What a pal.

Once the poppadums had been cleared away, and Hanna had asked if she could keep the tray of chutneys, the conversation turned to work. Hanna had drunk a small bottle of Tiger beer while Shazia was drinking tap water.

'Shazia.' Hanna was leaning close to her friend. 'I've been asked to organize a life drawing class at the museum, as part of Art Week in May. Do you know anyone who might want to teach it? Or, you know, facilitate it in any way.'

'Why not just ask your teacher?' Iain interjected. Hanna had been sure that Iain was busy talking to Mary about the idiosyncrasies of the Pembroke College hot water system. She definitely hadn't meant for him to overhear this bit.

'Ah, well. They, um . . .' When she needed to be, Hanna was a prodigious, creative, cunning and entirely plausible liar. She had once managed to get out of an Oyster fine by persuading the 'revenue protection officer' that she was an undercover police officer about to take down a man for receiving stolen property. She'd pointed with a biro, held at thigh height, towards a man with a bad case of neck rash, reading the *Metro* in a red fleece. The inspector had nodded earnestly, wished her luck and moved on to the next block of seats. But Hanna was tired of lying to Iain. She had spent nearly a hundred pounds on pencil sketches from the woman in Frome, who had started to include little poems that Hanna absolutely had not ordered. Since things had gone sour with Tom, she'd started using her Thursday nights to go to a yoga class in Cowley, so it wasn't even like she'd been lying to cover up something particularly transgressive or embarrassing. Clearing her throat, Hanna looked over at Iain's folded hands on the white tablecloth.

'Actually, I don't do life drawing,' she said, a smile creeping uncontrollably up her face.

'I wouldn't say you don't do it, Hanna,' said Iain. 'And just because you're not very good, doesn't mean you're not learning something.' Hanna shot her eyes up to his face. Iain was grinning like a hyena.

'What do you mean, not very good? Those drawings are good!' said Hanna, too quickly. Iain was laughing. Outright laughing.

'Hold on. Do you already know?' Hanna felt like someone who had just unknowingly lost at chess.

'Know what?' said Iain, trying to pull his face into a credulous expression.

'Fine,' said Hanna. 'I admit it! I didn't do those bloody drawings. I bought them from a woman in Somerset who keeps asking me if I want her to read my tarot over Skype.' Shazia was laughing now too, and Mary was smiling over at them both. A rush of relief and embarrassment flooded up Hanna's neck. At last, she could drop the pretence. 'I only said I was going to life drawing so I could go out without you hassling me about who I was meeting,' Hanna continued. 'I'm thirty, for God's sake! I didn't want my dad knowing all about my sex life.'

'I always liked Tom though,' said Iain, looking sincere, if not a little too pleased at having cracked the case.

'What . . . what do you mean?'

'I said, I always liked Tom,' said Iain, leaning back as a waiter placed a clean spoon on the table in front of him. 'I remember when you and him were in that play together, where he played Isaac Newton and you were Oliver Cromwell's wife.'

'But. But how did you know I was meeting . . .?' Hanna was so distracted by this that she failed entirely to even look at the waiter who refilled her water glass. 'I mean, have you been following me or something?'

'Oh, come off it.' Iain sprayed a small cloud of spit across the table as he said this. 'I happened to be walking down Little Clarendon Street one night – I'd gone to pick up some building regs from Calvin – and I saw you and Tom outside that bar next to G&D's. I would say it was amazing you didn't see me but, well, you weren't exactly looking about at the time.' Iain smirked. 'I hope you'd brushed your teeth, that's all I'll say.'

Hanna flushed beetroot. 'Yeah, well, you can take the hat back to the shop, Cilla Black, because absolutely nothing is happening there.'

For a second, Iain said nothing, and yet his disappointment was palpable.

'You're not going out with Tom then?' he asked, at last.

'Not any more,' said Hanna. 'In fact, I'm not sure I ever really was going out with him. I thought I was. I wanted to be. But when it came to it, I think he managed to keep me at arm's length for four months.'

Hanna was surprised how calmly these words were coming out. What Tom did to her was embarrassing and unfair but no longer very upsetting. It had been a crap way to treat one of your oldest friends, but at least Hanna had got out when she had.

'What happened?' asked Mary, looking genuinely sympathetic.

'Well, I invited Tom to be my plus one at Phil and Vicky's wedding and he went entirely insane,' said Hanna, smiling sadly at Shazia. 'He told me that he "wasn't that kind of person" and that he "lived in the moment". He said he "doesn't make plans" and, well basically that he never wants a girlfriend or partner or wife.' Saying it out loud like this did make Tom sound like an absolute roaster, but Hanna managed to stave off any sense of self-recrimination for falling for his schtick.

'That man,' said Shazia, sighing. 'I wish you'd told me, huh. I've seen him do this before. He loves to be all romantic and woke and righteous, right up until the moment reality kicks in and then he runs home to his mum, with a trail of crying women in his wake.'

'I bet,' said Hanna. Although she was slightly put out at the idea that she wasn't the first person Tom had treated like an emotional dishcloth.

'Well, I'm sorry to hear that,' said Iain, leaning back as the waiter placed a large silver bowl of prawns in a green-flecked sauce in front of him. 'I thought it might be rather romantic to get back together with someone you'd known at school.'

'Yes, well,' muttered Hanna.

'And I always remember Tom being so funny and clever. And how you used to zing off each other. Maybe you two were just too much like brother and sister or something. Or maybe he'll come round—'

'No, Iain,' Mary, amazingly, interrupted him. 'This man sounds like an emotionally stunted commitment-phobe who seeks out the validation of women without ever considering their lives or feelings.' Hanna looked over at this woman in her beige polo neck and tortoiseshell earrings and regretted how long she had underestimated Mary. In fact, she'd been outright hostile to her at first, and all because she felt jealous that Iain had found someone when she hadn't. 'I've known plenty of Toms, and they play the same old games for decades, until suddenly they're fifty and alone and starting to sag, and the whole roaming-soul thing starts to smell a little like emotional immaturity.' Hanna felt like she was hearing the blast of a ship's horn coming over the waves in the middle of the night. Mary was right. When she was with them, both Tom and Joe had been grinding towards the same pitiful, delayed, unfulfilled future. Both were furiously suppressing any attempt at emotional maturity. Both were using Hanna as a dam against the inevitable current of time. And yet, in Joe's case, once Hanna was taken out of the picture, his whole life had apparently slotted into place at lightning speed. Why did she keep doing this? Getting involved with men who seemed to not want to grow up with her, and fought against her attempts to grow up too?

'Well, maybe you just needed to give him a bit more time,' said Iain, spooning rice on to his plate before anybody else's meal had yet arrived.

'No, Iain.' There was Mary again. Hanna really liked her this way. 'She gave him more than enough time. More time than he deserved, it sounds like. What we need is to stop teaching little boys that they are Peter Pans, here to have fun and stay young, and that little girls are all Wendys – waiting by the window, growing old, on pause for them. My generation let their men act like children. And it's done a lot of harm.'

'I'll drink to that,' Shazia said, lifting her glass of water.

'Yes,' said Hanna, although the lump in her throat and the sudden rush of something to her eyes stopped her from saying any more. Mary was right. She was sick of child men. And Iain, despite his mortgage and his former marriage and his daughter, had a heavy dash of the Peter Pan about him too, with his music and his shorts and his silly gadgets. Perhaps it was no surprise that Hanna had kept trying to find immature men to fall in love with her; Iain had taught her how to do it from her Moses basket. She'd been trying to get his focus, win his affection, hold his attention since the day she was born.

'We need to teach our children – however old they are – that loving people is not a sacrifice but a freedom in itself,' said Mary. Hanna was struck. This was like watching an evangelical preacher. Who knew Mary had it in her? 'We aren't goldfinches flying through life alone, trying not to get caught or tied down. We are an interconnected tribe; a forest. Our roots keep us all standing and we must grow or die. If I'd had a son, I would have told him: growing up is the only option. Everything else is just killing time.'

'OK, OK, I'm outnumbered,' said Iain, holding his hands up like someone in a bank heist. 'Well, I'm sorry it didn't work out. And I'm sorry that you felt you couldn't tell me at the time.' He spooned a mountain of food into his mouth. 'But at least you can stop buying all those terrible pencil drawings of wrinkly old naked men now.'

'Oh God, I know,' laughed Hanna. They were all laughing now. The cheese-wire silence that had greeted Mary's deft takedown of modern masculinity had given way to hooting relief.

'I was a bit worried about some of the old lads,' Iain said, smiling just enough to reveal the partially chewed rice at the corners of his mouth. 'Judging by their meat and two veg, she wasn't heating the studio very much.' Hanna began to laugh far more than the joke deserved. Perhaps it was relief. She felt so glad to have finally heard Mary lay it all out so clearly; to let go of all that resentment. She was also relieved to have seen Tom for what he was, to understand that she could never have made Joe happy, and to finally peel back the cling film around her heart. Her laughter was also a cheer.

About halfway through their mains, as Shazia asked

for another roti and Hanna cracked into her second beer, Iain turned to Hanna and, taking Mary's hand on top of the tablecloth, said: 'Hanna, Mary has something she wanted to bring up with you.' *Oh God*, thought Hanna. *Here it comes. The reprisal.*

'All right, Iain,' said Mary, giving his fingers a short squeeze and then letting go. 'No need to be quite so formal. Now, Hanna.' She adjusted briefly in her seat. 'As you may know, I have a boat moored along the canal at Wolvercote that I use as an office and for holidays. It's got fairly rudimentary plumbing and obviously no Wi-Fi.' Hanna wondered if she was about to suggest a family holiday. 'But it's a good size and very cheap to run, and the mooring is only £42 a month. You have to pay a bit to the Environment Agency for the licence, but it's still only about £100 in all.' Iain and Mary looked at Hanna as if they were trying to guess the width of her head in centimetres.

'Right,' Hanna said, giving the word at least two syllables.

'And so I wondered – it was all my idea, not Iain's – if you might want to take it on,' Mary continued. 'It would mean you could move out of your dad's flat and have your own space again. There's no rush. You'd probably want to wait until the winter cold has really passed. But anyway, it's there and I'm not using it as much as I did when Remy was alive.'

'I don't, uh . . . I mean, that's incredibly kind.' Hanna pictured herself on top of the roof, watching the mist rise from the canal, hearing the cows lowing on Port Meadow, smoking a roll-up and drinking a cup of coffee made on her small gas stove. She'd wrap herself in her mother's old Welsh woollen shawl and read books in the evenings, and stoke the fire and smell of woodsmoke. She would do the crossword in the *Guardian Weekly* and split logs and wear heavy cashmere sweaters and know about things like starter engines. She would fall asleep with the smell of grass and May blossom on her pillow, and haul coal and be able to touch the ceiling. She would, in fact, become her ideal man. 'Mary, I would love to. If you're absolutely sure. Obviously I would pay you to rent it. And you could have it back for holidays and things—'

'Hanna, be sensible. It's a boat. I don't want rent – just cover the mooring costs and bills.' Mary smiled her small, tight smile. 'And it would give both you and Iain some much-needed privacy.'

In that moment, Hanna was so grateful that she didn't actually care that this woman was suggesting she live with a chemical toilet and no heating, just so Mary and Iain could have loud sex up against the kitchen table. In fact, she hardly pictured it at all.

'Obviously you could still come back to mine for a bath and to use the washing machine,' said Iain. 'And if it doesn't work we can try something else. But it sounds like it might be a pretty good stopgap? Until you can buy somewhere?' Bless her parents' unshakeable faith in house buying, thought Hanna. Despite all evidence that the only people her age buying houses were having houses bought for them. Still, if she was only paying a couple of hundred pounds a month in rent and bills, maybe she could actually manage to save something that, if you squinted hard enough, might look like a deposit. This wasn't London, after all.

'Well, it looks like you never needed my spare room after all!' said Shazia, her smile twinkling at Hanna across the table.

'Just as well,' said Hanna, looking down at her meagre, poppadum-flecked cleavage. 'I would have made a terrible wet nurse.'

22
Corner Cupboard

As Hanna pushed the wheelbarrow down to the canal, loaded with bedsheets, a toaster, nightlights, her nest of saucepans and winter coats, all held down by a large wire drying rack, she wondered for the hundredth time if she was really cut out for boat living. Would she keep it warm? Would she remember to fill the water tank? Would she be tidy enough? Did she have enough jumpers? She had visions of herself crawling through a rabbit warren of old newspapers, paint tins, Jaffa Cake boxes and huge, evil-looking cactus plants.

Mary's barge was long but not wide. At one end, under a roof hatch, was a double bed, taking up the entire width of the boat. For some reason it reminded Hanna of the beds Julie used to make her in the back of the car when they drove home from their summer holidays in the evening; an enclosed nest of pillows, a stack of blankets, hard walls. There was no wardrobe but along one wall was a ceiling-height set of box shelves, like the boating forerunner to IKEA's Kallax, in which Hanna would have to store all her clothes, make-up, accessories, shoes, underwear, bedding and towels. The floor and most of the walls were wooden, but Julie had offered to bring down some of her father's old wool rugs to cover the floor-boards. Hanna imagined square patches of wool the shape and colour of Brillo pads, attic-smelling and full of moths. But at least they would be warm. And would stop her worrying about staining Mary's floor polish with dropped perfume bottles or spilled nail varnish. Between the bed-room and main living space was one of those funny little plastic concertina doors that supermarkets used to put over the wine cabinets on Sunday mornings. Hanna couldn't envision using it much. The whole point of this boat was that it was her space, that she could do any-thing, at any time, with nobody else looking. It was a huge privilege, she knew, to be given this chance. Thanks to the wealth and generosity of someone who wasn't even a blood relation, she was able to live on her own, in a ludi-crously expensive city, almost rent-free. Thanks to Mary, she was starting her new life, away from Joe, away from Tom, away from Iain, and on the water. She was unlikely to start closing the bedroom door every time she changed her tights.

The living space was taller than Hanna had first im-agined and thankfully lighter. There were little round windows all along both sides as well as two large raised roof hatches made of clear plastic. In her child mind, these looked to Hanna like something from a light-house. Standing on a chair, she could put her head right in the middle and look out across the weeping willows and passing ducks, like a cabin boy. The wood panelling came up to shoulder height and gave the interior a strangely 1930s college feel. It meant there was no room to hang pictures, of course, but Iain had promised that she could store those back at his flat for now. The kitchen was beautiful, like something from a beach house. All 1950s cabinets in pale turquoise and cream Formica worktops. Mary had apparently picked them up from a *brocante* in France in the 1980s. Hanna imagined herself making pasta and thick tomato sauces at the stove, with herbs she'd grow in pots on the roof.

The strangest thing was the sight of people's feet passing along at head height outside. It was like living in a sunken bath; a not entirely unpleasant experience, Hanna supposed. Dogs would come and sniff at the kitchen window when she toasted crumpets. Perhaps she would look up on a quiet Tuesday morning to see her old English teacher walking to his allotment, whistling the *Coronation Street* theme. One day a handsome tree surgeon would spot her lying on the sofa smoking and reading a Doris Lessing novel, as he knelt down to start his chainsaw. It would be the beginning of a heady and sawdust-smelling romance. Or not. Perhaps Hanna would take a break from romance, she thought. Or just romance herself, as the dildo adverts said.

The bathroom sat under the wheelhouse and was surprisingly big. Mary said that Remy's only proviso for the boat had been that it came with a bath. He absolutely would not use a shower. Not even in hotels.

And so, they had taken off one of the side panels to haul the bath in through the actual wall, with a crane, as it would never have fitted down the stairs into the boat that way. Which meant that the bath was here to stay; hammered in for life. Hanna was thrilled. Not only did it give her somewhere to soak (if she could get enough water on board) but somewhere to wash her underwear between visits to Iain's. She'd never liked cleaning her knickers in the sink – too splashy, too much hitting the taps with the back of your hand. In the wheelhouse, Hanna genuinely felt like a pirate captain. Despite the fact that she had no intention of moving the boat from its mooring very much, Hanna loved the idea of sitting on the barstool seat and putting her hands on the big, old-fashioned wooden steering wheel. It was half the height of her and looked just like something from a children's book. From here she could look out to the fields on one side and a high grassy bank on the other. It felt like the countryside, even though Summertown was just a few metres away. This was liberation, independence, privacy; all floating on a couple of thousand cubic metres of duck shit, silt and brown creeping water.

It was a surprisingly warm day, with no rain or mist to deaden the sound. So, as Hanna pushed the barrow along the towpath, she heard Julie's voice clang out across the canal like a foghorn.

'She said she needed furniture, Iain. And I think she'll

find this very useful. I've been keeping my whisky glasses in it but she could use it for egg cups, saucers, anything short.'

It was still odd, somehow, to hear her parents talking to each other like this; without them knowing she could hear. It felt like spying. Actually, it was spying. But just as Hanna had always wanted to listen in on what her friends said about her when she was out of the room, so she'd always wanted to know what secret relationship her parents slotted into when she wasn't there. Were they more polite? Did they slip into old in-jokes? Did they slag Hanna off? Just as she was wondering, hovering behind the low-hanging branch of a willow tree, Julie saw her.

'Hello, darling. Well, isn't this lovely? Your very own little floating house.'

'Hello, Mum.' Hanna set down the wheelbarrow to hug her mum, who was wearing a huge red coat and a pair of shiny black DMs. They looked like liquorice. 'Yes, it's great, isn't it. Just please don't ask me about the—'

'What are you going to do about the toilet? Is it one that you have to get emptied or can you—'

'Mum, please.' Hanna raised her voice, just a touch. 'Can we just not talk about the toilet right now?'

Julie rolled her eyes as though Hanna had just suggested they try speaking in whale for the next forty-five minutes.

'Julie's brought you this corner cupboard,' Iain said from the top of the boat. He was pointing at an enormous piece of oak furniture tied to a removal trolley with enough rope to lasso a large semi-detached house.

'What's this, Mum?' asked Hanna.

'It's a corner cupboard, Hanna. It was Uncle Eric's but he passed it on to me and I thought you might like it for your new boat.'

'But Mum, it's huge,' said Hanna. 'I'm not sure we'll even get it down the stairs. Like, it's such a weird shape, and look, it's almost as tall as me.'

'It's an heirloom!' said Julie, a little sharply. 'I thought you'd be touched. It must be at least two hundred years old – they took it from Cotteringham when they sold the house. And you must have plenty of room in there, if it's just you.'

'Mum,' said Hanna, walking towards the enormous oak lump. 'Has this been in your storage unit all this time? The one you said you needed to clear by the end of the financial year?'

Julie narrowed her eyes. 'What exactly are you saying, Hanna?' They were skidding towards a confrontation that neither wanted.

'Fine, nothing. I'm not. OK. Well, if Mary is all right with it, let's just see if it will even go down the steps.'

'Mary?' asked Julie.

'Yes, Mary. Dad's partner.' Since she'd provided Hanna with a place to live, Mary had been promoted from 'girlfriend' to the heady title of 'partner'. 'The one who is letting me stay on this boat. It's hers. I thought you knew all this.'

'Oh, all right. You don't need to use that tone,' said Julie, pulling at one of the red nylon ropes. 'I was only asking who Mary was.'

'She's coming down in a minute to help, actually,' said Iain, scuffing at some dried bird shit with the sole of his boot. 'I thought it might be nice for us all to meet.'

'Oh, right,' said Hanna, looking a little uneasily at the giant corner cupboard. Other people in other situations might have been able to say a quick hello, but with Iain and Julie in the mix there was no guarantee that someone wouldn't suddenly bring up premature ejaculation or the state of the Labour party as Hanna tried to unpack her mugs.

'Well, if you've told her I'm here and she still wants to come, then that's up to—'

'Mum,' interrupted Hanna. 'It's her boat. She's been incredibly supportive.' Julie let out a noise like bread being cut with a blunt knife, but said nothing more. 'I think, if Iain and I start with the kitchen things, maybe you could carry the clothes and bedding into the bedroom, Mum?' said Hanna, looking at the spray of laundry bags, cardboard boxes and loose detritus covering the towpath. It wasn't that her mother could only carry light things; rather that Hanna knew Julie would enjoy making her bedroom cosy. She was good with that sort of thing, while Iain would probably relish the task of organizing the kitchen in the most space-efficient flow system that meant Hanna was less likely to bang her head on a cupboard door every time she tried to pull out a jar of pesto and a spoon in quick succession.

'Sure thing. I'll just fire up the tunes and we can get going,' said Iain, pulling a little mobile speaker out of his rucksack. Well, this was a sure-fire way to ingratiate herself with the neighbours, thought Hanna. A blaring soundtrack of B.B. King and Afrika Bambaataa as two divorcees and their adult child hammered saucepans around a kitchen the size of a garden shed. Although, looking around, the nearest neighbour was a good swimming pool's length away and they had an anarchist flag attached to their rudder.

After about an hour, Mary turned up on a pale blue sit-up-and-beg bicycle that made her look a bit like a midwife. There was even a huge straw basket attached to the front.

'Hello, Hanna,' Mary said, flicking the kickstand with her foot so the bicycle stood upright on the grass verge. 'How are you settling in?' It was typical of Mary, thought Hanna, to direct her remarks to Hanna, rather than Iain. To ingratiate herself not by stepping back but by being direct.

'Oh, it's amazing, Mary, thank you.' Hanna was gushing. 'The kitchen is so beautiful, and the view!'

'Yes, I always rather liked the fact that you could have a bath at duck height.' Mary pulled a red tartan-patterned tin and a large blue thermos out of the bike basket. 'I brought a flask of tea and some cake. I suspected you wouldn't trust the oven until I'd been to explain the gas situation.'

'Did somebody say cake?' Iain was rubbing his hands like someone in an amateur dramatics production. 'We've not been allowed so much as a dry crust and cup of water all morning.'

'Actually, Mary, I did want to double check about the water,' said Hanna, talking over Iain. 'Can we drink out of the tap?'

'Well, you can either fill the water tank with drinking water up at Wolvercote or bring your own onboard overland,' said Mary. 'Because I wasn't often staying on here, I usually just brought bottles but it's up to you. And if you go on to the river at all, you can filter the water there for washing and things.'

'And what were you saying about the oven?'

'Ah yes, well, that's connected to a gas bottle in the wheelhouse. I turned it on for you last week and always keep a spare for when it runs out. You're not really meant to but everybody does. There's a fuel barge that comes up every month or so, with coal and gas – actually Mike's branched out to wood and chocolate bars and homebrew too now – you want the nineteen-kilo propane bottles. They're red.' Suddenly Hanna wanted to ask Mary to come and babysit her on the boat once a week. There was so much to learn. 'I did actually make a little user's manual once, when a cousin borrowed the boat for a holiday up to the Caledonian Canal. It should be in the cupboard by the bathroom.'

'I'm spitting feathers here, Hanna. Is there any chance we could take a stroll up to one of those nice little bakeries in Summertown and get a cappuccino, or . . .?' Julie's tangle of cinnamon-coloured hair popped out from a porthole down at the far end of the boat. 'Oh.' Mary and Julie locked eyes. There was a microsecond of silence in which you could have parked a P&O ferry. Iain, naturally, was standing like a piece of cold garlic bread on the running board, doing nothing to ease the tension.

'Mum, this is Mary. She's brought us some tea and cake. Mary, this is my mum.' Then, realizing that this probably wasn't what Mary would call her, Hanna added, 'Julie.'

'Hello, Julie,' said Mary. 'Nice to have you on board.' *What a bloody power play*, thought Hanna. She didn't know whether to be impressed or terrified. *My boat, my partner, my domain*, Mary was saying. *Take that, Julie.*

'Oh dear, is the cake gluten-free?' Of course Julie was going to pretend to be coeliac now, thought Hanna. Perhaps it made her feel special; refined, delicate, sophisticated. Maybe it was an anxiety thing. Whatever the reason, Hanna had lost count of the number of allergies, headaches, ethical objections and religious strictures that had got between Julie and the real world over the years.

'It is, actually,' said Mary. 'I made it with ground almonds and polenta; I always prefer that when you make an Italian orange blossom cake.' She smiled. 'I got the recipe when I was working for the university in Perugia.' *Game, set and match to Mary*, thought Hanna.

High above the boat, three crows were swooping and darting around a red kite. The weed on the bottom of the canal was still cut low by the winter cold and there were yellow catkins like fat, dead caterpillars hanging from the bare branches. Hanna, Iain, Mary and Julie had all shuffled on to the bank, drinking from mugs that Hanna hadn't seen for a year. Holding a blue-and-white spotty cup which had once hung on a hook in the kitchen she'd shared with Joe, she felt like a time traveller, an archaeologist, a moth breaking out from its long pupation. This was her mug. In that wheelbarrow were her saucepans. Her bedding was tucked around her duvet. She might be squatting on a floating office that belonged to her dad's new partner, but wasn't that better than being an adjunct to another man? She'd spent enough time living with a boyfriend; hanging his towel, buttering his toast, stacking his shoes in the hallway. And she'd certainly spent enough time living with her father; both as a gap-toothed child following him to the newsagent's and as an adult, creeping past his bedroom in the early hours, smelling of sex and cider and someone else's sweat. She had done her time as the female assistant; she had chalked up her hours in intergenerational claustrophobia. Finally, she was going to be living in a space all her own.

'So how did you two meet?' asked Julie, unlacing her left boot.

'On Tinder,' said Iain, smiling through a mouthful of half-chewed cake. 'I signed up just before Hanna came back. Couldn't have her being the only free agent in town.' Hanna's smile hung on her face like a cheap suit.

'What, you waited until your only daughter was moving back in with you to start online dating?' Julie had turned right round to look at Iain, who was sitting very close to Mary, practically nuzzling into her neck.

'Well, actually that's not true, Iain.' Mary was, somehow, managing to retain eye contact with Julie despite having Iain clamped to her side. 'You joined Tinder nearly two years ago – I remember seeing it on your account. But we met perhaps three months before Hanna came to live in Oxford.'

'I feel sorry for people who have to meet online,' Julie said, as though this were a throwaway remark. 'To have so little faith in the human connection, no sense of community or opportunity to actually meet people in the world.' Hanna briefly considered rolling headfirst into the canal.

'Ah, so have you met someone out there, in the world?' asked Iain, briefly pulling himself away from Mary's lavender wool shoulder.

'I've met thousands of people in the real world, Iain, and formed important bonds with many of them,' said Julie. So nice to think of her mum receiving this parade of sexual suitors, thought Hanna; like the embalmed body of Lenin being kissed by visiting disciples until eventually his waxen ear fell off. 'But most importantly, I've finally learned what it means to love yourself.' Hanna prayed that they weren't about to get an insight into post-menopausal masturbation.

'I think I might get some tomato plants when it's warmer.' Hanna's voice echoed off the concrete bank across the water. 'And maybe even try to grow potatoes in a bag.'

'You'll need manure,' said Iain.

'I had a jasmine plant around the door, once,' Mary said, in an uncharacteristically sing-song voice. 'But Remy said the smell kept him up.'

Julie had done a wonderful job on the bedroom. The relief of walking into this tiny, tidy little space and seeing all her clothes folded away, her bed made, flooded Hanna with sunshine affection for her mother. This was, after all, the woman who had blown Hanna's nose, washed her clothes, read to her each night, brushed her hair, spent hours making plasticine figures or painting clay sculptures, and always told her she was exceptional. When Julie had been born, Hanna had been born right inside her; an egg already living in her mother's body waiting to one day come down the chute. The fact that that had happened when Julie was still only in her twenties had of course meant something. Julie had sacrificed some of her best, most elastic years to Hanna. She'd managed to sustain a career with Hanna quite literally crawling across her body. She'd cooked dinner and scrubbed the blood out of Hanna's PE kit and wiped the kitchen table and sung in the car and very occasionally let Hanna sit beside her and watch her sign a cheque, all while her own friends and contemporaries travelled the world, slept their way through whole football teams, studied for second degrees and spent long nights dancing. Julie deserved her own decade, now. She'd given at least three over to Hanna already. And Hanna felt ready to have her own decade too. One not defined by her relationships to other people but by her own sense of self-worth.

Out in the main body of the boat, Iain was boxing in some extremely complicated-looking wiring above the fold-out dining table. The silver of his earring was glinting in his reflection in the window. He had a mouthful of tacks and was doing that sort of slow, shallow breathing of someone deep in concentration. Hanna felt grateful to him, too. He'd been twenty-five when Hanna was born. All the football games he'd never played, the gigs he'd never watched, the parties he'd missed, the people he'd never met; all because he'd been a parent. And a fairly dutiful one at that. He'd done night feeds and rocked her to sleep and walked her to school and helped with her homework and made her sandwiches and taught her to ride a bike and painted her bedroom floor black when she'd wanted him to and taken her to get her ears pierced and bought her sanitary towels on holiday. The last one was perhaps a bad example; the pads he'd brought home from the corner shop in Devon had looked like something you'd use to lag a hot water tank, and it had felt like Hanna was balancing on a surfboard every time she sat down. But at least he'd done it. His little physical tics, lack of shame and hunger for attention were all hard work when taken in large doses, of course. But they weren't entirely foreign to Hanna either. She'd picked her nose sitting on enough toilets and danced on the bar at enough parties to know that she was Iain's daughter. And yes, he was led by his libido, but Hanna was hardly without appetite herself. That Iain wanted fun and diversion no longer felt like a slight against her own chances of happiness. He was her father but that didn't stop him being a man. He wanted his own freedom and so did she.

Perhaps all it took for you to forgive your parents, thought Hanna, as she shook a blanket across the little, low sofa, was to stop hoping they might change. Of course Julie had turned up with a vanload of furniture she didn't want to pay to store any more; of course Iain had invited his girlfriend along; of course they'd both spent the afternoon manoeuvring a little awkwardly around each other. But they were both here.

'Right, I think this is just about done,' said Iain, sliding his hand along the top of the wooden boxing. 'Mary can talk you through the electrics, but I'm pretty happy none of this is going to trip out or burst into flame in the middle of the night.' And there was that, thought Hanna. He may have been a foghorn in work shorts sometimes, but Iain was handy. Both Julie and Iain got shit done. 'Shall we just see about this cupboard?' he continued, gesturing towards the wheelhouse. 'Mary can help take the weight too.'

'Yes, let's get it in here,' Julie barked, coming out of the bedroom with her mug clanking against her string of beads. 'I think it'll look lovely next to that funny little stove thing.'

Up on deck, the sun was beginning to burn through the cloud, painting a milky light across some of the bare, bone-like trees. *Spring doesn't happen all at once*, thought Hanna. *Even the seasons take their time.*

'I think if Hanna and I get over on that side and take the weight,' said Iain, 'and you and Mary help guide it in . . . I've taken a look at the dimensions – I'm not sure it'll have the clearance at the bottom but we can try.'

'Mum, can you really not just pay for another year's storage?' said Hanna. 'It is massive.'

'It's not about the storage, Hanna!' Julie's voice was brisk. 'This is your first proper home and I want you to have Uncle Eric's dresser.'

'It's not my first home, Mum. Remember my house in Brockley? With Joe? I lived there for four years.'

'Yes, exactly. With Joe. This is *your* space.' Julie was speaking to Hanna as if she was a child refusing to put on her shoes. 'And it'll look so nice with the curtains and dining chairs I've brought.'

'Mum.' Hanna looked nervously over at Mary. 'I don't want dining chairs or curtains or any other furniture. I mean, you've literally been inside; it's already got everything I need.'

'Well, yes, perhaps,' said Julie.

'OK, on three we'll tip it that way and Hanna and I will get underneath,' ordered Iain.

'I didn't bring gloves,' said Mary quietly. It was an extremely half-arsed attempt at getting out of this, thought Hanna. But she didn't blame Mary at all. She was already going above and beyond what was expected of her by loaning this boat. She shouldn't have to haul furniture too.

'You don't need gloves. It's got good grip.' Iain was now squatting halfway down the steps into the boat. 'Right. One, two aaaand . . .' The corner cupboard weighed as much as a washing machine. It might as well have been made out of concrete. 'All right?' Iain was shouting now, even though the canal was almost silent. 'Now, Hanna, if we lift from here and try walking back. On three. One, two, thr—'

There was a horrible crack. Somehow the cupboard had tilted on Hanna's side and was now wedged diagonally in the door.

'Oh, for fuck's sake.' Hanna ground her forehead into the great wooden lump in front of her.

'It's all right,' shouted Iain. 'I think if we slide a blanket or sheet or something down the side we can right it without scratching the paint too much.'

'It really is too big for a boat this size,' said Mary quietly, stepping away from the cupboard.

‘Well, if Hanna hadn’t let it fall . . .’ Julie interjected.

‘Don’t blame me for this, Mum.’ Hanna sounded terse. ‘You’re the one who decided to offload a ton of furniture on me without any warning.’

‘I’ve driven all the way here to help.’

‘I didn’t want this sort of help!’ Hanna could hear the snappy fifteen-year-old in her voice. She cleared her throat. ‘Can’t we please just push it back up and give up? I don’t want a massive oak corner cupboard. The shelves are too small; I won’t be able to fit anything on them, and anyway, this is only meant to be a temporary thing. Until I get my life sorted and can hopefully move into a flat or house or something.’ Hanna could feel her throat turning hot. ‘I mean . . . I don’t know. Maybe I’ll find a cheap one-bedroom place to rent or something. Whatever. I don’t want to have this conversation now. Can we please just get this cupboard out of my boat.’ She halted. ‘Mary’s boat. Sorry. Can we please just push it back out?’ Nobody said anything for a few seconds. Then Julie exhaled like a heavy goods train pulling into a station.

‘Fine. Fine. I’ll take it back. But Uncle Eric would have loved you to—’

‘Please, Mum,’ Hanna said, in a quiet, determined voice.

‘OK then,’ said Iain. ‘If I take your side, Hanna, and give it a bit of a shimmy. Aaand . . .’ Iain braced his legs on the floor and bottom step. ‘Everybody go on three. One, two—’

'Are we pushing or pulling?' shouted Julie.

'Pushing!' shouted Hanna.

'Pulling!' shouted Mary.

'You're pulling and we're pushing,' said Iain after a second. 'Right. On three. One, two, three.' There was another gruesome screech as the cupboard edged back out of the entrance and up the step. 'Keep it going, keep it going,' shouted Iain, walking the cupboard back into the wheelhouse and on to Julie's trolley. 'There we are.'

'Hooray!' said Hanna, a little surprised at her choice of words.

'Well done,' said Mary, brushing her hands together. 'Well, now that's over I think we could probably all do with a drink. Hanna, do you have any wine?'

'Tight squeeze, was it?' A man on the towpath was standing watching them. His small terrier the colour of loo roll was straining at its lead. 'Best bit of live theatre I've seen in ages.'

'Thank you,' said Julie haughtily. 'It's a family heirloom. Eighteenth-century, probably.'

'And how do you all know each other?' Who the hell was this man? thought Hanna. Why was he asking these questions?

'This is my daughter, and her father and his girlfriend,' said Julie, flicking a stray tendril of hair behind her shoulder. All four of them stared at the man, daring him to say something. Channelling all the oddness of the situation on to him. *Go on, mate. Swallow that little conundrum.*

'So . . . you're not married?' The man with the dog gave Julie a rather leery smile, just as his dog started pushing its nose into a discarded green bag hanging from a thorn bush.

'Not at the moment,' said Julie.

'She is on the market, I think,' said Iain, far too loud.

'I'm not a house, Iain,' Julie snapped. 'I'm not on anybody's "market".'

'Well, I'll let you get on.' The man raised his eyebrows, as though this was the nicest little catch-up they'd had for years.

'Your dog is eating shit,' said Mary, a genuine smile spreading across her face. The man looked down, yelped and started pulling the plastic bag from between his dog's locked little jaws. 'Now, as I was saying,' continued Mary, 'I think some wine may be in order.'

'I might have a bottle of red somewhere,' said Hanna, heading towards the steps again.

'No need,' said Iain, hopping lightly on to the bank and retrieving his bike pannier. 'I thought, well, you can't move on to a boat without a bit of ceremony.' He pulled out two bottles. One of the very cheapest supermarket cava and another, tiny little bottle of prosecco. Around the black foil-wrapped cork of the smaller bottle was a length of green nylon rope. 'I think it's time we christened this boat properly.' Iain quickly darted a look towards Mary. 'If that's OK with you, of course.'

'Fine, as long as we can drink the other one,' Mary replied. 'There are champagne glasses in the cupboard,

Hanna. You probably saw them when you were unpacking.' Hanna hadn't. She'd let Iain unpack most of the kitchen, but hurried down into the boat to have a look. Glancing across the inside now, her books on the shelf, her pans hanging above the cooker, her blue wool blanket thrown over the bed at the far end, Hanna felt a deep surge of pride. This was hers. Well, not *hers* hers. But hers for now. It was a fresh start. She could begin a new chapter here. One on her own. Because she was on her own. Just her. No husband, no baby, no housemate, no eavesdropping dad in the next room. And that, for the first time, felt like freedom. She was going to be all right. Hanna had nothing and nobody to lose. Which meant, surely, that she had everything to gain.

'Can you find them?' Mary's voice came bouncing through one of the portholes.

'Yes, just coming.'

And there Hanna stood. On a patch of grass, flecked with cigarette butts and bits of gravel, holding a coil of green rope in one hand and a tiny bottle of prosecco in the other. Her mother, her father and her landlady. Her father's girlfriend. Her mother's ex-husband. Her dad's ex-wife. And Hanna: her father's daughter.

The bottle exploded like a firework. Broken glass ricocheted on to the bank. A ripple spread across the surface of the water. And time pushed on.

Acknowledgements

Firstly, I should thank Bill Frizzell, who signed off on the proposal and has supported the book ever since. I wouldn't have written it otherwise. Which isn't to say *Square One* isn't a total work of fiction; but it's nice to know my own father isn't going to sue me. Thanks too for all the babysitting, DIY and walks to nursery that made the writing of it possible.

Thank you to Sally Williamson for being such a calm, kind, insightful editor and for not being put off by all my innate grot. Writing a book during lockdown was strange, but being able to talk it through from our respective bedrooms was invaluable.

Thank you to my agent, Zoe Ross, for championing me and looking after me and making me laugh every time we talk.

Thank you to Becky Short, Sophie Bruce and Izzie Ghaffari-Parker for elegantly selling my ass all over again. Thank you to Beci Kelly for the cover design.

Thank you to my early readers for giving me hope and lending me support. You are wonderful.

Thank you to all the daughters who talked to me in the research for this book and delighted me with their stories of what it is to be fathered. I won't name you, but your secrets are sort of safe with me.

Thank you to my Wild Swimming Women; to Rachel, Zuhura and Miranda for keeping me sane and submerged, making me laugh and massaging my brain during the pandemic.

Thanks, as always and hopefully for ever, to Nick for being the third point in my triangle. I love you more than any fictional hero.

Thank you to my friends and family for making all those hours after 4.30 a.m. worth it: Mum, Boo, Tonie, Eliza, Alice, Molly, Jess, Amber, Ruby, Duncan, Caroline, Naomi, Hamish, Suzie, Jessica, Fia, Xander, Adder, Sharon, Alice, Raphi, Eleanor, Kirsten, Juliet, Nick Scott and all the rest.

Thank you to everyone who has ever looked after my son. There is no measure to describe how much that has helped me and meant to me. Shazia, Grace, Michelle, April, Katy, Tracy, Paris, Ursula, Basia, Liz Ellis and anyone else I called on for a few crucial hours while I worked.

Thank you to Sylvesters, The Covered Market, Bonners Fruit and Veg, Milk & More, Reg Taylor, Noor, the Natural History Museum, the Pitt Rivers, the River Thames, the Botanic Gardens, the Ashmolean, Boundary Brook Nature Reserve, Port Meadow and to my city as a whole for getting me through a global pandemic and a novel.

About the Author

Nell Frizzell is a journalist, writer and *Vogue* columnist. She has written for the *Guardian*, *VICE*, the *Telegraph*, *Elle*, the *Observer*, *Grazia* and the BBC among many others. Her first book, *The Panic Years*, is an exploration of bodies, babies and the big questions facing modern life. *Square One* is her first novel. She lives in Oxford, in a very small house full of pasta and bedding and bikes.